PRAISE FOR
MEMORTALITY

THE FIRST BOOK IN THE MEMORTALITY SAGA

"Punchy and fast paced, **Memortality** reads like a graphic novel. Its short chapters are exciting, well plotted, and compelling. Provost, a reporter, is a no-nonsense writer who delivers on the action . . . his style makes the trippy landscapes and mind-bending plot points more believable and adds a thrilling edge to this vivid crossover fantasy."
—*Foreword Reviews*

"A well-paced adventure filled with horror, mystery, fantasy and a touch of romance. A well-written novel with modern prose and social concerns, the complex idea of mixing morality and mortality is a fresh twist on the human condition. **Memortality** is one of those books that will incite more questions than it answers. And for fandom, that's a good thing."
—*Amazing Stories*

"Filled with action, conspiracy, and mystery . . . **Memortality** is a story that stays in your mind and satisfies the imagination. I do hope there is more to come with Minerva. This book is definitely on my shelf for re-reading."
—*Green Egg Magazine*

"Provost shows a complete understanding of his craft . . . If this is the kind of stories we can expect from him in the future sign me up."
—*Genre Book Reviews*

"Intriguing, captivating and mesmerizing. I loved it and would recommend it to everyone. The book was completely original, beautiful and gripping. I can't wait to read more from the author."
—*Booklove*

"**Memortality** takes a concept we've all dreamed of and turns it into our worst nightmare. Innovative terror at its best."
—Bram Stoker Award-winner **Michael Knost**, author of *Return of the Mothman*

"*Memortality* by Stephen Provost is a highly original, thrilling novel unlike anything else out there. From the haunting prologue to the thrilling conclusion, Provost has crafted an engaging, brilliant yarn that will keep you glued to the page until the very end. Stephen is clearly an author at the top of his game."
—**David McAfee**, bestselling author of *33 A.D., 61 A.D.,* and *79 A.D.*

"A rich and complex world, with an ever-twisting and an immensely compelling story, *Memortality* is a terrific science fiction thriller that imprints on your mind like an unforgettable snapshot."
—**John Palisano**, Bram Stoker Award-winning author of *Nerves* and *Ghost Heart*

"Fans of *The Running Dream* will love Minerva, a feisty protagonist with a special gift for helping the dead, who embarks on an action-packed adventure as she attempts to save her loved ones."
—**Alexandria Constantiova Szeman**, author of *The Kommandant's Mistress*

"*Memortality* was mind-blowing. There is no other way to explain what it does to the readers."
—*The Book Adventures of Annelise Lestrange*

"*Memortality* is one of those books that is strangely fascinating, curiously thrilling, and absolutely so much fun to read."
—*Jazzy Book Reviews*

"This story blew my mind away. I really enjoyed going on this adventure with Minerva. There was excitement on every page and couldn't wait to see what would happen next."
—*Books, Dreams, Life*

"*Memortality* is a fast-paced book with a great premise and great characters. It is a book packed with suspense, mystery, action, and the feels. And this book always made me think."
—*Erucchii's Books and Recs*

Paralucidity

The Memortality Saga
Book II

Stephen H. Provost

Pace Press
Fresno, California

Published by Pace Press
An imprint of Linden Publishing
2006 South Mary Street, Fresno, California 93721
(559) 233-6633 / (800) 345-4447

Pace Press and Colophon are trademarks of
Linden Publishing, Inc.

ISBN 978-1-61035-318-2

135798642

Printed in the United States of America
on acid-free paper.

Library of Congress Cataloging-in-Publication Data on file.

Contents

For Samaire, with love.

Training

"How do you like being dead?"

Minerva scowled and exhaled hard as she rose from the floor. She extended a hand for help, but Amber shook her head. "You're a big girl. Do it yourself."

Minerva's scowl deepened as she got up quickly the way she'd been practicing, using only her feet. "Look, Ma, no hands," she quipped as she jumped up, making it look far easier than it was. "And being dead has its advantages. Like why do I have to learn all this self-defense stuff? My wounds just heal up anyway. The real danger's all up here." She tapped her temple with an index finger.

"That's the point, to make you mentally tough," Carson interjected, standing off to the side, near the bleachers. "The more challenges you face, the more prepared you'll be for the next one."

"Yes, Sensei," she said, putting her hands together and bowing slightly toward the government agent. Dressed in a Men in Black-style outfit, he looked like a younger, slightly less rugged Tommy Lee Jones. "Or should I call you Yoda?"

"The farce is strong with this one," Amber laughed. "Quit stalling. I've already killed you eleven times. And you didn't answer my question: How do you like being dead?"

"I was dead before you killed me, remember? That's what makes this whole thing a little pointless . . . ugh!"

She absorbed a sidekick to her midsection that sent her back to the ground.

"Twelve," Amber said. Minerva hopped to her feet more quickly this time.

"No fair. I wasn't ready," she shouted, genuinely angry as she whirled to face Amber.

"Will you be ready when one of Jules' goons jumps you?" Carson asked calmly. "She may be out of commission, but who's to say there aren't others out there? Not to mention your garden variety assholes, purse-snatchers, rapists . . . shall I continue?"

Jules was Minerva's nemesis, the person who had put her in this . . . situation. If it hadn't been for Jules, Minerva wouldn't have been killed, and she wouldn't have needed to go into hiding.

Minerva telegraphed a right that Amber deftly grabbed before it could reach her chin, throwing her attacker off balance and back to the blue wrestling mat, once again.

"Thirteen."

Minerva growled and hopped up. She wasn't about to let Amber beat her, even if the nimble, smarter version of Wonder Woman did hold black belts in two martial arts and a brown belt in a third, not to mention being an experienced kickboxer, skydiver, backpacker, and physician. Minerva, for her part, had spent most of her life in a wheelchair. Once she'd finally managed to overcome that particular constraint (with Raven guiding and motivating her), she'd promptly let herself be killed in a hail of police bullets (again, with Raven providing the motivation). Raven was almost as much trouble as Jules, but he was cute. And nice. That made all the difference.

Minerva smiled slightly and brought to mind the memory of her head hitting the mat hard a moment earlier, directing the thought at Amber. The ability to project her own memories into other people's minds could come in handy. Sometimes painfully.

"Hey!" her opponent said. "No fair."

Minerva shrugged. "If you can fight dirty . . ."

Amber shook her head. "Believe it or not, I was taking it easy on you, Sis. You're a beginner, that's obvious, but you're making progress. It's like a video game: You've got to start at the newbie level and work your way up. I'd say you're about at Level 3 now."

"Out of how many?"

"Oh, maybe 184. But who's counting?" She laughed.

"How's she doing?" Raven asked as he walked through the double doors at the far end of the gym.

"Well enough for a newb," Amber said. She knew the question had been directed at her; Raven rarely spoke to Carson or even acknowledged his presence. The man had killed Raven's grandmother.

Raven nodded approvingly. Whatever insecurities Minerva might have, he knew she was the toughest person in the room. He was here because of her sheer force of will. Her memory had brought him back from the no-man's land of death, and then she'd sacrificed herself to keep him here. The fact that they were both dead, yet still very much aware and functioning, could get pretty confusing. All he could do was accept it and enjoy every moment with the childhood friend he had grown to love.

Minerva was less accepting, but she had struggled her whole life, so that was natural. In fact, it was her take-no-prisoners attitude that made her as strong as she was.

"Ready for a break?" Raven asked.

Minerva shook her head. "I'm not done here." She turned her attention back to Amber and assumed a fighting stance.

Amber, who was standing about eight feet away, put her hands at her sides. "You don't have to prove anything," she said. "You're doing good. Raven's right. Take a break. You're not used to this."

"Yeah," Raven said. "This isn't like when you were remembering how to walk. You'd done that before. This is new."

Minerva didn't even look at him. Her eyes narrowed as she stared at Amber.

The other woman had to stop herself from taking a step backward. As varied and impressive as her skills might be, she didn't have the gift. If Minerva got really mad, there wouldn't be much she could do to defend herself. She'd already gotten a taste of that with Minerva's projected memory of her head hitting the mat. Amber hadn't thought she'd go there; now she wasn't sure.

Minerva saw Amber's muscles tense and realized what was happening. She didn't relax a single muscle but spoke a few clipped words of reassurance that sounded almost ironic through clenched teeth. "Don't worry, Sis. I won't hurt you, at least not that way."

Amber didn't really know what to make of this, but she put her hands back up in a defensive stance, as she had done before.

Minerva smiled ruefully. "Sorry, Sis," she said with a barely detectable shake of her head. And she moved forward, exactly as she had done the first time. Again, she balled up her right fist and drew it back before she reached Amber, cocking it to deliver a heavy blow. Again, Amber reached forward to grab it. But this time, instead of a right cross aimed at Amber's chin, Minerva ducked low to the mat and allowed the momentum of her swing to carry her in a somersault that took less time than it did for Amber to react. Before she could move to counter, Amber felt the force of a strong two-legged kick, amplified by Minerva's momentum, strike her directly in the stomach.

"Oof!"

Minerva rolled to her right shoulder and hopped to her feet, while Amber, noticeably out of breath, whirled to face her, just barely off her knees in a crouch.

"*Now* I'll take that break," Minerva said.

Amber smiled and winced at the same time. "Where did that come from?" she asked, rising to her feet. "I've never seen that move before."

Minerva shrugged. "I improvised. Based on how you reacted before." She tapped her forehead once lightly with her index finger. "Or did you forget my flawless memory?" She grinned, and Amber laughed.

"First rule of combat: Know your opponent," Amber said. "You passed with flying colors. Me? Not so much."

Minerva chuckled. "You'll get the hang of it," she teased. "Or maybe not. It's not something you can learn without the right equipment." Amber took a playful swipe at her with an open palm.

Minerva ducked out of the way. "Knew that was coming, too." She winked.

They walked up to Carson, who shook his head slightly. "Don't get cocky, Minerva," he said. "She's got a lot of moves you haven't seen." He looked over at Amber, allowing himself a rare smile, which she returned.

"And there are goons out there who have moves she doesn't use," Raven added. "You can't remember something you've never seen."

Minerva raised an eyebrow. "Thanks for the reminder," she said sarcastically. "I'd almost *forgotten* that."

Date

The first few weeks after Minerva and Raven found each other again were a whirlwind. Raven's kidnapping and Minerva's subsequent death truly tested their limits, but things had quieted down, and Jules remained safely locked away at the top-secret medical complex where Minerva herself had once been held. She was no longer a threat, thanks to the comatose state Minerva had induced in her.

For the past couple of months, the group of them had been living in a house Carson found for them in Salton City, which was very salty but not much of a city.

Envisioned as a modern Riviera-style resort, it was developed in the sixties, on the western shore of the Salton Sea, about sixty miles north of the Mexican border and a little over a hundred miles east of San Diego. Most of it had never been built. Streets curved this way and that in neighborhoods of empty lots. A few had houses on them, but most remained vacant, caressed by the hot desert wind that carried a stench of salt, polluted water, and dead fish.

It wasn't a sea, really, but a huge accidental lake created when the Colorado River burst through its banks and emptied into a natural depression.

Early attempts to create a resort had seemed promising, with the lake hosting speed boat races, a Beach Boys concert, and a visit from Frank Sinatra. But as time passed, the chemicals from the surrounding farmland washed down the hillsides into the below-sea-level basin, polluting it to the point that the fish started dying, washing up by the thousands to decompose on the shore.

No one wanted to brave 100-degree summer heat to live beside a sea of dead fish. Many of the landowners just packed up and left, abandoning their property to the dust and the vermin. Vacationers stopped coming, too, leaving their Winnebagos and Gulfstreams to rot and rust in the searing desert wind.

Carson, their nemesis-turned-ally, had decided it was too dangerous to stay at the old motel he'd used as his base of operations for the Federal Intelligence Network, or FIN, a more elite version of the CIA that was so covert almost no one knew it existed. Amber's Topanga Canyon cabin was secluded, but it wasn't secure enough to use indefinitely, so he'd purchased a vacant four-bedroom home through a third party and set them up there, reasoning that if someone stumbled upon their trail, they could retreat to one of the abandoned trailers up the road in Desert Shores.

So far, no one had bothered them.

Everyone thought Raven, Minerva and Amber were all dead—which, of course, they were. There'd even been a funeral for Minerva. The problem had been Henry Marshall, the doctor who had tried to help Minerva and Amber reach Raven when Jules was still holding him hostage. The police had arrested him for harboring fugitives, and their success in breaking him out of jail had made him a wanted man. He'd insisted on turning himself in for the good of the others, and after a heated argument, they'd finally agreed. Carson would work on a way of getting him out once things settled down.

Which they had started to do. The three of them were even able to go out occasionally without being recognized, although if they wanted to do anything fun, like have a nice dinner, they had to drive up to Indio or Palm Springs.

〜

Minerva walked beside Raven as they entered Esperanza y Gloria. The Spanish restaurant's name translated to "Hope and Glory," something Raven thought was appropriately uplifting for the occasion, even if the two owners had named it after themselves. Sisters Hope and Gloria Rogers weren't even Spanish, but the food was good and the atmosphere even better. That was what mattered.

Neither *had* to eat anymore, but they still enjoyed the taste. Even in their current state, the biting sensations of the salsa and the creamy decadence of the flan could make them swoon.

The heavy wooden doors reminded Raven of something you'd see at a winery or an old castle keep. Inside, they found themselves surrounded by adobe walls, their eyes naturally drawn to the skylights that admitted the glow of sunset. Candles on the table and some iron chandeliers with faux candles of their own kept the place warmly illumined as the sunlight faded. Potted ferns hung from the ceiling, giving them the sense of having entered some ancient grotto.

"Fancy," Minerva remarked as a host in pressed white shirt and black tie led them to the table. "What's the occasion?"

"Don't tell me you *forgot?*" Raven sounded hurt. But he was smiling, pleased he had surprised her. He'd begun to think it impossible.

Minerva looked up at him—he was about four inches taller—with a knowing smile. "Gotcha," she said. "It's the three-month anniversary of our meeting the second time."

Maybe a lot of couples didn't mark three-month anniversaries, but Raven and Minerva weren't your ordinary couple. Going through as much as they had together only made them more aware of how important their connection was, and of marking that connection. Beyond the sentimentality, this was another way of cementing each other in their memories, another touchstone. That was how memory worked: Big events seared themselves into your brain, and even when you had an eidetic memory, every little bit helped . . . especially when your very existence depended upon it.

His memory of her had kept her in this world despite her death, just as her memory of him brought him back from the other side. Each had the gift of memortality, as they'd come to call it, and each of them used it to sustain the other in a sort of symbiotic state that allowed them to go beyond the normal bounds of awareness, into a state of paralucidity.

Minerva decided on filet of sole, Raven ordered steak, medium-rare.

"You did good out there today," he said. "I was impressed."

"I still don't see what good this training will do. It's not as though I can actually be hurt anymore. I am dead."

"Yeah, but they can still take you hostage, like Jules did with me. Besides, what if your friends got into a jam, like I was, and you had to go up against some ninjas or something to help them out? You're better off having the skills to kick some ass, rather than being a victim."

"I will *not* be a victim," she whispered, her eyes narrowing.

"Didn't think so," Raven smiled. "That's why this training is a good thing. But I didn't bring you here to talk about that."

Minerva's frown vanished. It *was* good to spend time with Raven, just the two of them, to relax for a change.

"Before they bring the food, I have something I want to give you."

Minerva sat up a little straighter, and before she could stop herself, she blurted out, "You're not going to propose, are you, because . . . I don't think I'm ready for that. I mean, I love you, you know that, but it's just that . . . I've been alone all my life and, I'm not sure . . . There's that whole 'till death do us part' thing, and . . . it just scares me a little and . . ."

Raven reached a hand across the table and put it on hers. "Whoa, slow down, Min. Who said anything about marriage? Besides, I think we've got the 'till death do us part' thing covered. In case you haven't noticed, we're both dead—and we're still together."

Minerva laughed nervously, feeling a mixture of foolishness, relief and . . . was that disappointment? Had she actually wanted him to propose? She brushed the possibility aside and let herself relax again, looking him in the eye. "Sorry," she mumbled.

He caressed her hand softly with the tips of his fingers, then pulled them back again to retrieve a small box he'd been carrying in the inner pocket of his jacket. It was too big for a ring, but it *did* look like a jewelry box.

"What's this?"

"Open it," Raven prompted.

She did. Inside was a shiny silver necklace with a dazzling emerald in a teardrop setting.

"Emeralds are good for memory," Raven said, "or so I'm told."

"As if we need it," Minerva chuckled, smiling as she gazed at it.

"A little insurance never hurt."

"True. Where did you find it?"

"It was my grandmother's. She slipped it into my pocked just before we left the Between. She said I should give it to 'that special person' when the time was right—and I figured the time was right."

Minerva leaned across the table, and Raven did the same, their lips meeting in a soft kiss. She didn't think they needed any insurance. Either for their memories or their relationship—but it sure was a beautiful stone.

Dossier

Neil Vincent pulled at the corner of his mustache as he studied the dossier on his tablet. Nobody knew him by that name, except his wife and those who had known him in his previous life as a government official. To everyone who mattered now, he was Phantom, a code name he'd chosen for himself as director of FIN.

It seemed appropriate.

He knew he had only a few minutes before the information would disappear, erased by a program designed to remove all trace of what had been communicated. No nasty emails to be retrieved by congressional subcommittees. No paper trail for anyone to follow. He had to commit it all to memory in the next few moments, or it would be lost forever. It was ironic that someone like him, who lacked an eidetic memory, needed to work as hard as he could to muster some semblance of that gift in order to effectively track those who did possess it.

Carson (aka Anthony Biltmore, code name Triage3NxO1) had been busy trying to stay one step ahead of the agency he supposedly worked for. Phantom had allowed him to think that he was still in the agency's good graces—even that he was operating with the agency's blessing in protecting Minerva Rus and Raven Corbet. Of course, the man would always be suspicious; any good agent in his position would be, and Carson was better than good. Phantom didn't expect to remove that suspicion entirely. It would be enough to make Carson relax, to drop his guard just enough. Then, he would make his move.

Vincent shook his head. He didn't have the luxury of letting his mind wander like this. A digital clock at the top of the screen on his tablet was ticking: 45 . . . 44 . . . 43 . . . That was how many seconds he had to absorb what was left of the cyber-document before him. The title was compelling, if wordy: "Agenda: Create and Militarize a Force of Indestructible Soldiers for Use Against Enemies of the State, Foreign and Domestic."

An army of zombies, he liked to call it. He knew from studying Rus and Corbet that the memortals, like ordinary humans, had minds of their own and, as individuals with free will, they could be extremely dangerous. His job was to find a way to dehumanize them, to program them in much the same way a drill sergeant might break down a raw recruit in boot camp, then rebuild the person as an integral component of a killing machine. Such soldiers had one, and only one purpose: to follow orders without question. If he could find a way to harness the power of a person who couldn't die, whose wounds would heal almost instantly, and if he could multiply that power by thousands, he could produce a deterrent more effective than a nuclear weapon. Not only could a battalion of such memortals neutralize an entire army of common fighters, a strategically placed strike team could disrupt a terrorist cell like swatting a gnat.

This had been Jules' task: to find a way to assemble such an army. Others on the team would complete the process by breaking their will and reconditioning them to accept and follow orders without question.

He'd given Jules a lot of leeway in accomplishing her assignment. The reason was two-fold. One: the less he knew, the less it could be used against him. And two: she was the best at what she did.

Her apparent failure to neutralize and capture Raven Corbet had been surprising and regrettable, but it had produced an unexpected windfall: Minerva Rus' death and reanimation gave him another subject to study and, eventually, to form the cornerstone of the zombie militia he envisioned.

Amber Hardin-Torres could prove useful as well. Though she lacked the gift, Rus and Corbet were preserving her by using their memories. She was just as indestructible as they were.

All the information Jules had collected on the three of them was contained in this dossier, along with other data compiled by a variety of agents who'd been trailing them since Jules' unfortunate miscalculation in her encounter with the Rus woman.

Recommendation: Retrieve agent, code name JulesB6s4R, and equip to resume original mission. Priority alpha.

3 . . . 2 . . . 1 . . .

As he read the last line, it vanished.

Witness

"You're going to *what*?"

"I'm going to arrange to have you testify against Duke Malone."

"I heard you the first time," Henry Marshall said, pacing the few steps it took to get from one side of his cell to the other. "Problem number one: I don't know Duke Malone and I never saw him do anything illegal. Problem number two: your Mr. Malone is, as I understand it, the head of the Carlozzi-Sevchenko Syndicate. Kind of a hybrid Sicilian-slash-Russian operation. Bollocks, man! They're the biggest criminal enterprise on the bloody West Coast!"

Carson nodded. "That's why the feds are so desperate to take them down, which in turn is why this will work."

"So, let me get this straight: You want me to lie under oath so the feds can put away 'Special Delivery' Duke Malone, so his henchmen—you still call them that, right . . .?"

"Not really. Goons. Minions. Whatever."

". . . so the people who do his dirty work for him can rub me out?"

"They don't really say that anymore, either. You've been watching too many old *Untouchables* reruns. But yes, that's the idea. Except you won't get killed. The point is to make the feds think you're in danger of getting killed, so they'll release you into the witness protection program."

"I've heard of the Syndicate finding them anyway," Henry objected, biting his lower lip and scowling.

Carson stepped closer and lowered his voice. "Not when I'm in charge of the operation." It was true enough: The mob had never succeeded in tracing someone under his care once that person had been placed in witness protection. The inconvenient caveat was that he'd never *been* in charge of a witness protection case. He was FIN, not WITSEC, and he had no particular love for those jerks in the Injustice Department, as he liked to call it. Besides, they'd just gotten to the point that Jules wasn't chasing them, and now he wanted to pick a bone with the Syndicate and tell it to go play fetch? Not the smartest idea he'd ever had, but it was the best option he could come up with after Minerva had insisted they do something to get Henry out of jail.

Henry took a step backward.

Carson tried to modify his tone to sound more reassuring, something he wasn't very good at. "Think of it this way. Normally, the worst you'd get for evading an officer would be a year or two in jail . . ."

"But I wasn't evading anyone," Henry protested. "I pulled over."

"Yes, you pulled over . . . after which police determined you'd been transporting a fugitive and got involved in an OIS where someone—namely our friend Minerva—got herself killed. Cops don't like that. They have to go on leave, even if it's not their fault, while Internal Affairs investigates."

"And they get rattled. Cops don't like being rattled."

"OIS?"

"Officer-involved shooting."

"Ah . . ."

"On top of that, you broke out of jail." Carson could feel his tone getting harsh again. He wasn't used to talking this much. Explaining things to people who should be able to figure them out on their own wasn't his strong suit.

"Correction. The four of you broke me out."

Carson took a deep breath. "That's not how the court is going to see it. What it comes down to is you're looking at doing some serious prison time—right alongside people who *will* fuck you up just as much as Malone's people. And they will fuck you up, whereas Malone's goons won't, because I won't let 'em."

Henry cocked his head to one side. "Even if that's all true, it still doesn't solve problem number one: I didn't see Malone do anything illegal."

Carson relaxed a little. He was halfway there. "No one has to know that. Especially when you *did* happen to be working at Serendipity Medical Center on the night that Joe Kelly expired of not-so-natural causes in the third-floor recovery unit."

Henry didn't know who Joe Kelly was, but he figured he'd annoyed Carson enough with his questions, so he'd hear him out. The guards had only given him fifteen minutes of privacy with Carson (who'd identified himself as Henry's lawyer), and he didn't want to waste it.

"On the night of July 23 last year, when you were checking on a patient named Mike Thurber on the same floor . . ."

"I *do* remember him. How did you know . . .?"

"Yes. Well. A couple of rooms down from Thurber was a patient named Joe 'Shoeshine' Kelly, a compulsive gambler who owed Duke Malone a lot of money and also happened to have shagged—that's how you Brits say it, right?—Duke's girl. He'd done it before Duke met her, but it didn't matter. Revenge is retroactive. That's what they say in the mob. So, Duke had his godson, Jeffy Lomeli, dress himself up as an orderly and sneak into Shoeshine's room to put a nice, fluffy pillow over his face—for an extended period."

Henry opened his mouth, but Carson didn't give him a chance to object.

"I know, I know," he said. "You didn't see any of this. But there was someone who did, a nurse who was on duty that night and can place Lomeli at the scene, going into and coming out of Shoeshine's room just before he coded. Naturally, she doesn't want to testify, which is where you come in. You tell her story in court, Jeffy gets put away and maybe, if the feds get lucky, they can pin an accessory charge on Duke himself. Everybody's happy." Carson exhaled as though he'd just run a marathon. His mouth was dry, and he was getting a headache. Talking was extremely overrated.

"Everybody except the Syndicate."

"Which is what we're counting on."

"Right."

"It gives us an excuse to put you in witness protection. It's your get-out-of-jail-free card."

Henry shook his head. He didn't like it, but he didn't like the alternative any better: years in prison, if he could last that long, just for helping some new friends and letting them help him in return. Granted, helping one's friends didn't typically involve harboring a fugitive (even an innocent one) or breaking someone out of jail. But his friends weren't really typical, were they?

"All right, then. Tell me what I need to know."

Inside

Darkness. Perpetual darkness surrounding a keen consciousness, impris-
oned like a genie in a bottle. Jules was aware there was absolutely nothing to
be aware *of*, and the very fact of that awareness was maddening. She imagined this must be what it was like to be claustrophobic—except without
being able to feel any constraints. The blankness itself was a constraint of
sorts. She could walk as far as she wanted in any direction and still feel like
she was in exactly the same place . . . nothing changed. Maybe she wasn't
walking at all. Maybe there were no directions, as such. She opened her
mouth to scream, but nothing came out.

Think, dammit, think!

She still had her memory. There was that much, at least. And memory
was the key to everything. She just had to find the lock that it fit.

Minerva had somehow projected this darkness into her mind and
trapped her here. That meant Minerva must have experienced the darkness
herself. She needed a specific memory to use as a weapon.

If Jules could identify that memory, it would be a start. It wasn't hard.
There had been that time when she caught Minerva by surprise, and
Minerva had forgotten not to meet Jules' eyes. She'd sent her reeling back-
ward into a dark abyss.

Somehow, Minerva had escaped, but how? If Minerva had left any fragment of the memory when she projected this blackness into her, that fragment *would* hold the answer. Minerva was still inexperienced at this game
she was playing—immensely powerful, but undisciplined. If she had been
careless enough to leave even the slightest hint, Jules would find it.

She had to.

There was no light here, no way for her to see anything, if, indeed, there
was anything here to see. Clearly, Minerva had no memory of anything

visual during the period she'd projected onto Jules, but perhaps there was something else: a sound, a touch, maybe even a scent. If Jules could latch onto any sort of sensory memory at all, she might be able to use it as an anchor to pull herself out of this purgatory. It wasn't the real world, but it wasn't the Between, either.

She forced herself to calm her mind, which wasn't easy. The unending, brutal emptiness would have driven a lesser person mad long before this. It was only Jules' discipline and tenacity that enabled her to hold on for this long.

How long had it been? She had no way of knowing. With no external stimuli to mark the passage of time, it might have been thirty seconds, thirty minutes, or thirty years.

Embracing the void that surrounded her, she became one with it, willing herself to be as vacant as this place she'd been consigned to. The emptiness rushed in on her like a tidal wave, threatening to engulf her altogether, to absorb her. She bent with it like a palm tree in a gale-force wind, allowing it to flood in, to seep into every recess of her mind.

At first, there was nothing. Pure emptiness. But at some point, she heard the distant echo of a voice.

"Neurogenesis."

She didn't recognize the voice; it didn't belong to Raven or Carson or anyone she knew. The tone was clipped and clinical. A scientist, perhaps, or a professor. Or a doctor.

What did it mean?

Jules allowed her thoughts to expel the emptiness once again as she focused on that single word. It was easy to decipher: "neuro" related to the nervous system, and "genesis" meant origin or beginning. In the mouth of a professor, it might have meant something about the origins of human consciousness, but Minerva wouldn't have been in a classroom when she was sealed off in this dark existence. She could, however, have been in a lab, or a hospital . . . which meant the word likely came from the lips of a doctor or some other medical type.

Something must have been happening to her nervous system while Minerva was in this state. Some kind of new beginning. Jules knew that cells could regenerate, but in the central nervous system? Once you were paralyzed, there was no way to grow back cells so you could walk, except

. . . Minerva had been paralyzed. Somehow, using the gift, she'd been able to walk again. That's what the doctor had been talking about.

Still, the doctor would've had no way of knowing that Minerva had once been a paraplegic. The gift left no scars, no physical traces of healing. That was its nature. Everything was "as good as new."

The doctor must have seen continuing evidence that this t was taking place and Minerva must have had some awareness of what was happening or she wouldn't have been able to hear his words.

Jules wondered, *if Minerva had used the gift to reverse the paralysis in her legs, perhaps she had also unwittingly used it to generate new brain cells.*

Maybe being in this state even accelerated the process.

She didn't know, but the possibility allowed her to breathe a little easier, figuratively speaking, while she probed for the anchor that could get her back to the real world. Unfortunately, no matter how she strained her ears, she was met with only silence. Either she was somehow too deep inside herself to hear what was going on, or she had been left totally alone. Neither thought was encouraging. She felt the panic that had been stalking her scrape its claws against the doorway of her mind.

Again she blocked it out. There had to be a way out. There was always a way out. It was just a matter of finding it. When she did, Minerva Rus wouldn't know what hit her.

Anchor

The noise wouldn't go away. In a moment of clarity, Jules realized that the scraping noise wasn't panic, but an actual sound.

She'd been focusing so intently on finding an anchor, she didn't recognize it when she'd heard it. It hadn't been what she'd expected. It sounded like an animal clawing at a wooden door.

"Who's there?" she called. No words came out of her mouth because she was locked inside herself.

There was no sense of space here, but she hoped that by focusing her attention, she could will herself to approach it—or beckon it to come to her.

As she concentrated, a sliver of light appeared just above her and, once noticed, the scratching changed to a banging noise, accompanied by the sound of wood cracking and splintering. A moment later, light flooded her confines. Realization came that she was lying flat on her back in a box that, for all intents and purposes, was a coffin.

A woman's face, lined with age, stared down. The wrinkles didn't conceal the anger that lurked behind her eyes. In her arms she held a plump orange cat that purred insistently as she rubbed it behind the ears.

She recognized the face at once.

"Mary Lou . . ."

"Corbet. Yes." The woman Carson killed, on her orders some twenty years ago—the mother of Jimmy Corbet. Raven Corbet's grandmother.

It was the woman Josef could never forget.

Jules had given herself entirely to him: her heart, her passion, her loyalty. It had never been enough. He'd eventually left Jules—her name had been Irene then—in the hope that the Corbet woman would take him back.

Jules felt her own anger flaring, rising up to meet the fury in the other woman's eyes.

"How did I get here?" Jules growled, pushing herself up on her elbows and sitting up.

Mary Lou's nostrils flared slightly, her eyes narrowed. "I brought you here, of course. Not that I wanted to, dear, but it became . . . necessary."

Jules climbed out of the box and looked around. As memories surged, she recognized this place. She was in the cellar of the thatched-roof cottage that belonged to Raven's parents. A cottage that existed in the shadowy realm between life and oblivion called the Between.

It was here that the dead could be contacted and worlds imagined, could be made manifest, if one had the gift ...

Jules had the gift, as did Mary Lou Corbet. The legacy of the man they had both once loved.

Josef.

"What was I doing in the box?" Jules demanded.

"We put you there for safekeeping." The voice from the doorway across the room belonged to Jimmy Corbet. Like Mary Lou, he and his wife, Sharon, were deceased, but unlike her, he didn't have the gift.

"Let me guess," Jules said. "I just sort of appeared out of nowhere, right?"

It all made sense. When Minerva had been unconscious, she'd materialized here, in Raven's manifestation in the Between. She had projected the memory onto Jules. It stood to reason that she would show up here, as well.

It wasn't the anchor that she'd been looking for, but it would do.

"So why did you let me out?"

Mary Lou stood closer. She was short, about five feet, and hunched over from the arthritis that had set in during her later years. The old woman drew herself up in an attempt to appear menacing. "Because you started all this," she said, "and now it's out of control."

Josef

"What do you mean?" Jules took a step backward in spite of herself as Mary Lou confronted her. "What's out of control?"

"You came here looking for Josef, didn't you?"

Jules crossed her arms in front of her. There was no use in denying it, but what difference did it make? Hadn't Minerva gotten to him before she could? Hadn't she, in her own words, sent him "straight back to hell"?

"I don't understand," Jules said.

A different voice answered: "Maybe I can help explain things."

Jules felt as though she'd nearly jumped out of her skin at the sound of the voice. She hadn't heard it in more than sixty years.

Its owner stepped through the doorway nonchalantly, as if he'd just gone outside a moment earlier to smoke a cigarette.

"You look like you've seen a ghost, dear," he said, smiling that gap-toothed smile she had once found oddly endearing. "I must say I like the new hair color, Irene. I always did like redheads." There was a mischievous twinkle in his eye as he shot a glance at Mary Lou, whose gray hair still held traces of its youthful orange-red. She averted her eyes in disgust, and the newcomer shrugged. "What can I say? Blondes are just too predictable."

Jules forced herself into an expression of composure. It wasn't easy, but she'd had plenty of practice, and it was paying off now. "What are you doing here, Josef?" she asked, as calmly as she could.

Josef looked wounded, but she knew it was an act. Such pretense comes easily to a sociopath. "I thought you wanted to see me?" he said in a faux pouty tone.

Flustered despite her attempts to maintain her composure, Jules sputtered, "Well . . . yes . . . I . . . but you . . ."

"Now that's the Irene I remember," he soothed. "Always at a loss for words. It was a privilege to 'educate' you, dear. And fun, too—until you stopped being interesting."

Jimmy Corbet spoke up. "Look, I don't know why you're here, but you've overstayed your welcome. I'm afraid you'll have to leave. Now."

Josef didn't even bother to turn to face him but waved a hand dismissively. "Is that any way to treat a guest in your house? Is that any way to treat your *father*?"

"You weren't invited here, Josef," Mary Lou said. "You'll have to leave."

"I'm sorry, Mary Lou, but I'm afraid you won't be rid of me that easily. I made the mistake of letting you go the first time, and I've regretted it ever since. I think I'll be staying a while."

Hearing his words reignited Jules' anger, and with that anger came a renewed confidence. "I asked you a question, Josef," she said, her voice cool. "What are you doing here? It was my understanding that an acquaintance of mine sent you off in an entirely different direction.

"It isn't that I'm not glad to see you, lover, just a little surprised."

Josef waved his hand again, as if swatting a gnat away from the side of his face. "Does anyone have a cigarette?" he half asked, half demanded.

"No," Sharon Corbet said firmly.

Josef sighed. "I've gone this long without one; I suppose I can wait." He turned his attention back to Jules. "And if by acquaintance, you mean that trifle of a woman who met me on my way here before, I assure you, she had no idea who she was dealing with. I merely let her think she had diverted me. You think I don't know how to deal with *Das Geschenk*? I all but invented the thing you call 'the gift.'" He laughed wryly. "And to answer your first question, I'm here because I want to be. You may think you understand this place, Irene, but its existence was something I discovered very early in my research. I was exploring the possibilities while you were still dreaming of bedding those SS idiots in Leipzig, Fräulein Schönbein."

Jules maintained her detachment. Fräulein Schönbein was a name he'd used so often, that it no longer had any effect. When they'd been married, it had been his way of dismissing her. She wasn't really his wife, he'd say. He should have married the American girl, Mary Lou Corbet. It was all too far in the past for her to care—at least that's what she told herself.

"Why couldn't I summon you when I tried?" she asked. "What did you do to me? Are there wires in my head someplace that you forgot to pull out?"

Josef threw back his head and laughed. "Oh heavens, no, my dear. Nothing that drastic or complex. A simple hypnotic block I placed to keep your memories of me from fully kicking in. You'll notice, even now that I'm here in front of you, that you can't quite get a fix on me, can you? Try looking directly at me, and you'll see what I mean. Go ahead. I won't bite— we're past that point of our relationship, I'm afraid."

"That's enough," Jimmy said. He had no love for Jules, but he had no intention of seeing his home turned into a sparring ring. Stepping up behind Josef, he put his arms around the man and gripped him in a bear hug—or tried to. Jimmy had been a wrestler in his high school days, and even in death he appeared a formidable adversary, with a barrel chest and biceps that looked as if they belonged on a circus strongman. But when he went to clamp his arms around Josef, they passed right through him as if he wasn't even there.

Josef looked over his shoulder, annoyed. "Really," he said. "You're dead. I know this. I may be dead, too, but I understand how this place works. I advise you not to try that again."

Jules, meanwhile, was testing what he'd said. She tried to look straight at him, but whenever she did, he seemed blurry, shifting position, fading in and out of perception like some demonic will-o'-the-wisp. The only time he seemed clear was when she saw him from the corner of her eye. The instant she tried to look at him straight on, she lost focus.

"Now you see me, now you don't," he said, chuckling.

"Very funny," Jules said. She wasn't laughing. "Well, now that you're here, perhaps you'd like to accompany me back to the world of the living. We have some work to do that I think you'll enjoy."

"Work?" he said, pouting. "I thought you might have something more interesting in mind."

"No such luck," said Jules. "But, I think you'll enjoy this. There's just one little complication: I'm stuck here thanks to that 'trifle of a woman' you mentioned. Any ideas on how to get us back."

Josef shook his head. "I really should have taught you better," he said. "I can see I *do* have some work to do."

Salton

The sun drew itself up over the purple hills east of the Salton Sea basin and gazed down on a land that time forgot. She fixed an angry eye upon it and unleashed a silent tempest of heat and more heat, baking the ground into a hard, cracked wasteland. The edges of the so-called sea drew in upon itself, exposing thousands upon thousands of dead and rotting fish.

Birds flew overhead, oblivious to the creeping carnage that had become a way of life. Oblivious, that is, until they swooped down to feast on one of the fish that managed to survive in the toxic cesspool. The poison in its body would be transferred from prey to predator. The birds would perish, as well.

The Salton Sea had long been a way station along the Pacific Flyway, a migratory path for birds that wintered in the south, then in summer headed north. Now it was more a death trap. The birds kept coming and dying. They knew no other way. Pelicans and kites. Cranes and ospreys. Storks and plovers.

Sometimes the only sounds that could be heard in the all-but-abandoned "resort" town were the soft, incessant lapping of tiny wind-driven waves against the shoreline and the cries of gulls circling overhead.

When they'd first arrived, Minerva decided to take a walk along the shoreline, intrigued by some romantic idea of the inland sea. It was as if ghosts long departed had left their memories behind. Memories of barbecues and boat races.

Memories of before the sea turned sour. Whether they were real or her own romantic notions, it was hard to tell. She didn't think she could reach into the minds of the deceased and retrieve their memories the way she'd done with Amber—at least not when they'd been gone so long; turned to dust, the way the bones of the fish that washed ashore fell apart and turned to sand in the baking sun, creating "beaches" of bone fragments. This is what had greeted her when she'd reached the shoreline, this and the acrid odor of decaying fish against the fainter scent of toxic ruin.

She hadn't stayed long. She returned to their compound with the idea that once was enough.

Everything was unnatural here, from the dreams that had brought vacationers in the mid-twentieth century to the death and decay that had followed, all flowing from the accidental sea itself. It felt like a city of the dead. How appropriate, then, that three dead refugees should call this twisted oasis home.

The morning sunlight seeped like liquid sulfur through the window shades as Minerva gazed over at Raven, eyes closed, unmoving, and seemingly at peace beside her. She was jealous that he could sleep so soundly when her own dreams were filled with nightmares. Of her childhood. Of the police unleashing a shock wave of bullets as she stood there, inviting it. She could still feel the agony of them ripping into her flesh, her muscle, her organs. But that nightmare was easier to take than the one where Raven was taken from her, over and over, as he had been by the car accident in their childhood, and then again by Jules when she had kidnapped him. The nightmares with Jules were the worst. Each time she saw the woman's face in her mind's eye, she feared she was being sucked back into the Between, and that this time she wouldn't be able to find her way out.

Minerva was glad the dead didn't need to sleep. For Raven, it was a luxury; for her, it would be like diving headfirst into the Salton Sea.

Minerva pushed herself up on her elbows, then to a sitting position on the edge of the bed. She felt tired, but she chalked it up to the toll of the emotions that had been assaulting her these past few months. The dead didn't get tired. At least, they weren't supposed to.

She found her way to the kitchen and switched on the coffee maker. It wasn't as though the caffeine would do her any good, but maybe the taste would remind her of the morning jolt she used to get from a strong black cup of java.

"Good morning, Sis."

Minerva looked up and saw Amber sitting at the kitchen table, a faux-wood Formica-top model on spindly metal legs that looked like something straight out of the period. A lot of things here looked like that. The kitchen countertops were Formica, also. The cabinets were simple particle board with flat, no-nonsense doors and drawers. It was on a foundation, but it seemed more like a mobile home in a lot of ways, which made it the perfect fit for a ghost town where so many of the "buildings" were abandoned travel trailers and double-wides.

"What are you doing up?" Minerva asked.

Amber tilted her head to one side. "Who needs sleep?" she said. "I never liked it when I was alive—too big a time-waster. I'd rather be out doing things. Now that I'm dead, I don't need it, so why bother?"

"You've probably already done your morning run and workout."

"Twice." Amber laughed. "Not much else to do. Sometimes I feel like, when I died, I went to hell."

"Tell me about it." Minerva poured herself a cup of coffee and offered Amber one, but she met the offer with a wince and a quick shake of her head.

"If I wanted to drink poison, it'd be whiskey," she said. "I'd rather drink that crap out there than that stuff." She motioned vaguely toward the polluted shore.

"Suit yourself."

"I hate this place," Amber said. "I want my old life back." It wasn't like her to complain, she usually made the best of her circumstances. The fact that she was voicing displeasure now meant she really *did* hate it.

"At least we're all in it together," Minerva said.

"I guess." Amber looked away from her and out the window, where the sun was just now breaking free of the low-lying hills. "You have Raven. I don't have anyone like that."

This really *was* unlike her. Amber never complained about being alone. In fact, she seemed to relish it.

"I thought you liked being on your own."

Amber shook her head. "I don't like someone else complicating my life, no. But now my 'life'—or whatever this is—has so few complications, I'm bored out of my mind. No job. No future. I mean, what is there for me, Sis? At least if I had a partner in crime, it might be halfway bearable. Even someone like Carson."

"Carson?"

"Yeah, why not? Not that I'm saying I'm interested, it's just . . ."

Minerva shook her head and rolled her eyes. "I can just see it. You two would be arguing all the time."

Amber laughed. "Even arguing like cats and dogs is better than feeling like there's no one there for you."

"What about us? Raven and me? We understand each other, and we don't argue. Much."

"You both have the gift. I don't," said Amber. "Do you know how that feels?"

Minerva had to admit she didn't. She'd never thought about how Amber might feel as one of the revived who lacked the gift. She had no idea what to say. Consolation had never been her strong suit. "I'm sorry," was all she could think of.

Amber flashed a wicked smile. "Don't be. I don't want your pity. Just wanted to vent. I'm good."

Minerva didn't know whether to believe her or not. Should she take Amber at face value, as this superwoman who could bounce back at a moment's notice, or was it all an act designed to keep people at a distance? That, was something Minerva could relate to. She'd been doing it for most of her life. Except with Raven.

"Training today?" Amber asked.

"Sure," Minerva said. "We don't have anything better to do."

Testimony

Henry had never envied Raven and Minerva, but it sure would have been nice to have their eidetic memories about now. He remembered studying for his exams during sixth form back in Britain and cramming as much information as he could into his head during med school here in the States, but there was more on the line now. He had to pretend to be someone else—to swear an oath and get up there in front of everyone and lie as convincingly as he could. They'd already spent hours deposing him, so everything would have to be consistent with what he'd said then. Thank God they hadn't made him take a polygraph. He only hoped no one would see him sweat as he stepped into the witness stand, raised his right hand, and promised to tell the truth.

"You may be seated."

Henry placed his palms flat against his thighs, something he'd done since he was a child whenever he found himself in uncomfortable situations. He'd gotten in the habit of gesturing wildly whenever he got excited, and during a visit to his grandmother's home—adorned throughout with her prize collection of Hummel figurines, Russian nesting dolls, and music box dancers—he had once knocked a ceramic owl from its perch in an open display case. It had come crashing down onto a ballerina in a pink tutu perched atop what seemed to be an iceberg. The music box, which played the theme to *Titanic*, listed to one side and thereafter played a warped version of the already melancholy tune. After that, he'd learned to keep his palms pressed firmly against his thighs as a way of controlling himself. It was probably just force of habit, but it seemed appropriate here, too.

Dutifully, he recounted for the prosecution how he had seen a man dressed as an orderly entering the room of a patient named Joseph Kelly and emerging a few minutes later. He further recalled that, as he stood at the nurse's station filling out a report, he had seen a nurse enter the same room and, a moment later, call for a code, meaning the patient inside, Kelly, was unresponsive.

"Can you identify the man in the orderly's uniform?" the prosecutor asked him. "Is he here in this courtroom today?"

"Yes."

"Identify him for us, please—the man you saw."

"He's the man sitting at the table over there. The defendant." He pointed to Jeffy Lomeli.

The prosecutor nodded and turned briefly toward the judge. "Nothing further, Your Honor." He walked back and resumed his place behind the prosecution's table.

Now comes the hard part, Henry said to himself. He willed himself not to swallow and pressed his palms more firmly against his thighs. The defense attorney, a woman with deep-set, dark eyes and curly brown hair, rose and approached the witness stand. Her eyes appeared to be searching his face for something. A weakness. An opening. He didn't know what, but in answer he made an expression that was as placid and unreadable as he could manage.

"Now, Dr. Marshall," she said, "it has been your testimony that you were at the third-floor nurse's station filling out a report when the events you've recounted occurred."

"That's correct."

"Was anyone else there with you? One of the nurses?"

"Not that I recall."

"Isn't it standard practice to have a nurse on duty at every nurse's station in Serendipity Medical Center at all times?"

Henry nodded slightly. "Yes, it is."

"Would you say it was unusual, then, even notably so, and against protocol that there was no nurse at that station when you say you observed the defendant entering the room?"

The prosecutor rose. "Objection."

The judge, a bald, bespectacled man with a passing resemblance to Mickey Rooney, nodded. "I'll allow it. But please, counselor, one question at a time."

"Yes, Your Honor."

"The witness will answer the question."

Henry looked from the judge back toward the attorney. "Unusual, yes."

"And against protocol?"

"Yes."

"What if I were to tell you that there's no record of that nursing station going unstaffed on the night of Mr. Kelly's death—that, according to the staff report, there was a nurse on duty at all times?"

"I'd say everyone's got to visit the loo," Henry said, shrugging enough to pull his hands up from his thighs for just a moment.

A wave of subdued laughter passed over the courtroom, to which the judge banged his gavel and called for order. Henry happened to look at Duke Malone just then: the Duke was obviously not amused.

"Very well, Dr. Marshall. But if there were not nurses at the station, where did the nurse come from who entered Mr. Kelly's room?"

"Well, if she'd gone to the loo . . ."

"Come now, Dr. Marshall, you have no way of knowing she went to the bathroom."

"Of course, I don't," Henry said. "I have no way of knowing where she was. I'm not in charge of the nursing staff and, the last time I looked, I don't have eyes in the back of my bloody head."

The prosecutor turned to the judge, who admonished Henry, "A simple 'yes' or 'no' is sufficient."

"Your honor," the prosecutor interjected, "I have to object. This entire line of questioning calls for speculation on the part of the witness."

The judge nodded. "Sustained. Counsel will please confine her questions to matters about which the witness can be expected to have knowledge."

"Yes, Your Honor." She turned back to Henry. "Now, Dr. Marshall, can you tell me which patient's report you were attending to when you alleg-edly saw the defendant enter Mr. Kelly's room?"

"I can't recall."

"Yet you can recall very clearly the defendant's face, even though he was—by your testimony—dressed in a very different manner, as an orderly, than he appears in this courtroom today? Is that correct?"

"Yes."

"And you can recall the nurse . . ."

"Ms. Blomberg."

". . . Ms. Blomberg, who entered the room and called the code. Is that also correct?"

"Yes."

"And the fact that the patient in the room was Mr. Kelly. You recall that, too, correct?"

"Yes."

"Don't you think it's a bit strange that you can remember all these details, yet you can't recall the name of your own patient, whose report you say you were filling out when all this happened?"

"Good God, woman, I've had dozens of patients at Serendipity, and this was all over the bloody news the next day. I'd be an idiot not to remember it!"

The judge looked over at him with an expression that usually went with a waggling finger. "Yes or no, Dr. Marshall," he said, simply but firmly.

The judge then turned to the prosecutor. "Please wrap up this line of questioning and move on, counsel."

"Of course, Your Honor. I have only one more question for the witness."

"Proceed."

"Isn't it true that you yourself are presently in custody for transporting a fugitive, obstructing a police officer, and escaping from a county holding facility?"

"Yes."

"And isn't it also true that you have been promised leniency in those charges against you in exchange for your testimony here today?"

"It is."

"No further questions, Your Honor."

"The witness is excused."

Verdict

"I'd say that went rather well, wouldn't you?"

Carson looked at him blankly. "You never know," he said. "I could have done without the bathroom comment, though."

Henry shrugged. "Got a laugh."

"This isn't a comedy club."

True enough. Whatever the verdict, it wasn't his problem now. The court had accepted his testimony. Now all he had to do was wait for the jury to return the verdict and, once the bureaucratic hoops had been navigated, reclaim his freedom. He'd been taken back to his cell, but Carson had assured him it was just temporary. Everything had been arranged for his release and transfer to witness protection as soon as the verdict was in. This was essential. Carson knew that the moment the case was over, Duke Malone would have people looking for Henry. Even before the verdict, he'd been in danger. Hence, the need for a cell separate from the general population. Even his meals were brought to him, "like room service without the fancy silver tray," he had joked.

The jury's deliberations dragged on for the better part of the day; when that happened, it often meant the jury was having trouble reaching a decision. Carson used the time to coach Henry on the finer points of California-speak.

"You'll stand out worse than Johnny Rotten at the Bolshoi Ballet," he said.

Henry didn't bother to ask who Johnny Rotten was. Probably someone from before his time, or maybe an ogre from a children's book he hadn't read. But he was a bit disappointed: The ladies all seemed to like the accent . . . except for Amber, who wasn't impressed by much of anything. Still, he knew better than to argue the point with Carson.

"To start with, no more talking about going to the loo, okay? Just call it the restroom or the facilities. That'll get your point across."

"Right."

"It's not a 'lift,' it's an elevator. It's not a 'motorway' or 'M road,' it's a freeway. Got it?"

"Look, I'm not completely lost about this. It's not like I hopped across the pond just yesterday, y'know?"

Carson scowled. "It's not a 'pond,' it's a goddamn ocean. Are you *trying* to make this difficult? I have other things I could be doing."

Henry looked away in mock sheepishness. "Sorry."

"You've got to take this seriously. These guys will kill you if they figure out who you are, which is why we've got to beef you up about forty pounds, add some facial hair, and give you a new name."

"Got one picked out? You're an expert at this alias business, Mr. Carson. Or is it Biltmore? Or . . ."

Carson ignored Henry's needling. "As a matter of fact, I do," he said. "As of this moment, you're Eric Daly. That's so simple even you can remember it."

"Do I have a middle name?"

"William."

"As in the Conqueror. I like that."

The sound of footsteps halted their conversation, and a moment later a guard came around the corner, flanked by a man in a dark gray suit.

"Who's that?" Henry whispered to Carson.

"Shut up."

The guard slid his key into the lock and rolled aside the barred door. "Verdict's in," the guard said. "Guilty."

"Time to get you out of here," said the man in the gray suit.

"Excuse me," said Carson. "I don't believe we've met."

The man extended his hand in a single, sharp motion. "And we won't, formally at least. No names. Those are my orders. I'm with WITSEC. I'll take him from here."

Carson ignored the proffered hand, leaving it stuck there awkwardly as though it had been frozen in time. The nameless man finally withdrew it. "I'm his attorney," Carson said. "I was told I'd be handling the arrangements."

"You were told wrong," the man replied. "Now if you'll allow me to escort our friend here."

Carson knew his options were limited. He couldn't make a scene while they were still in the jail, or it would attract the kind of attention he was trying to avoid. But he couldn't just let the nameless man walk away with Henry. For all he knew, the guy was one of Malone's people, who could be counted on to dispose of the good doctor before Carson was able to track him down again. But if Carson didn't want to make a scene, chances were this guy didn't, either.

"I'll just tag along with you for the time being," he said, "to make sure everything's in order."

The man stared at him for a moment, then put one hand in his pocket and gestured with the other toward the door. "All right, but be quick about it. We don't have a lot of time."

Blackout

Never turn your back on someone you don't trust. It was one of the first rules he'd learned, even before he entered his present line of work. That went hand-in-hand with "Don't trust anyone unless you have to."

Carson wasn't thinking when he walked through that door ahead of the nameless man—and he wasn't thinking a moment later, after he felt a sharp pain in his temple where the man had hit him with something very hard. The next thought that entered his head, when he came around again, was a question: Why was the same prison guard still here, but Henry and his visitor were gone?

"You must have blacked out," the man said.

"Blacked out, my ass. That jerk you brought in here with you cold-cocked me."

The guard shook his head slowly. "I'm afraid I don't know who you're talking about. When I arrived, the door was open, and the prisoner was gone. I'll take you to the infirmary, but I'm afraid we'll have to hold you for questioning."

"You think *I* let the prisoner out of here?" *Of course not. Someone told him what to say.* Carson didn't have time for this. He'd put together this entire scheme to get Henry off the hook for escaping, now he was being accused of helping him escape again . . . all to get him out of the way. If the man in the dark gray suit was one of Malone's men, Henry was probably dead already. He had to hope something else was going on, but he had no idea what it could be.

He'd play along for now, let the guard take him to the infirmary.

෮

"I only left him alone for a minute. I swear." The security officer who'd been left to watch Carson was staring at the empty restraints on the hospital bed where the man had been lying just moments earlier. "They were secure when I left him."

The young man, barely out of his teens, hadn't been on the job more than a couple of months. Such recruits were often compliant but, unfortunately, just as often incompetent. The older guard raised himself up so he towered over the boy. "I told you to watch him, idiot, *not let him escape!*"

"I'm sorry, sir. Should I make out a report?"

"There's no point in that. He wasn't even here long enough to check in!" That wasn't the real reason the senior guard didn't want a report made out. The shorter the paper trail, the better. He wasn't working for the Los Angeles County Jail on this one; he had someone else to answer to. That someone wouldn't be happy when he found out Carson had slipped through their fingers.

He hoped the consequences for him personally wouldn't be as severe as he feared they might, but there was nothing he could do about it now. He turned away from the young security officer without saying anything more. At this point, it was out of his hands.

Fatigue

Minerva didn't want to keep up with her training, but she knew it was necessary. Carson insisted, and Amber seemed to relish it, even with Minerva memorizing her moves and, increasingly, fighting her closer to even.

Carson seemed even more demanding since Henry had been whisked away. He'd pursued what few leads he could find, but whoever took him was good at covering their tracks.

After a half-dozen or so dead ends, Carson had concluded he'd be better off returning to Salton City to make sure no one else went missing. He put out the word among his street contacts to keep an eye out for any sign of Henry. At the moment, he couldn't think of any other options. If someone that adept got his hands on Minerva or Raven, the results would be far worse.

Amber had been the most shaken by Henry's disappearance. As much as she liked to pretend he was a nuisance, he was the one link she still had to her former life. They were both doctors. Healers. They cared about helping people.

But they were different, too. She was dead, and he was alive.

At least, she hoped he was still alive.

Minerva sighed. "Do I really have to do this?"

Carson had them training with long bamboo sticks. He had gone over several moves with Minerva in slow motion, showing her how to parry an attack and use the energy of an opponent's offensive to her own advantage. How to strike down suddenly on her combatant's stick to dislodge it, and how to thrust effectively. Amber then demonstrated the lightning-fast method of twirling the stick in both hands to create both a defense and a distraction.

"That's all very cool," Minerva said approvingly. "But do you really expect me to carry around a six-foot bamboo stick in my purse in case some nimrod wants to come at me?"

Raven laughed, earning a scowl from Amber. "It's all about reflexes," she said to him. "And viewing a weapon—any weapon—as an extension of yourself. You can use it to absorb your opponent's energy or make it an extension of your own. Even if you don't have a weapon, training with one can help you learn your body's limits. And expand its capabilities."

"Okay, okay," he said, putting his hands up in front of him. "You're the expert here. I'm just a guy who played tennis in high school."

"Which taught you some of the same things," Amber said. "The racket was an extension of your hand, and you learned how to balance, shift your weight, attack and defend against your opponent's shots. This really isn't all that different."

"I suppose not," Raven admitted. "But you're making me tired just watching you."

"Now that you mention it, I'm a little tired, too," Minerva said. "Can I get a rain check here?"

If I'm dead, why am I tired?

"Not a chance, Princess," Amber chuckled. "Defend yourself!" She came at her swiftly, her stick spinning like a psychotic windmill, up over one shoulder, around her back, and out in front again in a blur.

Minerva lifted her own stick, but she was far too slow. Amber's weapon caught her on one shoulder, knocking her off balance. Before she could right herself, Amber thrust the end of the stick into her gut, doubling her over. She hadn't hit her hard, but she tumbled backward, dazed and out of breath.

"Sorry," Amber said, reaching down to help her up. "I thought you were ready."

"Well, I wasn't." Minerva glared up at her and hesitated, then took her hand. "Look, I really am beat. I don't know what's wrong with me, but I'm just not feeling it today."

"No worries." Amber smiled and pulled her to her feet. "Happens to everyone."

It doesn't happen to me. Minerva hadn't felt tired at all since she'd . . . died. Until now, which was odd. As she got to her feet, she felt dizzy, and she reached out to steady herself by putting a hand on Amber's shoulder.

"You okay, babe?" Raven asked, stepping out onto the mat toward her.

Minerva bent over and put her hands on her knees. "I don't think so," she said. "This is really weird. It's like I'm exhausted."

"I'm kind of tired myself," Raven said, putting an arm around her as she stood up straight. "Which is weird because—

"Because dead people aren't supposed to get tired," Minerva said.

"Yeah."

"Well, I feel fine," Amber piped up, "so whatever's going on, it's not affecting me."

Carson studied Minerva. Not only was she not feeling good, she wasn't looking good. She seemed pale and looked like she hadn't slept in several days. She still ate and slept, though not as much as she used to. It was familiar, and who doesn't enjoy the taste of a good shrimp dinner now and then? A good night's sleep held the same attraction. A soft pillow, a puffy comforter pulled up over your shoulders, a warm body to cuddle with— Minerva and Raven had learned the attraction hadn't faded one bit in their afterlives. But food and sleep weren't strictly necessary. Minerva shouldn't have dark circles under her eyes and her skin shouldn't look blanched, as though she had a fever.

"Something's wrong," Carson said simply.

Amber looked worried. "Yeah, I think so, too. We should have you checked out."

That was Amber's natural response. She was a doctor, after all.

"Where," Minerva quipped. "In a hospital for dead people?"

"No," Carson said. "But she's right. We need to figure out what's going on. We'll take you to the facility where we're holding Jules. That way we can make sure that situation is secure and check on you at the same time."

"Not *that* place." When she did bother to sleep, Minerva still had night-mares about the government medical lab where Carson had locked her up before he'd switched sides. Fortunately, the agency he worked for didn't *know* he'd switched sides. She hoped.

Regardless, she didn't want anything to do with that hellhole. She'd been held there against her will by that psycho psychiatrist Dr. Fitzgerald, who had tried to make her forget Raven. That had not gone well . . . for the doctor. He'd been the first one Minerva had used the gift against, as a weapon. Fitzgerald had wound up paralyzed, and two government goons who'd gone after her had ended up dead, courtesy of Carson's Baby Glock. None of that was anything she wanted to be reminded of.

Carson nodded once curtly. "It's secure and it's where FIN's scientists were studying the gift. It's the best place for you, under the circumstances."

From the look on Raven's face, it was clear he wasn't convinced. "Are you *sure* it's secure, Carson? Or are you just taking us back there to lock us up like lab rats? How do we even know whose side you're on? I'll give you this: You're good . . . at betraying people."

Carson stayed silent. In a way, he felt, he had that coming. He never expected to be forgiven for killing Raven's grandmother, and he *had* changed sides. But it had been a matter of conscience, not self-interest. Raven couldn't see inside Carson's mind to know what he was thinking, and his ability to play one role or another depending on the situation was one of the things that made him such an effective agent. It was a double-edged sword, though: You might be good at keeping your enemies guessing, but you'd have a hard time earning the trust of anyone who knew the truth about you.

He didn't have the luxury of wallowing in self-pity, and he wasn't inclined to, anyway. It was a distraction that limited one's effectiveness when dealing with the situation at hand. And the situation, in this case, was troublesome: Not only did Minerva look sick, Raven wasn't looking good, either. He wasn't as pale or weak as Minerva, but he definitely wasn't his normal, energetic self.

"We'll need to look at you, too," he said.

"How convenient," Raven snorted. "Take us both there on some pretext, lock us up, and you'll be killing two birds with one stone."

Minerva was staring at him. It was one of those looks that said, *I don't like this either, but he could be right—and what other options do we have?*

"I get it," Carson said. "You don't trust me. But Amber doesn't seem affected by whatever's hit you, so she can stay behind. If something goes wrong . . . well, if you had to choose anyone as backup, you couldn't do much better than a daredevil martial arts master who's also an M.D."

Amber smiled a self-satisfied smile. Carson didn't hand out compliments often, and Minerva's look changed a bit. This time, she spoke to Raven through her thoughts, something they'd discovered how to do when they'd been separated from each other thanks to Jules. *He's got a point. You may not trust him, but we both trust Amber. I feel like hell right now, and we need to figure out what's going on.*

Okay. I'd feel a lot better about this if Amber knew how to get in touch with us this way—through our thoughts—but she doesn't have the gift, so . . .

So, we'll have to trust her all the more. I don't have a problem with that.

Raven knew that made sense, but he didn't have to like the idea of going along with anything Carson suggested. *Neither do I. All right, I'm in.*

"Will you two please stop with the think-speak?" Amber said. "I might start thinking you're talking about me behind my back."

"Actually, we were, Sis," Minerva said, mustering a smile despite her fatigue. "But don't worry. It was all good."

Leipzig

Jules and Josef were walking through the streets of Leipzig, as they had when they first met. They'd never had what anyone might describe as a normal relationship, but in the first days it had at least seemed like something she could live with. And be happy.

Those days hadn't lasted long, with the war looming and the Führer demanding results from Josef's laboratory. Josef had held back the results of his most important work—his work on human memory—despite the danger of doing so. He thought his mastery of the gift would give him the leverage he needed to climb to the highest levels of the Reich, and he wasn't about to just give it away. So, he had stalled Hitler and his cronies by pursuing other avenues of experimentation on human subjects. Hideous and perverse "examinations" of "patients" that often led to their death, mutilation, and dissection, not necessarily in that order.

It was all part of a smokescreen, he told her in confidence, a necessary "unpleasantness," he called it, to ensure he preserved his position and protected his work.

As time went on and they grew apart, he confided in her less and less, no longer sure that she wouldn't reveal his subterfuge to the Reich. She was convinced this was the reason he had kept her around for so long: He was afraid she would betray him if he rejected her.

"Why have you brought us here?" Josef asked her, his tone devoid of his usual charm.

"This is where it began," she said. "And if I must endure your company, the least I can do is create a place, here in the Between, that holds some semblance of fond memories."

He shrugged. "As you will. It makes no difference to me. I will say you've conjured up a fair likeness of the place. It must have made quite an impression."

She ignored the remark.

"Why the hypnosis?" she said as they came to a small park. In another lifetime, they sat together on a bench amid the lime and linden trees from which the city took its name. "Why did you want me to forget you?"

Josef looked her in the eye. "I asked you to leave with me. You refused," he said matter-of-factly. "I knew then that you could not be trusted with my legacy."

Jules looked away from him. "Your legacy?" she spat. "How many people did you kill at Auschwitz with your 'experiments'?"

"As many as needed to die," he said. There was no emotion in his voice. He really was a sociopath. "It was all for the greater good, Irene. I told you that, but you wouldn't believe me, even after the gift I gave you. Tell me, Irene, where would you be without me? Rotting away in the cold ground like the others."

"Swine. That's what you called them. 'Little rats scurrying around, eating the crumbs of our glory,' I remember you saying."

The edges of Josef's mouth curled upward slightly and Jules' lips tightened. "You did me a favor," she whispered, "by clouding my memory."

"Oh, how self-righteous you've become, Fräulein. You know as well as I do that the gift is more than worth the price, or you wouldn't have come. You wanted me then, back when we were . . . intimate. You may not want me anymore, but you *need* me, Irene." He grabbed her by the shoulders and spun her around, forcing her to look at him.

She tried to wrench herself away, but he held her firm.

"Going somewhere?" he taunted. "Where will you go? You've already said you need me to get back to where you came from—back to the world of the living. Relax, Fräulein, we have all the time in the world to get to know each other again."

Jules ducked down suddenly, using his leverage against him and forcing him to release her. In the same movement, she tumbled backward onto the ground, somersaulted, and sprang to her feet, facing him in a combat stance.

Josef brought his hands together slowly and rhythmically in an exaggerated clapping motion. "Impressive, Fräulein," he said, nodding his head slightly in mock deference. "But our mutual predicament remains: Each of us is stuck here in limbo."

"So why don't you get us the hell out of here," Jules growled.

Josef smiled that gap-toothed smile of his. "I'm working on it."

Suggestion

"Are you sure this is going to work?"

"No."

Josef had been working on an idea ever since he'd been called back from eternal sleep.

Thanks to Minerva, he might have found a way to make it work. When she'd confronted him on the path to the Corbet house, she hadn't exactly sent him "straight back to hell," as she had so arrogantly put it in recounting the details of their encounter to Jules.

She'd inadvertently projected one of her memories onto him: the feeling of being drunk on Jack Daniels as she celebrated her twenty-first birthday alone in her bedroom. She'd gotten sick and blacked out. It hadn't been pleasant, but it came up short of hell by a good distance.

Minerva hadn't realized, while she was projecting that memory, that he was hitching a ride on the connection and sending something of his own. A hypnotic suggestion triggering her subconscious to remember him. By doing so, he ensured that she would unknowingly preserve his existence in the Between. Something, eventually, would trigger a conscious memory in the world of the living. That memory would bring him back.

All the way.

Jules seemed unimpressed. "That all sounds way too complicated," she said. "Wouldn't it have been simpler not to hypnotize *me* in the first place? If you hadn't put that block on me, I would have been able to bring you back myself."

"In case you forgot, you declined my invitation to join me in South America, Fräulein. We were still married at the time, and your decision wounded me. I was bitter." He shrugged. His nonchalance belying the intensity of his tone. "And since you chose to reject me, I didn't want you to have any additional hold over me.

"Besides, I didn't trust you. I still don't."

"The feeling is mutual."

"Nothing like a common goal to erase old grievances, eh Fräulein?"

"Ours was always a relationship of convenience." She laughed. "Now what do we do?"

"We wait for the trigger."

"Which is?"

"You, my dear. The minute she sees you again, she'll remember me in such vivid terms that—Presto!—I'll be back among the living."

Jules still wasn't impressed. There was no reason to believe that Minerva would ever have any reason to lay eyes on the comatose Jules. And if she did, who was to say Josef wouldn't just leave her in the Between to rot once he had returned to the living? Or that Minerva wouldn't find a way to banish him once she realized what was happening? She considered the last for a moment, then shook her head slightly. "She may not know you well enough to bring you back. Besides, she's too weak, too untested. She doesn't know what she's doing."

"Untested, yes," Josef said. "But she's far from weak. She did manage to put you in your current state, now, didn't she, Fräulein?"

Jules wanted to slam her fist into his smug expression. "I wouldn't brag if I were you. At least I'm still alive. You're dead, Josef."

"Not for long."

Lab

The medical complex was as Minerva remembered it, minus Dr. Fitzgerald and the two dead musclemen Carson had shot.

White, sterile-looking walls almost glowed in the fluorescent light. Mostly empty hallways led to examination rooms, labs, and who knew what else. It was a top-secret government facility. You wouldn't expect to find a lot of people wandering around.

Carson brought Jules here after Minerva locked her away inside herself and, she hoped, thrown away the key. She'd done that as much for her own benefit as everyone else's: Minerva had no desire to have anything more to do with Jules. Ever.

"Are you sure it's secure?" Raven asked.

Carson nodded. "I'm never 'sure' of anything. But everything I've been able to find out about Jules indicates she was working alone. Her motive seems to have been personal: a vendetta against your grandmother and everyone in her family. That's why she engineered the assassination, and why she wanted Minerva to forget you, so you'd go back to being dead."

Raven just stared at him. *An assassination you carried out, asshole,* he thought, but didn't say it. He'd said it often enough before, and no one ever seemed to listen. Minerva and Amber seemed ready to trust Carson as though he were the pope. Infallible. But not only had Carson killed Raven's grandmother, this supposed sharpshooter had missed a clean shot at Jules—he'd admitted as much. And now he'd lost track of Henry. He'd even been behind bringing Minerva to the lab in the first place, with the intent of forcing her to forget Raven and consigning him back to oblivion.

He was trying to keep me alive.

The voice in Raven's head was Minerva's. She'd overheard his thoughts. Again.

You want to be a spy just like him? Raven snapped. *Just because you can read my thoughts doesn't mean you get to do it without my permission.*

Sorry.

And while we're at it, yeah, he was trying to keep you alive . . . by killing me.

There was a silence inside his head. Raven couldn't tell if it was because she felt guilty for invading his thoughts or was pissed at him for going off on her. He got his answer soon enough.

"Well, I guess we won't be the kind of couple that goes around finishing each other's sentences when we get old," she said under her breath, but loud enough for Amber and Carson to both hear.

The others turned their heads slightly toward her on reflex, then turned away, pretending they hadn't heard.

Hey!

Minerva ignored him and raised her voice a little. "Hey Amber," she said. "Remember when I took a bullet for this guy here?" She motioned toward Raven with a slight tilt of her head without looking at him. "A bunch of bullets."

Amber shifted uncomfortably as they stopped in the corridor. "Of course, I do."

Minerva, this isn't . . .

"You'd think he might be as concerned for my life as I was for his, wouldn't you?" There was an edge to her tone as it moved beyond irritation. But there was something else there, too: a raspiness that hadn't been there before. Her voice seemed weak, a surreal contrast to the outrage she was voicing.

"Chill, Sis," Amber said. "You're not looking so good."

"That's why you brought me here, isn't it?" Minerva said. "Can we just please get on with it. If Mister Bossy-butt has no objection." She shot a steely glance at Raven, who met her eyes but failed to hold them. She wasn't acting herself. She'd always had a tough side that surfaced when she felt threatened, but she had never directed it at him. She wasn't looking herself, either. The fatigue she had shown during training was sapping her strength; maybe that was what was causing her to lash out.

Come to think of it, Raven thought to himself, *I'm feeling tired and edgy, too.* It wasn't as obvious as Minerva, but he could tell something wasn't right. He kept going over it in his head: Dead people shouldn't feel sick. He'd never felt sick since Minerva had brought him back, except . . .

They were walking again, following Carson through a pair of double doors and down another corridor that looked just like the last one. A few paces onward, they came to another door on the right that was shut and protected by a locking mechanism.

"What's in there?" Minerva asked.

"She is," said Carson, as he entered a six-digit code. One of two lights just above the keypad turned green, and a six-inch-square silver door below slid quickly open, revealing a flat strip of transparent material.

"Shouldn't we try to help Minerva first?" Amber said.

"I *am* trying to help Minerva," Carson said as he pressed his thumb to the surface of the material. "The more I think about it, the more I keep coming back to the conclusion that Jules has to be the cause of this. You needed to establish a connection to lock her inside herself, and she—or the connection to her—is draining you. Sapping the life out of you."

Carson pulled his hand away from the key mechanism. The door wasn't opening.

Raven stepped in front of him, into the narrow space between him and the door. "And you were going to tell us this when, exactly?"

Carson backed up a step, but he was more worried about the fact that the door wasn't opening.

Raven stepped forward, closing the space between them again. "How do we know you haven't brought her here as part of some trick to revive Jules?"

"Something's wrong." The statement wasn't directed at Raven, or at anyone in particular.

Carson heard the sound first, and the others turned a moment later to face the hallway they'd come down. The footsteps became corporeal a moment later in the form of six men, dressed in fatigues and outfitted in tactical gear, approaching them at a brisk pace.

"Now what?" Minerva said, her voice almost a drawl she seemed so tired, but the anger seeping through nonetheless.

A man who looked to be about six-foot-four with a military buzz cut strode up to them at the head of his companions. Ignoring the two women and Raven, he stopped directly in front of Carson, punctuating his arrival by planting his feet firmly on the ceramic flooring. He was not about to be moved.

"I'm afraid your clearance has been revoked," the man said in a clipped tone that sounded more commanding than informative.

Carson didn't flinch. "By whose authority?" he asked calmly. No wonder the fingerprint sensor hadn't worked. The key code, which was universal for all agents at his clearance level, hadn't been tampered with, but his own personal access had been denied.

"Classified, sir," the sergeant said, his rank clear from the triple-striped chevron on his arm.

"I want to speak to your superior officer, whoever he is," Carson said calmly.

"No, sir. Our instructions are that we obtain the assets from you and escort you from the premises."

"Assets?"

He nodded once toward Minerva and Raven, ignoring Amber.

"Assets my ass." Minerva's tone would have sounded intimidating had it not been for slurred speech that made her sound like she's just emerged from a dive bar after last call.

The sergeant ignored her.

"Over here, sailor," Amber waved at him. He obviously wasn't a Navy man—from his uniform, he was Army Special Forces—but Amber was trying to get his attention, and insulting him seemed like the best approach. There was no way in the world she could take on six trained Green Berets, even with her martial arts training. Numbers didn't lie, but she could. As much as she hated to use her looks instead of her brains, there were times when those brains demanded she resort to baser methods. And since she had her own "assets"—in the form of her toned figure and long legs—it would have been foolish not to use them.

"Hey, Mr. Squid guy." If she could distract him for a moment, Carson might be able to think of something. She had no idea what, but it was better than doing nothing.

The sergeant ignored her, but she noticed two of his men looking toward her out of the corners of their eyes. She smiled at them and tried to keep them distracted.

"Corporal, secure the assets," the sergeant commanded.

"Yes, sir!"

The corporal stepped toward Minerva, who had become so unsteady on her feet that it seemed she might fall over at any minute.

"If you'll come with me, ma'am," he said, reaching out to take hold of her arm, as he looked her squarely in the eye.

She caught his gaze.

"Don't 'ma'am' me," she slurred, but her eyes were razor sharp.

"What the . . .?!" He released her arm and stumbled backward, suddenly blinded. Arms flailing as he lost his balance and tumbled into the sergeant, who in turn lost his footing and fell into the two men who'd been distracted by Amber.

It seemed like a cross between an old Three Stooges short and a game of human dominoes. Minerva had projected the same blinding darkness onto the corporal that she'd used on Jules, except she had neither the strength nor the desire to make it permanent.

The two remaining Green Berets stepped forward to be met by Amber and Carson. The odds were more even, at least until the others recovered, which wouldn't take more than a few seconds. Amber pivoted as the first soldier advanced and wheeled a back-kick into his midsection, knocking the wind out of him. Carson, meanwhile, delivered a straight-arm to the throat of the second man, who fell to the floor gasping and grabbing at his neck. *They didn't teach you that in basic, soldier?* he said to himself, at the same moment swinging around to face the sergeant, who had pulled himself up off the floor and was lunging at Carson like a mountain lion springing up from a low crouch. Carson had no time to react before the sergeant's full weight slammed into the wall.

Raven ran toward Carson to help, but it was like his legs were stuck knee-deep in mud. He felt light-headed and dizzy. The last thing he saw was Minerva falling to the floor a few feet away.

The sudden wave of fatigue that encompassed him spread to Amber. She fell to her knees as she prepared to follow up her first blow. She'd been fine, but suddenly, whatever had been affecting Minerva and Raven hit her, as well.

Amber was all but unconscious.

Carson, thrown backward against the wall, reached into his shoe and pulled out a short blade, which he thrust upward into the chest of the sergeant, who screamed and rolled aside. Carson sprang to face the rest of the armed escort, only to see them in full retreat, the unconscious bodies of Minerva, Raven, and Amber draped over their shoulders.

The fate of their comrade was a secondary concern to the completion of their mission: the procurement of the target "assets."

The sergeant was just as expendable to Carson, who had only one use for him at this point. If he had the same level of clearance Carson had enjoyed—before it was revoked, that is—his fingerprint should provide access to the lab where they were keeping Jules, feeding her through a tube and pushing air into her lungs to keep her alive. Anyone assigned to this facility should have been given top clearance, at least temporarily.

It was worth a shot.

Carson dragged the sergeant up to the door and lifted the man's hand, pressing his thumb flush against the security reader.

He was in luck: The locking mechanism released and the door slid open. Lined with a few white cabinets on the left wall for medical supplies and equipped with a heart monitor and IV station, there was little to distinguish it from your standard hospital room, except that it had no chairs. With no visitors, there was no need for such niceties.

The bed itself was standard issue, as well. There was only one thing to distinguish it: It was empty.

Jules was gone.

Fading

Colors swirled through Raven's awareness, lights sparking and winking out against a backdrop of pinks and purples, reds and oranges. It was the way he'd imagined a nebula might look if he were traveling through some distant galaxy, probably based on some old rerun of *Star Trek*.

Min, are you there?

Her presence seemed more remote, more tenuous than usual, but she was there. He felt her.

At first, she didn't answer. He wondered whether she was still giving him the silent treatment. Then, finally, came a faint reply: *Mmm-hmm.*

Min, I need you to focus on me. If you don't, we're both dead.

Mmm-hmm, Raven. So tired.

I know. Me too. That's what this is about.

This?

C'mon, Min, focus. Please. She seemed to be slipping further into the void. The closer he got, the faster she'd slip away.

He could not exist without her, any more than she could without him. It was this reciprocity that kept them alive. Now it was on the verge of doing just the opposite.

Yeah, Raven. I'm here.

Good. There was still time. There was still a chance. But they had to act quickly.

Listen to me, Min. Listen carefully. Carson was wrong about this weakness being tied to Jules. It doesn't have anything to do with her. It's us.

What do you mean, it's us?

I mean we're fading, Min, and if we don't stop it, we'll be gone.

I don't understand . . . There was a brief pause, and Raven couldn't tell whether it was because she was thinking about what he'd said or because she was so weak. Then: *I haven't stopped thinking about you for a second. Not since I died.*

I know. I haven't stopped thinking about you, either, but it's the only explanation. We can't get sick, Min. You know that. And this is exactly how I felt when Jules was holding me captive and you were unconscious. It's the only explanation.

But how? Why?

Raven couldn't answer. He hadn't figured that part out just yet; the more important question was how to stop it. The colors kept swirling, and the lights kept flashing like sparklers on the Fourth of July.

What about Amber? Minerva's mental voice was, for a moment, stronger, more urgent.

She was right. Without Minerva, Amber would fade away, too. Raven remembering her didn't do much good; he'd only known her a short time. Minerva had entered her mind in the moments before her death, and in that brief time had learned as much about Amber as the woman herself knew. This extensive knowledge enabled Minerva to form a photographic memory of who Amber was. Using her gift allowed Minerva to preserve Amber's life so it would continue beyond death.

But now, she wasn't just keeping Raven alive, but Amber also. Was that somehow unsustainable? Was the strain of keeping two people sustained too much for Minerva? Was that why she was fading? Why they all were?

I think so. Maybe.

Minerva had been listening to his thoughts, but this time, he didn't mind. If they were going to figure this out, they needed to stay connected. Privacy wasn't an option. How ironic that he'd been wishing for it just a short time ago. Now he was thankful he *didn't* have it.

I think I have an idea, Minerva told him. *What if we go back to the Between?*

Why?

The more we fight . . . to stay in the real world . . . the more energy we use. Even her thoughts seemed ragged, coming in fits and starts, as if she were out of breath. *If the Between is halfway from life to death . . .*

Then we'll be using half the energy. Maybe less. We can make it last longer.

Minerva gave a mental chuckle. *I guess I was wrong about us not finishing each other's sentences. I'm sorry, Raven . . .*

No need, Min. It was good to see she still had her sense of humor. *I'm gonna start thinking about my parents. Just follow my thoughts, and I'll see you there.*

But Raven . . . what if we can't get back?

He didn't answer. His thoughts were already focused on his parents in the world his mind had created in the Between. The first time, he'd needed Jules to help, but he was sure he could find his way back.

Minerva sensed his confidence, and it made her relax, just a little. They couldn't stay here in the waking world, anyway. What was it Carson had once said? "Sometimes the best plan of attack comes after a strategic retreat." Carson had been wrong about a lot of things lately. She could only hope he was right about that.

Protection

Henry squirmed against the ropes that bound his hands behind his back, as he shifted position in the back seat. He didn't know the make, model, or color of the four-door sedan. The blindfold tied securely around his head wouldn't allow it. But if he ever found out, he made a mental note to cross it off his test-drive list. The seats had zero lumbar support, and the leg room left a lot to be desired. That probably had something to do with the fact that his hands were tied behind him and he continually felt the need to shift his weight from one "cheek" to the other.

"Where in bloody hell are you taking me?" he demanded.

The answer came from a voice filtered through what sounded like a ham radio. "If we told you that, it wouldn't do much good to put you in witness protection, now would it, Mr. Daly? And lose the British accent. It's a dead giveaway.

"And I do mean dead."

Eric Daly was the name Carson had given him, and Carson had told him to "lose the British accent," too. But these people couldn't be working with Carson. One of them had clubbed Henry over the head back at the jail; then they blindfolded him and hustled him into the car.

Whoever these men were, they'd gone to great pains to hide their identities. The only face he'd seen was the one belonging to the man who had ambushed Carson, and he'd been wearing dark glasses. His appearance had been about as generic as you could get. Clean shaven. Dark, close-cropped hair. Standard navy-blue suit, impeccably fitted and pressed, without even the hint of a wrinkle. He had no idea who was driving the car, the only voice having come from a staticky two-way radio.

Henry guessed from the stop-and-go traffic that they'd been on a freeway for most of their trip. After four grueling hours, the car swung off the road. Their speed became steadier and the road rougher.

Even behind his blindfold, Henry could tell from the light bleeding through that they were either facing the sun or out in the desert someplace. He felt sweat dripping down the back of his neck. Then he heard someone flip a switch, followed by an exhaling hum and the welcome feel of cool air circulating through the car. It was early fall, so wherever they were taking him was one of those places where the heat outlasted the summer. Maybe Palm Springs or Indio, from the length of the drive. Or maybe, if they'd gone farther than he thought, Las Vegas. At least there would be something to do there . . . but Duke Malone owned one-third of the city. It probably wasn't the safest place to be.

Maybe they'd taken him to the Mojave Desert, or even Death Valley. No one would think to look for him there, and there was a reason they called it Death Valley—a reason Henry didn't want to think about.

The car traveled a few more miles on the uneven surface, then pulled over, accompanied by the crunch of tires meeting gravel.

Henry heard the sound of the door opening, and felt the rush of heat from outside.

Grabbing him roughly by one arm, someone pulled him from the back-seat and shoved him away, nearly knocking him into the dirt. The dust swirled up into his nostrils. Wherever he was, it hadn't rained in a long time.

He half-expected his assailant to kick him in the shin or drive a fist into his face, but as he waited—and winced—he heard the sound of tires peeling out on gravel and the sound of the engine growing fainter in the distance.

Not knowing what else to do, he just stood there. The sun baking his skin with a dry heat. One that makes you feel like you're coated with residue of caked-on sand.

"Hello, Eric."

Henry pivoted at the sound of the woman's voice. "Hello?"

"Turn around again, will you? I need to untie you."

He did. The woman took hold of the rope that bound his wrists, digging between the coils to loosen the tension. Pulling it through the first knotted loop. Then the second. Then a third. His captors had wanted to be sure he was secure.

"They always overdo it," the woman said. "They don't seem to get that they're helping you, ya know? Why would you want to go anywhere?" She laughed.

The rope finally came loose and he flexed his fingers. A moment later, Henry felt her fingers at the back of his head, loosening the blindfold. He squinted as the glare of the late-afternoon sun hit his eyes. His view was toward the east, where a row of low hills met a bleached-blue sky. It lacked the smog of the L.A. basin but seemed just as dead and stale.

He was standing on a stretch of seemingly abandoned road that might have been paved, though it was hard to tell under the layers of dust and dirt. He could tell where the car had dropped him off alongside the road, but he saw no sign that other cars had been this way recently.

The face of the woman who'd untied him gradually came into focus. It was nearly level with his own, and she was sporting a pleased-with-herself grin. Her hair was naturally dark, he could tell from the roots, but she'd colored it purple, cut in short bangs across her forehead but ridiculously long in the back, flowing down nearly to her beltline. Her eyes were dark and her face was round; in fact, *she* was round, what you might call Rubenesque. The most distinctive aspect of her appearance was the multitude of tattoos that seemed to cover most of her available skin. Around her neck was a spider web with a teardrop ruby at the base of her throat. Her right arm was covered with fine lace, embedded with small images of skulls, animal heads—a panther, an owl, a wolf, a bear, a dragon—set in among scattered hearts and jewels. Her left arm bore a series of symbols ranging from a stylized pentacle to a pair of theatre masks to a dagger, all connected by a winding scarlet ribbon. There was something on her chest, as well, but he couldn't make it out, most of it spreading beyond her exposed cleavage.

He realized he was staring.

"What's the matter? Never seen a BBW before?"

He shook his head and looked her in the eye. "BBW?"

"Big beautiful woman. That's me, kiddo."

"I'm sorry, love. Didn't mean to stare."

"Love?" She smiled broadly. "I like that, but . . ."

"I know, I know, I have to lose the British accent."

The woman threw back her head and laughed. "That's not what I was going to say, 'love.'" She drew the word out teasingly for added effect. "I was going to say, no need to be sorry for staring at the ladies."

"Ladies?" Henry was confused. He stared at ladies all the time. It was one of his favorite things to do, in fact. Discreetly, of course.

She jiggled her breasts at him. "You know, the *ladies.*"

"Oh." Henry hoped he wasn't blushing. "I'm afraid I didn't catch your name." He stuck out his hand, but the woman ignored it.

"Paige Marie Daly," she said as she moved a step closer. He felt her arms winding their way up his back. "Your wife, remember?" She leaned in and pressed her lips against his; and it wasn't just a friendly peck on the mouth.

"There," she said, pulling back again. "That should help jog your memory. Or create one," she laughed loudly. "We have to put on a good show for the locals."

Henry looked around. There wasn't a car in sight, and no one in their right minds would be out walking in this blistering heat.

Daly. There was that name again.

This woman was obviously part of his "new life." His new identity. He wondered if she was in the program, too, or whether she was here to keep an eye on him.

He looked up and down the road. It was lined with largely abandoned double-wides and camper trailers interspersed among vacant lots. He and Paige were standing outside one of the mobile homes, which seemed to be hugging the ground like a scorpion hunkered down in the desert heat.

"That's our place," Paige said. "Nifty, ain't it? C'mon, let me show you." She grabbed his hand and started tugging, signaling that she expected him to follow.

"And where are we, exactly?" he asked.

"The middle of nowhere," she laughed. "Welcome to Bombay Beach, kiddo."

Hack

Carson looked at his watch and wondered about his next move. Maybe it should be to ditch the watch. Who needed one in an era of smartphones synced to the nanosecond via GPS? Still, it was a Rolex, and he'd grown attached to it. What he hadn't grown attached to was the idea of losing, something he'd been doing far too much of lately. He'd lost Henry, and now Minerva, Raven, and Amber—all through his own carelessness.

Worse still, he had no idea where to start looking.

He also didn't know what had happened to Jules.

He went over it in his mind again and again: If Jules had been moved, it meant someone had a use for her, perhaps thinking she could be revived. That didn't narrow things down much. Anyone who knew of her gift would be eager to exploit it.

But only one organization had access to the complex: the government. Specifically, FIN. Someone inside FIN wanted Jules moved; someone with the authority to not only make that happen, but to revoke Carson's personal clearance. So, the "someone" in question had to be near the top.

That's where the trail got harder to follow. The way FIN was designed, no one really knew who was in charge. Orders were filtered through regional contacts, using agreed-upon codes to confirm their authenticity. It was like the old speakeasy, where you had to know the password to get in but didn't necessarily know who ran the joint. Money was laundered, as were identities. Everything, it had to be assumed, was a front for something else.

The modern equivalent was a computer system. You had to keep changing your password every sixty days to avoid someone hacking your bank account or email.

"Please use a minimum of eighteen characters, including at least one numeral, one uppercase letter, one special character, one symbol from the Rosetta Stone, one from the Voynich Manuscript, and one from the Klingon alphabet."

It wasn't quite that complicated, but you had to make things more and more complex if you wanted to ward off hackers.

That was the answer.

If he could hack into the system, he could not only follow the e-trail back to its source, he could also find Raven, Amber, and Minerva. And, most likely, Jules.

Maybe Henry, too. His mistake in looking for him had been relying on informants. Whoever had taken Henry was too good. Information would never make it to the street.

Carson was good at breaking into data systems. Very good, in fact. But FIN had managed to disable his access to Grail, the program he had designed to infiltrate other networks—a fact that only exposed its limitations. Even with it, he wasn't sure he could have broken through whatever firewalls lay between himself and the elite of FIN.

For that, he would need help. And he knew just the man for the job.

Carson had known DeJohn Sutcliffe since they were juniors at Calabasas High. Back then, Sutcliffe had dreamed of being the lead guitarist in an arena rock band. The next Eddie Van Halen. That was John. He'd even added the "De" to the front of his given name to create the kind of stylistic moniker he thought would stick with record company executives, fans, and, of course, girls.

"You know, like Dennis DeYoung," he once said, ignoring the fact that DeYoung was the guy's last name and that he'd been kicked out of Styx.

As it turned out, Sutcliffe never got to meet a record company exec; never was even in a band, as far as Carson knew.

Like so many stoner-loners who became very good musicians no one had ever heard of, Sutcliffe was more interested in staying in his room, noodling around on the Stratocaster his parents bought him, than in dealing with the human race. "My fans have to like me; I don't have to like them," he'd told Carson. Only problem was, he wasn't particularly likable. He never got any fans, at least for his guitar work.

Not that he wasn't good. His parents never did complain about the quality of his playing, even if they did grouse about how loud it was before they finally broke down and bought earplugs. By that time, it had become clear that Sutcliffe's fascination with the guitar wasn't just a phase. At least they hadn't wasted the $599 for the Fender on a passing fancy.

As much as he loved the guitar, it wasn't something an introvert could make a living at. When he realized he'd have to actually join a band and go out on tour, the dream ended. The home studio he eventually bought himself was an indulgence, not a means to any career, purchased with money he earned doing the other thing he was really good at—even better than playing guitar, it turned out.

Sutcliffe was what people commonly called a hacker, or a cracker: a black hat whose business was to crack security codes, infiltrate computer systems, and provide the means for his clients to make—or steal—money. As with FIN, everything was under the table and off the record, which made him the perfect person to infiltrate FIN's computer network.

"I didn't realize you had anything like this in mind," Sutcliffe confessed.

Carson smirked. "I know you like a challenge."

"Yeah, you're right about that. But this will cost you. You got enough cash?"

Sutcliffe was always straight to the point, you had to give him that.

Carson nodded. "Fifty grand."

They stared out over Los Angeles from Mulholland Drive. Couples came here to make out, but not during daylight. No one really came up here before sunset, especially on the dirt section that was blocked by a fire gate. Carson knew how to get around that. Beyond the gate, it was isolated, which made it a good place to meet when you were planning to infiltrate a government computer database very few people knew existed.

That was one advantage: If they did happen to get caught, FIN couldn't come after them—at least legally—without exposing itself to the public eye. That was the last thing it ever wanted to do. "Compromise everything except security and secrecy." That had been one of the agency's so-called ten commandments, drilled into him shortly after he'd joined. He'd never officially joined, because nothing was ever official with FIN. Employment wasn't a contract, it was an "understanding." It could be terminated at any point and without cause.

Carson wondered why *he* hadn't been terminated, either in terms of employment or literally. His security clearance had been revoked, but he hadn't been dismissed. Someone must have thought he still served a purpose, a task he'd be expected to perform, either willingly or unwittingly.

What that purpose was, he didn't know. Maybe Sutcliffe could help him find out.

Carson handed over a bulging manila envelope containing his payment, and Sutcliffe put it in the inner pocket of his jacket. He'd known Carson for a long time; no need to count the Benjamins.

"You have the keycodes?"

"Yes, but they don't work anymore. They've locked me out."

"Doesn't matter. Patterns, y'know? Electronic signatures, echoes, ghosts in the machine. That's all I need. You got the laptop?"

Carson pulled a MacBook Pro out of his briefcase, which he opened and booted up. "All yours."

"Part of the payment? Oh, thanks. Didn't expect that." He smirked.

"Very funny. Where do we go from here?"

"*We* don't go anywhere. *I* take this puppy back to my lair and hatch it. Then *you* better hope it's healthy or you'll owe me more currency so I can put it in intensive care, if you know what I mean."

Carson didn't. Not exactly, anyway. He knew some of the tools Sutcliffe would probably need, but not all of them, or he wouldn't have needed the help. He was good, but Sutcliffe was better. One of the first things you learned as an agent was to put aside ego and admit when someone had skills you lacked. Then you could exploit the talent—and learn a little something along the way. That's why Carson was mildly disappointed that Sutcliffe didn't want to bring him in on the process. But he understood. As long as he got what he was paying for, it was all good.

"Fair enough," he said. "When will you have something."

"Give me forty-eight hours. I'll have something for you by then."

"Sooner? If possible?"

"If possible." He shut down the laptop and flipped it closed. "Nice doing business with you, Corky," he said, using Carson's high school nickname.

"No one calls me that anymore."

"I do. It's part of the price." He said it deadpan, so that it was impossible to know whether he was joking or dead serious. Carson had the same talent; in fact, he had perfected it based on his friendship with Sutcliffe, if anyone could really be called Sutcliffe's friend. But one thing Carson knew about Sutcliffe is that he would do a job if the money was right, and he wouldn't stiff you. There was still honor, at least among some thieves.

Detour

Maybe Raven shouldn't have been so confident. Sure, he could get them back to his parents' home in the Between. No problem. What could go wrong?

Distraction was one thing that could go wrong—very wrong, as it turned out. As he focused his memory on his parents, he was reminded of a story his mother had read to him when he was young. His parents didn't just read him normal bedtime stories; they read him detailed biographies, historical accounts, ancient myths. The goal wasn't merely to entertain or send him off to sleep: They were ways to exercise his memory. His parents knew about his gift, and they needed it to stay alive, but they had also wanted him to know as much as he could about the world. "You'll have an entire library inside your head!" his mother had once told him.

It had seemed like a good idea at the time. And it had been. But now it had caused his mind to wander at precisely the wrong time. His parents had once read him a series of stories that seemed, in the present moment, to have diverted him from his intended destination to . . . here.

Just like the first time he'd entered the Between, he found himself in a forest. But unlike the first visit, when the forest seemed to shift and shudder, this one seemed very much like a real place. The ground felt firm, the sky blocked the sun with a shield of gray clouds, and beside him stood an enormous oak tree spreading in all directions.

"Okay, what just happened?" Minerva asked.

Raven shook his head as he looked around, trying to get his bearings. "I'm not quite sure, Min."

"Where are we?"

Raven didn't answer because where he *thought* they were didn't seem possible.

"I don't know, exactly," he said. "How are you feeling?"

"Better," Minerva said. "You were right. I think coming here might have allowed us to save some of our strength."

There was a rustling in the underbrush off to their right. Raven looked over in time to see a brown hare scurrying away. The hare appeared to have been startled by a rapid, rhythmic tapping from high up in a nearby birch: the sound of a woodpecker announcing its territory. A nuthatch in a nearby rowan tree abandoned its perch, as did a jay, which began chasing it for sport.

A moment later, there was another rustling nearby, and Raven realized it might not have been the woodpecker that had spooked the hare and the other birds. This rustling seemed farther away, but grew louder as something trampled on fallen leaves. The sound seemed to rip through the thick woods.

Raven and Minerva instinctively took a few steps backward, sheltering under the massive oak As they did, a twelve-point royal stag burst through a thicket off to their right, bounding past them in a rush of hooves and antlers. Raven found his back hugging the tree as he watched the animal fly past, turning his eyes again toward the place where it had emerged as he heard the sound of branches breaking. Something, or someone, was in pursuit.

An instant later, a small man wearing a dirty green cloak over a brown shirt emerged from the thicket. The horse he rode, an unremarkable light brown steed of average size, hadn't been prepared for the sight of Minerva and Raven just a few steps off its intended course. It reared and nearly threw the man from its back, breaking off the chase. It danced nervously in a circle, backing away from the two strangers.

"*Wearg rounsey!*" the man said under his breath in a voice that, even in just those two words, they could tell was thickly accented. He dismounted hurriedly and stomped to the place where his hat had landed in the dirt. "*Wearg haet!*"

The man seemed scarcely to be paying attention to them. Raven took Minerva's hand and started inching toward the other side of the tree. If they could get clear of his field of vision, they could perhaps go unnoticed. He obviously had a temper, and there was no use antagonizing him.

"What language is *that*?" Minerva asked, leaning in to whisper in Raven's ear.

"English, I think. He said something that sounded like 'hat,' and 'rounsey' ... I think that's a kind of horse."

The man walked up to the horse, which had calmed and stood minding its own business. He swatted at its hindquarters with the cap. The horse, taking offense, whinnied loudly and ran off.

Minerva continued her conversation with Raven mind to mind. Better not to draw any more attention than necessary. *That's not like any English I've ever heard. What does "wearg" mean?*

Probably dammit, or maybe something worse.

"*Incer! Astende!*"

The man had turned and was staring straight at them, pointing with a drawn sword. He approached in a measured stride that was as ominous as it was methodical.

Minerva looked at Raven.

I have no idea. Either he wants us to stand where we are, or he thinks we're astounding. Maybe both?

"No comprendo," Minerva ventured.

That won't work. He's not speaking Spanish.

Well, it's the only other language I know any words in. You got a better idea?

Raven had to admit he didn't. What was bothering him was the fact that he'd obviously taken them someplace in the Between where he didn't know the language. That meant this place somehow existed independently, at least to some degree. It was more a destination than a creation, which meant he had less control than he would have if they had landed in his own memory.

The man stopped a few paces away, looking them up and down. The anger seemed to have drained from his face as recognition dawned.

"By the beads of the blessed Mary, thou art one of those!"

Now he's speaking like Shakespeare, Minerva offered.

Maybe he's bilingual?

"I'd attempt no escape, were I thou. Anon, mine own men hast encircled this clearing."

"We mean no harm," Raven said, putting his hands down and opening his palms in front of him. "I don't even know how we got here."

"You got here by remembering, lad." Now his language was closer to modern English, but still with the same thick accent. He stroked his scruffy chin. "I'd say . . . southwest side of the New World, about the nineteen-hundred and eightieth year of our lord."

"Close," Minerva said. "L.A. area, 2016."

He put his cap back on without bothering to dust it. It was plain from his body odor that he'd gone without bathing for days. Or weeks.

"Can't get 'em all right," he shrugged. "The gifted and revived come here from all times. We try to make sense of their tongues when they land, and we do a fair job of it. Those of us who are gifted pick them up quickly enough."

So, he's gifted, Minerva commented.

Guess so. Looks like there are more of us than we thought.

The man turned and put two fingers to his lips, letting go a shrill whistle. Almost at once, three men emerged from the undergrowth. Two of them were shorter than Raven and Minerva, barely five and a half feet, but the third was a bear of a man who looked a full foot taller and significantly bigger around than either of his companions.

The man they'd been talking to, who appeared to be their leader, stepped toward Raven. "I believe introductions are in order," he said, extending his hand to grip Raven's. "I'll begin with myself. Roger is the name, and these are my lands." He made a sweeping gesture with his hand.

"Roger," said Raven, more than a hint of skepticism in his voice. "I would have sworn your name would be . . ."

Minerva finished the sentence for him: "Robin Hood?"

The man scowled and released Raven's hand. "Everyone who comes here does," he said, spitting off to the side into the dirt. "The shire-reeve who thinks he owns the woods pinned that name on me, but you will never hear me use it. If you value your life, you'll keep it from your lips, as well."

Raven thought it best to change the subject. "Aren't you worried about your horse?"

"He's not my horse, technically speaking. Stole him off some dead nobleman. I won't tell you how the man got to be dead, so don't ask." He winked. "Besides, Trelaine always finds his way back. Not that he's worth keeping, but I'm used to him."

This brought a laugh from the others, who acted like they were gathered around a table in some English pub for a pint, except that they'd gathered around Raven and Minerva. It was an uncomfortable feeling, no matter how jovial the group seemed. Each man had his hand on the hilt of his sword. That didn't help.

"I'm John," the big man said, doffing his cap and taking an exaggerated bow toward Minerva, ignoring Raven completely.

"William," said one of the others, touching the brim of his own cap.

"Miller," said the third, seeming reluctant and somewhat distracted. He looked to be the youngest, shuffling his feet and staring at the ground.

"You're no miller," the big man scoffed. "Your *father* is a miller. He made a good, honest living. You didn't have to go about poaching in the Shire Wood."

"We've been over that," the smaller man snarled. He seemed to have even more of a temper than Roger, and despite his short stature, he looked to be no weakling. Like Roger, they all seemed able to speak modern English, even if it was spiced with occasional words from an earlier age.

"Tangle with me, would you, lad?" the big man answered, puffing out his chest. "I'd think better of that if I were ye."

The man who'd called himself Miller glared at the big man and seemed to be restraining himself from lunging.

"Or go on," John said. "If you think you're so much. You ain't so much a miller, son. You ain't so much at all."

"Too much for you," the smaller man breathed in a voice low enough that Raven could tell he couldn't decide whether he wanted the bigger man to hear him.

"Enough!" Roger said, sticking out his sword in the small space that separated the two men. "Be quiet about it or I'll send ye both to the fountains and let our friend the friar put the fear of God in ye."

Miller backed up a step, but John held his ground and shot a warning glance at Roger. "I'm not afraid of getting wet, Robin. I'm not scared of your friar, and I'm not afraid of ye!"

In a flash, Roger jumped between the two men, shoving Miller roughly out of the way, pressing himself against the larger man's barrel chest. "That's not my proper name, John, and I'd thank you to take it back and apologize."

The bear-man threw back his head and laughed.

"You think this a comedy, little man?" Roger said. "We all know why they call you a *little man*, do we not?"

John's laugh vanished into less than an echo and, reaching out with both arms, he snatched Roger up off the ground in a bear-hug.

"Gentlemen, gentlemen, please," William said. "Our code requires that such disputes be settled by a test of skill. A trial with the longbow, to be exact. Shall we therefore adjourn and reconvene at our encampment an hour hence, where we might decide this issue with honor and decorum?"

The big man laughed again, dropping Roger roughly. "Honor? Decorum? We're outlaws, Will."

"We still have a code," Roger said. "And we'll live by it. Mother of God, we'll live by it."

"What's wrong, Robin?" the larger man said in mock sympathy. "No stomach to settle things like a man?" He raised a fist and shook it, half-playfully. "Who's the little one now, eh? But I've beaten you before with the bow. I'll beat you again, by God!"

Are these people who I think they are? Minerva asked.

Raven just nodded. There was a rustle in the trees nearby.

"Wearg, ye men!" Roger hissed. "Haven't I told ye to keep quiet? Now the shire-reeve may have found us. Disperse now and we shall all meet back at camp."

John nodded. He was willing to challenge Roger in single combat, but he also seemed ready to take his orders, if it came to that. "I'll take these two," he said, grabbing Minerva by a wrist and clapping a giant hand around the back of Raven's neck.

I was hoping they'd forgotten us, Minerva said in her thoughts to Raven. But it wasn't Raven who answered. It was Roger.

We have been at this for hundreds of years, now. We forget nothing. It is our business to remember.

Aim

Roger pointed to a birch tree about twenty paces from where he stood.

"Child's play," John scoffed. He nocked an arrow, took aim, and let fly. The arrow struck the trunk of the tree square in the center.

"Some refreshment, milady?" It was William, who had retrieved a water pouch from a tent in the encampment and filled it from a nearby stream.

"Thank you," Minerva said, taking a drink and passing it to Raven. William's eyes never left Minerva's face. Raven had noticed that Minerva received a lot more attention than he did. It wasn't surprising. She was, as far as he could tell, the only woman there.

"Did John say he beat Roger in an archery contest?" Minerva asked. "I thought Robin Hood never lost."

William laughed and shook his head. "That's what he'd like you to believe, just like he'd like you not to remember that name the shire-reeve calls him."

"Sorry."

"Robin Hood's more of a title than anything. There've been dozens of men called that around the shire and throughout the midlands. A badge of dishonor, if you will."

"Like a scarlet letter?"

William laughed again, this time ruefully. It was the title of a story written six centuries after his time, but he'd heard another visitor mention it. It hadn't been funny then, and it wasn't now. Roger wasn't the only outlaw whose name got butchered.

"Very funny, Miss. It's a good thing you're so comely, or I'd have to challenge you on that one, the way John did Roger. The name's not Scarlet, Miss, it's Scadlock. Not as euphonious, I grant, but my father's name is one of the few things I'm proud to have kept in this life. It's the same with Much the Miller over there, although he says he hates his father."

"Much?"

Will shrugged. "I'm not sure why we call him that. But there is much more to him than he'll let you see at his first encounter."

Minerva looked Will up and down. Of the bunch, he was the best dressed, wearing a long-sleeved shirt, gold-trimmed jerkin, and navy blue cloak. It wasn't scarlet, as the tales described it.

I guess you can't believe everything you read.

No, you can't. The voice in her head was Scarlet's . . . er . . . Scadlock's.

"You have the gift, too, then?"

"Aye, me and Roger. That's why he's the leader of our merry band. Not everyone with the gift can hear another man's thoughts, but we've had hundreds of years to practice."

"But John doesn't have the gift? Or any of the others?" Minerva asked.

Will nodded. "That's why Roger has the advantage," he said. "All things being equal, John's his better. He once knocked Roger into a river during a battle of staves and, yes, he has defeated him with the longbow—although that's not a regular occurrence—even without the gift. That's how good he is. If Roger didn't have the gift, he'd have no chance against John Lyttel."

As they spoke, the contest continued. Having taken his shot, John stood aside, and Roger planted his feet in the exact same spot where the big man had taken up his stance. He nocked his arrow, took aim, and, without the least hesitation, fired. The arrow found its target within an inch of John's.

"See, Milady?" Scadlock said. "Roger studied every detail of John's aim and delivery, and he reproduced it with near perfection. A thing of beauty, is it not?"

The contest seemed like a game of H-O-R-S-E in playground basketball, with one difference: The first man got to call his opponent's shot in the outset, rather than having to make it first himself.

"Now John gets to call the shot, and Roger will lose his advantage," Scadlock explained. "But even if he cannot see an opponent shoot first, his skills are still exceptional."

John returned to the same spot, but this time, he gestured to a large oak that looked to be a hundred and fifty yards away. "Third branch up on the right," he said confidently.

Roger stepped to the mark, shaking his head.

"That's how John beat him the last time," Scadlock whispered. "Called out a target too far away. Roger might have the gift, but John's got something even the gift can't match when it comes to distance. Brute strength."

Roger took aim, steadied his hand, and waited a moment. Then he let the arrow go.

It landed in the grass, some ten paces short of the target.

John slapped him across the shoulders as Roger yielded the mark to him. "Not such a *little* distance, eh, Robinhod?"

Roger said nothing, but stood back and waited patiently as John took his stance and set his own sights on the target. He wasn't as sure of himself this time, drawing a bead, then angling his longbow up slightly, then somewhat to the left. Finally, when he seemed satisfied, he released the arrow.

Raven and Minerva watched it fly farther than they would have believed possible. There was never any doubt that it would surpass the distance covered by Roger's shot. Instead of striking its intended target, it flew a good two feet above the branch, hit a clump of smaller branches and tumbled harmlessly to earth.

"You aim too high, little one," Roger joked, returning John's pat across the shoulders as the larger man shrugged and walked away.

"Worth a try," he said.

William chuckled, took a drink from the pouch, then returned it to Minerva.

"Where's Maid Marian?" she asked as she took it.

William shook his head. "Everyone asks about *her*. There is no such person. I asked someone who passed through once where they got the notion that we had a woman among us. He said he'd read it in a romance. He said people performed what he called 'Robin Hood Games' on the village green every May Day. Someone must've fancied Roger had a girlfriend, but look at this place. Does this seem like somewhere a well-born lady would make her home?"

Minerva looked around her. It wasn't so bad. At least it was better than being cooped up in her bedroom, the way she had been most of her life.

Raven spoke up: "Robin's . . . I mean Roger's devotion to the Virgin was well known in the tales my parents read me. Maybe someone mistook that as romantic love for a real woman."

William considered and nodded. "Perhaps. From what we have heard from people who've traveled this way, any number of false tales have been told about poor Roger. As I said, there were dozens of outlaws and vagrants called 'Robin Hood' in our time—some more notable than others. Roger was the most accomplished of the lot, but tales about some of the others must have crept into his legend as it grew."

"Many in our time consider him *just* a legend," Raven said.

While they were talking, Roger had set a new mark and indicated a new target about forty paces away. John struck a glancing blow off a large rock embedded in the earth, and Roger followed with a straight-on strike. Nonetheless, both agreed that John's shot was sufficient for the contest to continue.

"You said others have been here?" Raven asked. "Roger said something about that, too."

"Aye, that's how we learned your tongue. We've been visited by men and women across centuries. Scores, perhaps even hundreds. We've turned into kind of a—what do you call it in your time—a 'theme park' in this place between life and death. They all want to see the famous Robin Hood, and I have to stop Roger from running them through every time he hears that name. There were two named Shakespeare and Bacon, both of whom had the gift, although the latter claimed the other man stole his work. They were so annoying that we made them shoot to determine which of them was to be believed."

"Who won?"

There was a glint in William's eye. "We agreed not to tell."

"I didn't know the Between had been here that long."

"Only people who have the gift and those they bring here ever see it, and it is what we make it, after all. The holy mother church knows about it but, like everything else, Rome has fear of things she doesn't understand. The cardinals and archbishops think it's a kind of witchcraft, so they call it Purgatory—where they send people to be purged of their sins. Of course, that doesn't happen. The church doesn't send anyone here, and there's no purging going on . . . although we have run across a few people we would like to purge from our midst!"

He winked, as if he thought they'd understand.

"But if the Between has been here for centuries, that means Josef didn't invent it," Raven said.

"Did you say 'Josef'?" The gleam in Scadlock's eye fled as if it had never been there.

"You know him?"

William nodded. "He came poking around the shire a few days ago. Told us he wanted to do some kind of experiments to 'enhance' our gift. Went on about how this place was really something called the collective unconscious and that we could all control it better if we worked together—under his direction, of course. When we told him we were managing just fine without him, he started getting nasty. Roger showed him the door."

One corner of Minerva's mouth turned up in a half-smile. "I did the same thing."

"Good," William said. "We may be outlaws, but we do what we have to." His face brightened and he winked again. Raven wasn't too happy about the winks being sent in Minerva's direction—but he kept his mouth shut. Scadlock had a roguish quality that made Raven uneasy, but what did he expect from an outlaw? Besides, he was feeding them valuable information, and he didn't want to let his jealousy get in the way of that.

What he questioned was Roger's ability, or even Minerva's, despite the strength of her gift, to put Josef in his place for long. Josef might not have invented the Between, but he'd made studying the gift his life's work—an obsession, even. That meant he knew more about it than Minerva, or perhaps even Roger, who seemed more interested in shooting his longbow and reliving past glories than finding out more about how to use the gift.

The archery contest continued. John had identified another long-distance target for Roger, a beehive in a large oak about seventy yards away. Roger shot him a look like he was crazy.

"Are ye afraid of some puny insects a-way over there?" he chided. "Come, come, now. That's my target for ye. Shoot for it or forfeit the challenge."

Roger gave him another look that suggested John was even crazier for suggesting a forfeit. The big man responded with one of his belly laughs.

Roger stepped to the mark, took aim, and launched the arrow with less hesitation than before. It sliced through the air, its feathers steadying its path, its bowman's aim directing it precisely where he had wanted it to go. The beehive swung backward with the force of the arrow, and a cloud of frenzied insects rose from it. For a moment, it seemed as if the hive were suspended in midair. Then it came crashing to the ground. The bees swirled in a miniature tornado.

"That settles it then," Roger said, resting his bow against the trunk of a nearby birch.

John drew himself up and threw his head back. "It settles nothing," he said. "I've not had my turn yet!"

Roger smiled at him. "There is no turn to have, Little One. With the hive dislodged, thy shot would not be the same. So, the match is forfeit . . . unless you'd care to cross yon meadow and restore the hive to its previous place."

John looked across the clearing, where the angry bees were still circling around their ruined home.

"What is this?" William called out at him. "Is the mighty, fearsome John afraid of a few little insects?"

John turned toward him. "Not if the insect is a maggot with a blue cloak and a dull wit." The big man's irritation vanished as something caught his attention and he wheeled about.

There, across the meadow, a half-dozen men on horseback broke through the trees and began riding straight toward them. The bees, in their fury, buzzed at the men's backs and around their heads as their arms flailed and they pushed their horses at a gallop.

"The shire-reeve and his men!" John shouted.

"No time to pack up camp," Roger said. "Get what you need and get out of here. Now! We'll meet up at Barnsdale in a fortnight."

He turned to Raven and Minerva. "You two are on your own for now." He bowed, doffed his cap briefly and turned away, shouting over his shoulder as he went: "I would advise you to move quickly. You will not find the shire-reeve as gracious a host!"

Minerva grabbed Raven's hand and they turned to run, heading through the trees away from their pursuers. No sooner had they eluded the men chasing them, than they found themselves face to face with a man standing directly in their path, brandishing a sword. If they hadn't been right on top of him, they might have avoided him. He was garbed in a horsehide cloak that hid him well beneath the trees and clouded sky.

He said something neither of them could understand. All they could make out were the last three words: "Guy of Gisborne."

Minerva stepped in front of Raven, looked at the man's sword, then raised her eyes to meet his. "I don't have time for this."

The man didn't flinch, a devious smile crawling across his thin lips.

Raven tried to stop her. *Min, I wouldn't. You don't know what . . .*

Her focus was entirely on the man in front of her. *Think that little pointy thing's going to stop me? Welcome to the twenty-first century, moron.*

She unleashed one of her most potent memories. The memory of being gunned down in a hail of police bullets. It had killed her. While she might have hesitated to use it under normal circumstances, it wasn't exactly normal to have the point of a sword inches from your chest.

She waited for the man to fall back on his heels.

But instead, all her focus, all her mental concentration produced . . .

Nothing.

Except a sudden feeling of wind howling through her body, scraping at her core, as though it were tearing her apart from the inside out.

Child!

The word was thought, not spoken. She understood it perfectly, even in the midst of her agony. *A taste of your own foul brew will suit you nicely, witch.*

Minerva stumbled backward and fell to the ground, as the man stepped forward to glare down at her, his sword still pointed at her chest.

Until Raven tackled him from behind. The man who'd called himself Guy had been so intent on repelling Minerva's assault that he'd forgotten about Raven, who sent the sword flying from his grip and planted a fist squarely in his face. Then another. Then a well-placed knee to the groin, causing the man to curl up like a potato bug.

Before the man could recover, Raven kicked him in the face and, to his amazement, the man's head came off.

Then, something even stranger happened. The head spoke.

"*Dysig!*" It was a word in the old tongue, but that's all that was said before a whooshing rose through the trees and the head fell silent, its body three feet away on the forest floor.

Raven knelt beside Minerva, who was shaking her own head repeatedly back and forth, as if trying to dislodge something. "I wonder what he said. Min, are you okay?"

She blinked twice and stared up at him. Then, slowly, an odd smile crept across her lips. "Your word for '*dysig*' would be fool." The voice was hers; the person behind it wasn't. "And you can call me Guy."

Shot

Phantom sat next to the bed in a large travel-trailer parked in a picturesque but largely empty campground on a sheer cliff overlooking the Pacific. It was secluded enough that it didn't have a tollbooth, just a lockbox where campers were expected to deposit the overnight fee. But it had electrical hookups, and that was as important as the seclusion it provided.

Ideally, he would have returned to New York, but time was of the essence.

Phantom seldom became personally involved at ground level in these operations, but this one was too important to entrust to anyone else.

On the outside, the trailer looked perfectly normal. Curtains were drawn over the back widows and a thick cloth divider had been pulled across the width of the vehicle behind the front seats, sealing the interior off from prying eyes. Beyond that curtain, things were anything but normal. The interior was set up as a portable hospital room, complete with heart monitor, IV bag, and a host of medical supplies that could last for some time.

He had two companions: Dr. Friesen Hoyt, who specialized in comatose patients, and Marina Escobar, a nurse practitioner. Both were FIN agents, and neither one knew who he was . . . just that he was their designated contact and lead operative on this mission. He'd given it the code name Operation Revival. The goal was to pull the fourth person in the trailer—the woman lying on the bed—out of what seemed like a coma. Phantom knew it was something far more complex.

"Progress?" Phantom asked Hoyt as he stared at his clipboard.

He shook his head. "Nothing, that I can see. I've looked at everything conventional. None of it would cause what we see here. All her readings are stable. Her heart rate is steady, her breathing is clear, her blood pressure is stable. It's as though someone put a lock on the doorway to her mind and scrambled the combination."

"Well, if she's not responding to conventional treatment," Phantom said, "we need to try something unconventional. What do we know about how the Rus girl was treated when she fell into a coma?"

"We were able to access the records from Serendipity hospital."

"And?"

"It seems she received a shot of adrenaline to the heart right before she lapsed into her coma."

"Before? That doesn't help us. We need something to bring her *out* of a coma, not put her in one."

The doctor looked up from his clipboard. "I know. But there's something else here that doesn't add up. The adrenaline shouldn't have rendered her catatonic, but it appears to have done just that. And that's not all. Something else happened that shouldn't have. The hospital records show an accelerated pattern of brain cell regeneration. We call it neurogenesis. It's not abnormal by itself, but the rate at which it occurred is like nothing I've ever seen."

"Could the records be wrong?"

Hoyt shook his head slowly. "No. I don't see how. The notes are detailed and quite specific."

The heart monitor was beeping in a perfect cadence in the background. Blood pressure 122 over 79. Heart rate 76 beats per minute. The numbers stayed consistent, barely fluctuating.

"So, if we were to inject this patient with adrenaline, what do you think would happen?" Phantom asked.

"Well . . ." Hoyt hesitated. "It's risky. There's a high risk of brain damage."

"But if we do nothing, her muscles will atrophy and . . . How long will she stay this way?"

"Indefinitely. And yes, her muscles would atrophy. Presumably, her organs would start to deteriorate and, eventually, she would die. She is far older than she appears. I've started to see some degradation of the flesh, minor changes in hair coloring and so forth. None of it is natural."

Phantom wasn't sure what to make of that, but it wasn't his primary concern. "If you administer the adrenaline, what are the chances she'll wake up?"

"I have no way of knowing. It could bring her out of it, but as I said, there are fairly substantial risks."

"Yes, yes. I know. Do you think it would induce the same effect in our subject that occurred with the Rus girl?"

"It's impossible to tell. I wouldn't have expected to see it there—or in anyone. But if the two subjects' physiology and brain structures are similar, who knows?"

Phantom looked at Escobar. "I assume we have adrenaline available?"

She nodded. "We do." She was already holding a syringe with an extended needle containing a dose of clear liquid.

Phantom nodded. "Go ahead then."

The nurse practitioner stepped forward and plunged the needle into the patient's chest, squeezing the syringe and removing it.

For an instant, nothing happened. The monitors remained steady for one beat. Two. And then the patient gasped, her eyes flew open, and she threw her head back in what seemed like a convulsion. Her heart rate rose, along with her blood pressure. She gasped again and arched her back against the hospital bed. She sat bolt upright, then collapsed. Her eyes were still open, though, for a moment.

Then they closed and her body appeared to relax.

"What just happened?" Phantom asked, almost frantically.

"I'm not sure," Hoyt said. There was a tinge of frustration in his voice. "I think we may have just killed her."

Guy

Minerva remembered her mother complaining about her sick headaches, the migraines she'd get without warning, forcing her to turn out all the lights and bury her head beneath a pillow. Minerva had always imagined it was Jessica's punishment for the way she'd treated her. Karma and all that. She didn't know whether she really believed it or not, but it was comforting to think that mean people might somehow get what was coming to them.

Guy of Gisborne was definitely a mean person. That was an understatement. What kind of a sicko skinned a horse and wore its hide on his back? Seriously. Minerva remembered hearing that people who were cruel to animals usually behaved the same way toward people, and that was definitely true of this man. Whatever he'd done to that horse, he'd done worse to humans. He was an assassin.

She knew all this for one reason: Guy of Gisborne was inside her mind, fighting to take over. How this happened, she wasn't sure. The last thing she remembered was seeing Raven kick the man and his head go flying off. It all seemed surreal, but she was sure she hadn't imagined it. And she hadn't imagined the chill of the man's spirit—that's the closest thing she could think to call it—invading her.

Somehow, the disembodied Guy had managed to enter her mind, accessing her most sacred thoughts and cherished memories, not to mention her darkest fears. In doing so, he'd opened his own thoughts to her.

She knew him now.

And that knowledge gave her a means of fighting back.

Minerva knew he had once been paid to kill Roger. He had used the gift to get inside his quarry's head by way of his dreams. Raven had come to her the same way, but it had been her memories that had brought him to her, surfacing in her sleep from somewhere in her subconscious.

With Guy, it had been different. He'd never met Roger, yet somehow was able to project himself into the other man's dreams without ever making eye contact.

How did you do it? Minerva demanded. She imagined herself with her fingers around the man's throat, digging into his flesh, even though it was all inside her head.

He resisted, as she knew he would. He hadn't known she would be this strong when he'd invaded her mind, and . . . What was that? Just a tinge of regret? But it wasn't as if he'd had any choice after Raven kicked him in the head. There had only been a moment to decide. He needed to transfer his consciousness, his memory, into a new host before he faded into oblivion and his thoughts were dispersed across this artificial landscape conjured from a time long past.

Two choices had presented themselves: the man who'd dislodged his head or the man's female companion. Surely, she was the weaker—women were always weaker, or so he believed—and when it came right down to it, he was a coward. Despite his disdain at the prospect of taking on feminine form, he had in that split second calculated that it would be better to over-power *her* than to risk being repelled by *him*.

Not what you expected, am I?

He felt her pressing him, a mental vise grip that made him want to scream. He tried not to panic. There had to be a way to wall a part of himself from her as he kept fighting. If he didn't possess her, she would possess him, and he would be lost. Only his memories would remain, and they would belong to her. He'd had the element of surprise on his side when he'd attacked her. She hadn't expected it, hadn't known just what he was. But then she'd realized and steeled herself against him. Now, she was on the attack.

He felt her pulling the information, like a thread slowly extracted from his inner being without his consent. He fought her, but he felt her pulling, bit by bit, piece by piece.

I . . . am . . . a . . . dreamwielder.

What does that mean? Tell me!

He felt as if his head were about to explode, even though he no longer had a head. He tried to fight against the agony of her attack, demanding he answer, yet offering no relief if he did.

So, he told her.

Dreamwielders could use their gift to search out someone while the person lay sleeping. Anyone. They only needed to see the target once in waking, to have made eye contact, however briefly. Once the subject's "thought signature" was memorized, they could find the person again in slumber. If their target was weak, they could impose their will outright or disguise their thoughts to make them appear as though they were the sleeper's own. They could plant nightmares, so the dreamer became preoccupied, and terrified, of the fears that grew in response. Even among the strongest, who recognized their presence, they could succeed in planting a mental beacon of sorts that would enable them to find the person in waking whenever they wished.

Jules had done something like that to her once. Minerva wondered if she was a dreamwielder, too.

So, the Between exists in our dreams? She kept pressing.

Dreams are . . . a corner . . . of it . . .

If he had been speaking, his voice would have been hoarse, his breathing ragged. If she could maintain this pressure, he would soon be unable to resist. She could feel it, and it excited her.

This is wrong, she told herself, and in that moment loosened her grip just enough for him to rip his consciousness back out of her grasp. He drew himself up and they stared at one another across the imaginary ring of combat.

Your hesitation will be your undoing. He launched a mental assault that felt like a steel pole being thrust into her solar plexus. She felt herself falling backward. She couldn't even think about her next move without him knowing it, but she had the same advantage. She could sense his thoughts also. This was *her* mind, *her* body. She knew it better than he did—at least for the time being. She had to find a way to exploit that, and quickly. She could feel her energy begin to wane as she used it against the intruder, this Guy of Gisborne, a character out of what she had thought was a fairy tale.

His mission to kill Roger had ended badly. After Guy had provoked him in a dream, Roger had gone after him

Guy's arrogance, however, had gotten the best of him. Instead of lying in wait to ambush Roger, he had stood out in the open, confronting him directly before attacking with a knife. He'd managed to penetrate Roger's defenses and wound him slightly on the left side, but Roger had recovered and delivered a more telling blow. What happened next, however, seemed bizarre. Roger had taken hold of Guy's hair, pulled back, and used his blade to slash through his neck, severing the man's head.

He had done so by design. Once he'd seen the man in person, he'd recognized Guy as a dreamwielder. Not only was a dreamwielder able to invade other men's dreams, he could also survive almost any attack by willing himself into a lucid dream state. Once there, he could dream he was healing himself of any wound inflicted. The dream would become reality.

Roger had encountered one or two such men before. He knew the only way to destroy such a demon was to keep him from dreaming. That was accomplished by severing his head. Beheading would release his essence into the world at large, where it would dissipate like the morning fog.

Unless he found a new host.

A dreamwielder whose head had been severed could only survive by taking another's body.

When Roger had beheaded Guy, his essence had rushed to seek a new body. It had been frantic, scrambling to find refuge. Having sensed Guy in his own dreams earlier, Roger had known this. He had suspected that Guy would try to find sanctuary in his own body, and had set a guard against that very possibility. Something Minerva hadn't known to do.

Despite Roger's precautions, something had went wrong. Unbeknownst to Roger, John Lyttel had dispatched a young outlaw to follow and send for help if the need arose. The dying Guy had sensed the man's presence. The outlaw had no defense against the wraith-like being's assault. He succumbed, allowing his body to be possessed by Guy's consciousness.

As she sifted through Guy's memory, Minerva recognized the young outlaw, and as they struggled, each desperate to gain the advantage, she understood why Guy's head had come off at a single kick from Raven. It was a reflection of what had happened, all those centuries before. Guy lived out his life in the young outlaw's body before the man had died a natural death, and they had both wound up here in their original forms, each condemned to re-enact their own lives time and again in the Between.

The more time Minerva spent in the Between, the more she was learning. There were rules here, but they weren't hard and fast; you could shift them, especially in the corners of the Between that you controlled. But where they intersected with another's memory, there was no control. Things happened at the whim of the Between. Sometimes from your perspective, sometimes from another's.

Raven had described arriving at one such intersection the first time he had come here, a nebulous place of shifting waves of images that had made him feel seasick. Off balance. Disoriented. But his parents' home, the place he had created from his own memories, had seemed almost as physical as the "real" world.

Two kinds of people could come to the Between: Those with the gift, and those who were brought here by someone with the gift. That's how John had been brought here. By Roger. So had the other members of his band, except for William. But you had to know about the place in order to get there. Roger and William obviously had, but Raven apparently hadn't, which was why he'd needed her memories to revive him. Guy hadn't, either. Like most of the merry men, he'd been brought here by Roger, along with the young outlaw whose body he had taken.

Guy owed Roger his continued existence, and it infuriated him. He had been brought here for Roger's amusement, to play a role in Roger's fantasy of perpetually re-enacting his own adventures in this make-believe Nottingham. It had driven him to the brink of madness and beyond, and this madness now served as his greatest advantage against Minerva.

The mad will always defeat you fools who cling to sanity, he mocked. *We know how to take it from you, but you fear to absorb our madness!*

Minerva felt something like tendrils weaving their way through her, attaching themselves to her and squeezing. How had she let this happen? She had been winning. She had been on the verge of destroying him. She had let her focus slip, just as she had let it slip in her training against Amber. What would happen to Amber now, and to Raven, if this man took her and absorbed everything she was?

They would die.

NO!

Her mental scream ricocheted through the chambers of her mind, where her own thoughts were being seized from her, crowded out by the thoughts of the madman.

Believe the lies, he told her. *Only then will you survive.*

Raven! She called out with all the strength her withering mind could muster.

He didn't answer.

Yet dimly, somewhere beyond the cacophony that was raging in her head, an idea began to form.

She had no time to waste, no time to wonder whether it was her own inspiration or the product of Guy's madness. A few more heartbeats and she would be lost. She had survived being gunned down by police in the real world. She only hoped she could survive this as well. It was her only chance.

Raven! CUT OFF MY HEAD!

Nothing happened. She couldn't tell if he'd heard her. If he had, he was hesitating, and there wasn't time. He couldn't afford to wait.

Raven! NOW!

There was a sudden, deafening sound like a rushing wind inside her skull, and it felt as though she were being sucked up and out by the kind of tornado that had pulled Dorothy out of Kansas and dropped her into Oz. She wondered vaguely whether *she* would wind up in Munchkinland or the Emerald City, the way she and Raven had ended up in Nottingham. She had no time to wonder. Blind, she reached out to the only thing she knew could save her. She felt her thoughts fading as she struggled to focus them on Raven. If she lost her focus, she'd be dead.

Raven stared at Minerva's body beneath him, then at the sword in his hand.

A moment later, he was sent reeling backward by a force that hammered into him and swirled up inside like a furious gust of wind blasting open the windows of an old mansion. It careened through him, seeking out the core of his being, binding itself to him. But for all the chaos, the force seemed strangely reassuring.

As suddenly as it had started, the wind subsided. It was replaced by a familiar voice inside his head.

Hi there, handsome. Thanks for letting me hitch a ride.

Bombay Beach

A bead of sweat rolled down the side of Henry's forehead, just missing his eye and disappearing into what had grown into a full-fledged beard. He hadn't shaved during his time in jail, and he didn't have a razor here, either. He reached up with his napkin to wipe the sweat away as he stared down at the plate of scrambled eggs, ham, bell peppers, and cheese in front of him.

"The napkin's for your mouth, not your sweat, kiddo." Paige laughed, a sound he was becoming used to hearing. But most of the time, he couldn't tell whether she was mocking him or genuinely amused.

He nodded, smiled and shoveled a forkful of the eggs into his mouth, trying to keep his mind off how stifling it was inside the manufactured house that was, for better or worse, his home. A badly insulated metal box wasn't the best choice of dwelling for the middle of a desert, especially when what passed for air conditioning was more like a sputtering fan that blew lukewarm air. "At least it's a dry heat," Paige had told him. Yes, there was that. Any excuse to look on the bright side.

Henry swallowed the mouthful of eggs.

"Good," he said. It was a sincere compliment.

"Of course." Paige's tone fell somewhere between self-satisfaction and surprise that any other response was even possible. "How do you think I got this?" She stuck out her belly and rubbed it approvingly.

Not enough exercise? Henry said to himself, but he held his tongue. Belly or no, he found Paige attractive—and fun. The fact that she was a good cook didn't hurt, either.

They'd agreed to share all the household duties. She cooked four days a week and he cooked the other three, they alternated the dishes, and each of them did their own laundry. Paige didn't care much about housecleaning, so he did most of that, and she'd volunteered to do the grocery shopping—

which was a big sacrifice on her part, since there was only one market and it didn't, even in the remotest sense, qualify as "super."

She wouldn't have let him go, even if he'd wanted to. She didn't want him to so much as step outside the door. Their only vehicle was a Harley, and he couldn't have stayed upright on a motorized Hog any more than he could have on a hog you found in a pigpen.

She had the keys, anyway.

They'd been here almost a week, and he still hadn't figured out whether she was in witness protection, like him, or had been sent here by someone to keep an eye on him. One thing he did know, she wasn't one of Duke Malone's people. If Malone's "family" knew where he was, they wouldn't be keeping an eye on him, they'd be gouging both of *his* eyes out, if they even bothered with such niceties before putting a bullet in his head.

From what Paige said, she *was* in witness protection, just like him. And her story seemed convincing enough.

She said she had grown up in Oildale, a rough neighborhood just north of Bakersfield in the San Joaquin Valley. More recently, she'd been riding with the Lost Mountain Condors, a motorcycle gang that got its name because it collected "dead meat," as she called it; riders who were down on their luck and had nowhere else to go. The gang, she said, had given her life a purpose after she'd become pregnant and married the baby's father, a guy named Ted Frias. She'd miscarried and he'd forced her to find a job as a tele-marketer so she could support him while he sat at home, got drunk, and played online video games. He wasn't very good at it. Once he'd demanded that she play with him, he was so bad—or drunk—she beat him the first time, even though she'd never played "Warrior Caste IV" before.

That's when he'd started hitting her. He didn't stop for the next two years. It was only by chance that she'd met one of the Condors, Mike Gonzalez, at a gas station on her way home from work. He'd noticed her split lip, from one of Ted's particularly vicious backhands. Her "punishment" after forget-ting a bottle of Jack he'd demanded from the liquor store.

"Be glad it wasn't my fist," Ted had told her with a wicked smile.

She was. She was amazed by that point that she still had all her teeth.

This Mike Gonzalez had asked her what happened, and she'd told him.

It had been the right move. Gonzalez wasn't tall, maybe five-foot-eight, but he weighed nearly three hundred pounds, and what hadn't migrated to his beer belly was pure muscle. Best of all, he had a particular distaste for men who hit women. He made it his personal mission to pay Ted back for what he'd done to her. Not only was he "one genuine bad-ass," in Paige's words, he also happened to be one of the gang's leaders. He could count on his buddies to back him up, which is exactly what they did.

Mike asked Paige if she could be out of the house on a certain evening around seven o'clock. She agreed, offering to pick up a pack of smokes for Ted when the time came. She returned to find him lying naked on the floor, unmarked except for a knife wound in his chest. And a badly split lip.

Instead of calling the police, she'd run. Having nowhere else to go, she'd ended up at the Condors clubhouse, which was actually Mike Gonzalez's ranch east of Bakersfield. The police never thought to look for her there, and the murder remained unsolved. She learned to ride a Hog and became part of the gang. Mike's girl. Until four years after Ted turned up dead, when she happened to see one of her old neighbors in Coulterville during a run up Highway 49.

He saw her, too. And worse, he recognized her He tipped the cops to where she was.

They arrested her the next day in Angel's Camp for questioning. Mike made her promise not to take the fall for him. If it came down to it, she should tell the cops he did it and make a new life for herself.

"I can handle myself in prison," he told her. "Been there, done that. No big deal. I won't see my girl behind bars. No way. But they'll try to put you there for running away. Rat me out, testify against me. Hell, all you gotta do is tell the truth. But make them give you something in exchange. Make them drop anything they've got against you. Promise me."

She did. She told them that Mike was an old friend who had killed Ted in self-defense after driving him home because he'd been too drunk to drive himself. Mike had gotten six years for voluntary manslaughter, and she'd gotten a new life in witness protection because the cops were worried the gang would come after her.

That had been four years ago. She'd been living in Bombay Beach ever since.

"The cops must have figured I needed a man to protect me," she said. "No offense, Eric Daly, but I got a hunch I'll be doing more protecting than you will." She laughed.

"Hey."

"Like I said, no offense. I could do worse for a husband. You've got looks. You've got money. You've even got that sexy British accent. And between the two of us, you don't got to worry about changin' it around me." She winked at him. In spite of himself, he smiled.

"I could do worse for a wife, too, love."

We Are I

If Raven hadn't been comfortable with Minerva reading his thoughts before . . . *imagine how I feel right now.*

I don't have to imagine. I'm right here.

This can't be good for a relationship. Having someone literally in your head 24-7.

Are you trying to tell me you want to break up? It's a little late for that Sherlock, don't you think?

I'm not saying that. This will just take some getting used to.

For you and me both.

I suppose if we can survive this, we can survive anything.

What's that supposed to mean?

It wasn't like before, when Minerva could read his thoughts selectively. Now she was just *there*. All the time. The minute he even half-formed a thought, she knew what it was. It went the other way, too. It was like having multiple personality disorder, except both the personalities were there at the same time. And each was keenly aware of the other's presence. Talking to yourself took on a whole new meaning when the self you were talking to wasn't you.

Suddenly, Raven knew everything Minerva did. He hadn't realized her feelings for him were that strong. He'd suspected it, but she'd kept part of it locked away so he wouldn't suspect. She had a hard time trusting, even him, and she still wondered whether he was really the same person her childhood self had trusted without question. Before life and death and love had become involved in the equation.

He couldn't censor himself, either. The minute a thought popped into his head, it popped into hers. She was literally inside his head. All the way inside. Like some parasite.

Hey!

Sorry, Min, I . . .

Didn't mean it. Right. I know. Her usual sarcasm was there, but underlying it was a sense of understanding. She knew what he was going through. She was dealing with the same thing. There was no stopping her from reading his thoughts now, and that was scary. But it was just as scary to her as it was to him. More so. She'd spent so much of her life isolated from other people that just being in a room with too many others made her want to run. Dealing with him and Amber and Carson was enough of a challenge.

I can't blame you on Carson. He's an ass.

Are you ever going to lighten up on him?

Would you lighten up on someone who killed your grandmother?

Minerva could sense the hurt in Raven, and it wasn't just about this. Everyone he'd ever been close to was dead. His grandmother. His parents. Even her.

Please tell me I'm not going to lose you, too.

She could sense the sorrow behind that thought, and the worry. She'd never seen Raven worry outwardly before, except about her.

I'm not going anywhere. I think you're stuck with me.

What happens if we find our way back to the real world? Will we still be . . . like this?

Minerva saw an image behind the question. It made her smile. It was an image of her body, pressed up against his. They were holding each other and kissing.

Yes, I'd miss that, too.

Raven blushed. She literally felt the heat rise in his cheekbones. Not only could she hear his thoughts, but she felt everything he felt.

He recovered quickly. *One thing's for sure, we'll never have to worry about forgetting each other if we're like this.*

She laughed to herself and was surprised to hear Raven's laugh escaping his lips. Apparently, she could make his body react to her thoughts as readily as it responded to his own. *This could be fun.*

Don't get any ideas.

Too late, I already have them.

Raven's tone changed. *What's that?* He'd suddenly become aware of something else inside Minerva's essence, something that seemed very alien, almost insane. Not almost. It was. There were memories there that couldn't possibly be hers. But they were like dead memories. As though she'd read them in a history book and somehow made them her own.

That's him. She turned Raven's head toward Guy's headless body. *He was inside me, and he was about to take over my body. We were fighting, and he was winning. That's why I had you cut off my head. It was the only way to stop me from losing myself.*

Where is he now?

Dead, I think. I mean really dead. When you cut off my head, his spirit came flying out and needed a new host, just like mine. Thank God I found you before he did. With me here, he had nowhere to go.

But he's still inside you. I mean . . . us.

Raven felt his own head shake back and forth. It was an odd sensation when someone else made it happen without any warning. *No, he's not. Just his memories. The echoes of who he was. He seems to know a lot about Roger and the others, too. I guess if you hang around someone for a few centuries, you get to know them pretty well. If we can get past all his craziness, it might be able to help us. The hard part is telling what are real memories and what's delusion. He was one psycho SOB.*

Yeah. I can tell he hated Roger. Blamed him for bringing him here to live out some sick Sherwood Forest fantasy over and over again. Do you think there's any truth to that, or was he just nuts?

I don't know, but we should find out soon enough.

They looked simultaneously—because there was no other way for them to do it—across the clearing to see Roger approaching from the east.

"Ho there! Where did you two . . ." he began, then broke off his sentence and quickened his pace as he caught sight of the two headless bodies a few feet away from Raven/Minerva. "By the Holy Virgin, what devilry is this?" he said, crossing himself and kneeling next to the bodies. There was a wild look in his eyes that neither Minerva nor Raven had seen before. He stood abruptly and fixed Raven with a stare that could have fired arrows into his skull. He had the gift, and that could be dangerous; Raven made sure not to look him in the eye.

"Are these two dead by your hand?" he demanded, his voice shaking with a mixture of shock and rage.

Raven didn't know what to say, but fortunately Minerva had an idea. Raven felt his mouth move and heard the following words come out: "We overheard this man plotting to ambush you when you came looking for us," she said. "He attacked Minerva before I could stop her, and you can see what happened. But he didn't see me, so I jumped him from behind and knocked his sword loose. Then I used it on him the same way he used it on my girlfriend."

Raven felt his face contort into an expression meant to symbolize grief. *You can do better than that.*

Raven took over and made it more convincing.

Sorry.

You'll learn.

"Do you realize what you've done?" Roger's voice was frantic, as though he were more grief-stricken than Raven and Minerva together could pretend to be. "You've ruined everything. Everything."

Maybe Guy was right about Roger. Raven felt the point of Roger's sword on his neck.

Minerva . . . or Raven . . . gulped. *Maybe so.*

Tag Team

"Do not do anything hasty, Roger."

Roger didn't take his eye off Raven. He knew the voice belonged to Will Scadlock. "Guy's dead," he said, his voice a growl with a hint of panic. "You do know what that means, Will? Of course, you do."

"Yes." Scadlock's voice was measured and calm. "But none of this ever depended on Gisborne, Roger. It depends on us. You and me."

Raven and Minerva felt the point of Roger's sword shaking against their neck.

If he moves wrong, he'll carve a slice out of my Adam's apple.

What's the point of that thing anyway?

I don't know, but right now I'm thinking you can have it.

I already do.

"You know why we brought Guy here. We need a challenge. This is our paradise, but without a rival, who are we? What will become of us? We'll simply waste away, growing fat and slow and bored."

Scadlock didn't say anything. He didn't seem to have a good response to Roger's assessment of the situation. Minerva felt like she'd wandered into one of those historical re-enactments, where people went out to the park for a weekend and dressed up as famous figures from this or that time period. Roger and Will were doing the same thing, except they were reliving scenes from their own lives. Who knew how many times they'd matched wits with Guy of Gisborne since all of them died more than seven hundred years ago.

I've heard of reliving past glories, but this is ridiculous.

Roger was talking again. "What do you suggest now, old friend?"

"There's always the shire-reeve."

"That dimwitted buffoon? No challenge at all. He was never anything more than Henry's lackey, then Edward's."

Who's he talking about? Minerva wondered.

Kings of England. Raven replied.

As in Henry VIII, the guy who cut off all his wives' heads?

Not all. Just two of them. And no, not him. Henry I and Edward Longshanks. Remember that DVD we watched? He's the guy who chased Mel Gibson—I mean William Wallace—around in Braveheart. *Most people think Robin Hood lived during the time of King John and Richard the Lionheart, but he didn't. The earliest reference to him puts him in Edward's time.*

When did Raven become such a know-it-all? He'd been killed at the age of eight, but it was like he'd taken a college course on this stuff.

My parents read me all the old Robin Hood tales when I was a kid. That's probably why we ended up here, remember?

I remember everything, smartass. I just wasn't thinking.

"This one is to blame for it all," Roger was saying, his eyes still fixed on Raven. He and Minerva had no idea how powerful Roger was, but if he'd survived in the Between for more than seven centuries, they weren't going to take any chances—even with their own two gifts combined. Here, in their weakened state, expending too much energy could mean the end of them.

"If you are so sure of that, then just be done with him here and now," Scadlock said offhandedly. "Does he belong here? I would say not."

"Indeed," Roger snarled. "Let vengeance be thine, oh Lord, but let me be thine instrument!"

Minerva had an idea, and not a moment too soon.

"Stay your hand!"

Raven heard the sound of his own voice, but it was Minerva who had made his lips move.

Roger's muscles froze, but the sword remained inches from Raven's neck. "State your piece," he said finally, through clenched teeth.

"It appears I have outwitted you again, old friend."

Roger's eyes narrowed, but he said nothing.

"Do you not recognize the voice of your archenemy? 'Tis I, Guy of Gisborne."

Raven realized that the tone and inflections in his own voice sounded different. Slightly foreign. Antiquated. Minerva had found another use for her gift. Because she could remember everything exactly, it was possible, at least in theory, for her to *duplicate* it exactly, and that included speech patterns. She was putting that theory to the test. Raven could only hope it worked.

"How do I know you are who you say you are?"

"You defeated me in a contest of skill with bow and arrow, then I sought to kill you. I managed to stab you in the left side, but you did recover and beseech Our Lady for good favor. Then you delivered a killing stroke and cut off my head as I breathed my last."

"Everyone knows that story," Roger scoffed. "You could have heard it in your own time and come back here to retell it. Do I seem a fool to you?"

"Very well, then. I shall tell you something that surely no one but the two of us would know."

"Go on then."

"After you did slay me, I fled to the body of the miller's son and abode there the rest of my days. I did not destroy his spirit, but allowed it to abide there as long as he did not cross me. I suppose I felt a tinge of guilt of over using him in that manner. When he died, you brought us both here, where he could be restored to his own body and me to mine. He never forgave you for killing me and allowing me to steal his body from him. I would watch your back, if I were you."

"And now you've taken this simpleton in like manner?" Roger seemed skeptical, but also surprised that Raven had told him something only Guy could have known. He hadn't been happy about keeping the miller's son around, but John had taken a liking to the boy and had insisted on accepting him in their band. He and John had been at odds before. It was never pleasant. He hadn't thought it worthwhile to make an issue of this particular matter. Now, he was having second thoughts.

"What exactly do you think the miller's son might do?"

"When you were alive, he thought to kill you, but I never allowed it while I controlled him. He probably still wants to, but since you are, quite obviously, dead now, I have no idea what he might be planning. Maybe you should ask him."

"I just might do that," Roger scoffed. "But I am still not convinced you are who you claim to be."

"I let you win our archery contest to throw you off your guard so I could kill you."

Roger's face went blank, then contorted into a smile. "No one lets me win at anything!" he nearly shouted.

Raven smiled. "But I did. You might well have beaten me in any case, but you just proved my point, old friend. That oversized head of yours is your biggest enemy. Only someone who studied you, as I did, would know that."

Roger cocked his head slightly to one side and narrowed his eyes, studying Raven. His lips were pursed tightly together, as though holding back some unsaid words he feared might escape. Finally, he ventured, "You give away an assassin's secrets too quickly."

Raven shrugged. "Perhaps because I am done being an assassin. You and Scadlock have kept me here in your make-believe Shire Wood for a dozen lifetimes. More. And what do we do here? Run around the same place chasing one another and trying to fill up time with enough diversions not to bore ourselves to death. The lot of us are already dead, but this is worse, Roger. I cannot even really kill you. What use is being an assassin when the very thing that defines you is out of reach?"

Roger was shaking now. "We are not dead!"

"It only seems that way. You have wrapped yourself in this fantasy, in which the same scenes play out time and again. The exact way you have them scripted.

But you are stuck here, Roger. You can never go back to the real world. You are fated to live your echo in this shadowland you have created."

"Lies!"

Before anyone could argue, there was a rustling of leaves nearby and a solitary figure emerged from the underbrush, looking a little dazed and a lot disoriented.

"What the hell am I doing here?"

Raven/Minerva spun in their collective heels and turned around to look behind them. The voice was both familiar and oddly out of place here, in pseudo-Nottingham. Roger turned along with them, sword drawn.

"You've got to be kidding me," Minerva said through Raven's lips as recognition dawned.

The newcomer looked somewhat dazed but still managed a smile that was far more self-satisfied than mirthful.

Minerva rolled Raven's eyes. *Here we go again.*

Blackmail

Phantom stared at the message on his computer screen.

"ACCOUNT COMPROMISED." It blinked at him, its letters alternating silver and crimson, like the bloody edge of a knife twisting in his stomach.

He'd flown back to New York from the West Coast, only to be greeted with this. It had not been a good week, and it was only getting worse. The metallic glare of coppery sunlight slid under the mostly closed blinds and across the desk as he sat back and stared at the screen.

Reflexively, he pressed control-alt-delete.

Nothing happened. Of course, it wouldn't. It had been twenty minutes since the message first appeared and only a few seconds less since he had notified his IT people to trace the source and close the breach. They hadn't managed to do so, despite their vaunted expertise. The fact that the hacker had circumvented the significant safety measures installed to protect his account was bad enough. More worrisome was the fact that whoever it was had known his account was there in the first place.

The intercom blinked. He had a phone call on Line 2.

"Yes, did you trace the breach?"

But it wasn't his IT specialist.

"Is this the man they call Phantom?" The voice was muffled and distorted. It sounded like it belonged to an alien from an old episode of *The Outer Limits* being broadcast on an antique UHF signal during a thunderstorm. Whoever it belonged to was using some sort of voice-distortion software.

Phantom checked the caller ID. The screen was blinking zeroes. FIN's secure phone system had an automatic call tracer, but that wasn't working, either.

"Who is this?"

"That's an ironic question coming from someone who uses a code name." There was coarse laughter from the other end of the line. "I'll tell you mine if you tell me yours."

Phantom wanted to hang up, but only someone dangerous could have gotten his number and bypassed security, and he knew better than to ignore a threat. He had three tasks: identify it, determine its weaknesses, and neutralize it.

"I'll try again, then. What do you want?"

The coarse laugh was repeated, in what seemed to be exactly the same tone and duration as the first time. The person on the other end wasn't just using a voice-distortion device. He seemed to have recorded at least some of what was being said in an effort to further disguise its origins. The person orchestrating the call must have anticipated this latest question, because another recorded answer came in a different voice, speaking in a faster and slightly higher pitch.

"Here's what you are going to do," it said. "Restore access for Triage3NxO1. All security access. This will include fingerprint and voiceprint recognition. Then you're going to provide the codes necessary to confirm that you have, in fact, accomplished this."

Triage3NxO1. That was Biltmore's code name. Or Bradley Carson. Or whatever he was calling himself these days.

The voice changed again. Now it belonged to a woman, but the static and distortion were as pronounced as ever. "Next you will provide the location of Dr. Henry Marshall. The precise location."

So, Triage was behind this.

"What do I get in return?"

The voice changed again, back to the original, and from the way it answered him directly, he guessed it wasn't a recording this time. "For one thing, you get to keep your identity, Doctor Vincent."

Phantom froze. Nobody knew his real name. FIN's command structure, with its semi-autonomous network of cells and false identities, was designed to protect that.

The familiar laugh came through the phone line again, followed by yet another recorded voice. This one sounded like an old man's. "You have twenty-four hours to supply us with proof that you've complied with our demands regarding Triage3NxO1 and Dr. Marshall.

"Thank you for playing."

There was a click and a dial tone.

Neil Vincent sat down in his desk chair, feeling the cushion give way as he sank back against its dark leather folds. The coppery-gold stream of sunlight that had spilled across his desk was fading, leaving the desktop dark and empty. The "ACCOUNT COMPROMISED" message continued to taunt him as it blinked silently on the screen, appearing and disappearing in three-second intervals.

The phone rang again. It was IT.

"Anything?"

"We're still working on it. Trying to isolate the source of the breach, but every time we start to get a fix on it, it shifts somehow. The best we can figure is that whoever's doing this is modulating the frequency so that it's passing through different wireless towers or maybe even different satellite carriers. We can't track it through to its source. Every time we block it, it appears somewhere else."

"Well, keep working." He ended the call.

If IT couldn't isolate the breach, this was a problem. A big problem. The blackmailer hadn't promised to seal the breach if his conditions were met; he had only promised not to reveal Vincent's identity.

A good extortionist always kept at least one threat in reserve, should it be needed. Not only could he continue to hold Vincent's identity over his head, he also had access to his account. Vincent must have missed some small tidbit of personal information somewhere.

Phantom was a ghost—Neil Vincent was anything but. An Air Force colonel and nuclear physicist, he had been a top security adviser to the Joint Chiefs of Staff and had chaired the Nuclear Regulatory Commission after leaving the military. Then he had withdrawn from public life to pursue those famously nebulous "personal interests" everyone talked about when they retired. Except he hadn't retired. He'd just entered a new line of work as the head of FIN, a position so top-secret that even the president didn't know who held it. The only person who knew the leader's identity was the person who had appointed him, his predecessor. The level of security this process afforded outweighed the lack of oversight, or so the thinking went.

The fact that his own identity had been compromised was unacceptable, not just to him personally, but because it made him a security risk. Susceptible to just this sort of blackmail.

But something didn't add up. If Triage was behind it, as the demands indicated, why had he gone to so much trouble to mask his identity?

Maybe the blackmailer wanted him to *think* Triage was his man. Maybe they were somehow using Triage. Who else stood to benefit . . . unless Triage's account had been hacked the same way? And what about the demand for Marshall's whereabouts? None of it made sense.

In the final analysis, none of this would be Phantom's problem. His identity had been compromised—agency protocol demanded he name a successor and resign immediately.

It would be someone else's.

The question was, who? He'd had a successor all picked out, but something had happened to foil that contingency. He needed a second option.

He was about to start looking, when the phone rang again.

"Dad! It's me. Are you there, Dad?" The voice on the other end cracked in its transition from boyhood to adolescence. Or maybe it was panic. It was hard to tell. Like the call from the blackmailer, the sound was distorted, but it didn't keep Vincent from recognizing the voice of his thirteen-year-old son. Rudy didn't have this number; very few people did, but one of them was the blackmailer who'd called him earlier. Now, apparently, he had Rudy, as well.

Vincent heard his son's panic echoed in his own voice.

"Rudy, where are you?"

"I don't know. I can't see anything. Dad. Please. Help."

Rudy's voice was replaced by one he'd heard before. "Just some insurance to help you follow instructions. If you don't, you probably know what will happen."

The line went dead.

Phantom knew he wouldn't be transferring leadership to a new successor, not today at least. Protocols be damned. This had just gotten personal.

Integrity

Earlier that day, DeJohn Sutcliffe sat tied to an uncomfortable wooden chair and his mouth sealed with duct tape.

This was not how he'd planned to spend his Saturday. He'd hacked into CableView so he could watch the Ohio State–Michigan game, then thought better of it and decided to pay for it fair and square. Sutcliffe liked to think of himself as a straight shooter. A man of his word—especially when it came to his chosen area of expertise.

If he was going to do it, it wouldn't be to hijack someone's data for personal gain. That would be unseemly. It would be because a third party was paying him for the service. In his mind, that left him free of any responsibility. He was merely a tool; a cog in the machine. A necessary cog, but one that could be replaced by another hacker . . . if you could find one as good as he was. But that wasn't his problem. He wasn't about to apologize for being the best of the best. He'd worked hard to become this good. It was a point of pride, not something to be ashamed of.

Yes, Sutcliffe charged a premium price for his expertise, but he didn't allow bidding wars. If someone was paying him to do a job, he'd do it to the best of his ability, and he wouldn't flake out. He certainly wouldn't go back on an agreement with one party if someone came along offering more compensation to back out on or, worse, to undermine a client. Especially one who was also a friend.

So, when a "someone else" had come along with a briefcase full of crisp hundred-dollar bills—more than a thousand of them—he didn't blink an eye before saying "no." The "someone" in this case, however, was four someones, all of them significantly larger than he was and wearing pinstripe blazers over physiques that would have fit in perfectly on an MMA heavyweight fight card. Sutcliffe thought the leader had even introduced himself as Brock. Not the Brock he'd seen on pay-per-view, but every bit as imposing. It turned out he'd misheard the guy: His name was *Breck*. But whatever he was calling himself, it didn't matter. What did, was that he and his companions weren't about to take "no" for an answer. It seemed they had followed him out to Mulholland Drive, where he'd met with a client who'd paid him fifty grand to hack a government agency he'd never heard of.

He was usually more careful, but when an old friend from high school named Cary Abramowitz called to set up the meeting, he hadn't told him the particulars. Sutcliffe guessed it was probably something simple, like hacking into his wife's email or running a deep background check on a business associate. He hadn't taken the kind of precautions he normally would have, considering the circumstances.

His mistake. He'd started to suspect something when Abramowitz asked him to use the name "Carson" instead. When the nature of the job became clear, he'd thought about backing out. But a deal was a deal, and he always had liked a challenge. Not a 6-foot-plus, 280-pound challenge . . . times four. He'd be more careful the next time—if there was a next time.

The way it was looking, there might not be.

Breck appeared to be in his late thirties. He was a square-jawed behemoth with a receding hairline that seemed more pronounced because of his decision to comb it directly backward. It was held in place with too much styling gel, and tapered down in a ponytail. His eyes seemed to have been knit closer together by eyebrows that nearly met in the middle. The bridge of his nose had obviously been broken at least once. A splotchy purple-red birthmark stretched along his left jawline from beside his ear, down to his neck. It looked a little like a map of England.

"That went well," he said to nobody in particular, and it wasn't meant sarcastically. Sutcliffe wondered if Breck was even capable of sarcasm.

"Yeah, it did," said one of his companions, a man an inch or two taller than Breck but slightly leaner. His shoulders didn't look *quite* as wide as an eight-lane interstate.

Sutcliffe knew that none of the men were really in charge. The "man behind the curtain," so to speak, was someone a lot smarter. Smart enough to *remain* behind the curtain and let his "muscle" do the dirty work. When the monetary offer didn't work, they used other means of persuasion. Standard operating procedure for goons. Threats, escalating from the mundane to the disturbing, followed by the execution of those threats on various body parts.

Sutcliffe might have been a man of principle, but he was no hero. And no fool. His instinct for self-preservation (and aversion to pain) had clicked into high gear when they started talking about breaking toes, one by one, and sewing one of his pupils to its eyelid. He'd need at least one eye to complete his task, as well as his fingers, or they'd probably have threatened to break them, also.

The thought entered his head that, once they were done with him, they might break everything and toss what was left into the Los Angeles River. His head would be slamming into the same concrete Schwarzenegger had used for the motorcycle scene in *Terminator 2*.

Terminated. That's what he'd be. Whether he ended up there, in the Pacific, or in some shallow grave in the Angeles National Forest, it wouldn't matter at that point. Nothing would.

What mattered was not *getting* to that point. Sutcliffe chose to comply with their demands, on the off chance he could avoid that fate or at least bypass some of the pain associated with the journey. A slim chance was always better than none.

So instead of hacking into the government agency for his high school friend, he did it for these guys.

It hadn't been easy. There were firewalls, false fronts, and an array of defenses coded in ways he hadn't seen before. The process had taken him longer than expected. His visitors had lost enough patience to break two of his toes along the way. But he'd managed to get through and give them access to at least some sections of FIN's segmented database—the key component being the accounts belonging to a certain Neil Vincent, whose name he vaguely recognized from some news reports a few years back.

They'd also forced him to "clean up" a recording they'd made of Vincent's son, whom they'd obviously kidnapped as some sort of insurance. They'd made the kid answer a bunch of questions that worried parents were likely to ask under the circumstances.

"Are you all right?"

"Where are you?"

"Can you see anything?"

"Who's there with you?"

They'd wanted it digitized so they could key up any of the answers with the press of a button.

"What did you do with the kid?" he'd asked them, getting a punch to the gut for his troubles, accompanied by a single, clipped laugh from one of the goons. Sutcliffe took that to mean the kid was dead . . . or that they wanted him to *think* he was. If that was the case, it wasn't necessary. Sutcliffe was scared enough already.

But that didn't mean he had abandoned his code of honor. Not entirely, anyway. He might have betrayed Abramowitz, but if these idiots needed him to do a simple job like as digitizing a boy's voice, they obviously didn't know much about hacking into a complex computer system. They knew what they *wanted* him to do, but they hadn't the slightest clue about *how* to do it. They were smart enough to demand evidence that it had been done, but they weren't smart enough to know that he'd surreptitiously sent a duplicate of everything to Abramowitz.

Whatever else happened, at least he could say he'd fulfilled his end of the contract.

"Any more we need to do here, Jake?" Breck asked one of the others, who was using his laptop to check Sutcliffe's work. The hacker felt like he was back in middle school, waiting for the results of a pop quiz in algebra . . . except then he hadn't been sweating over the idea that he might end up dead if he failed. Or even if he passed, for that matter. Despite his best efforts to put on a brave face, he was still wincing in pain at those two broken toes.

The other man nodded. "All good here."

Breck looked back at Sutcliffe with a half-smile that allowed just one side of his mouth to curl upward.

"Then I guess we're done. Don't feel too bad about not taking the money. We weren't gonna let you keep it anyway."

He reached down and ripped the duct tape off Sutcliffe's mouth. "Any last words?"

"Yeah. Fuck you."

Reunion

What is she doing here? Raven asked Minerva.

You thought about her, remember? That must have brought her here.

But that would mean she's . . .

"Dead." Jules said the word matter-of-factly, clearly nonplussed by this latest turn of events. "I'm dead, aren't I?"

"It sure seems that way," Minerva answered.

That means we can get rid of her for good if we just stop thinking about her, Raven offered.

Yeah, like that's going to happen. Ever try to stop thinking about pink elephants?

"Who's she?" Roger asked, but Scadlock had already sauntered up to Jules, bowed low, and taken her hand in his own to kiss it.

"William, at your service, Milady," he oozed. "Welcome to the Shire Wood."

Jules curtsied slightly—curtsied!—and smiled a tight little smile while averting her eyes.

She's good, Minerva remarked. *She can blend in anywhere.*

She's showing off—and she's not as good as she thinks, Raven answered. I don't think women curtsied in Sherwood Forest.

Did guys kiss a girl's hand?

I don't know. Maybe Scarlet—er, Scadlock—invented the idea.

It's not a bad one. You should try it sometime.

If you ever get out of my body . . .

"Thank you, William. Now would you kindly tell me what I'm doing here?"

"I brought you here," Raven said, interrupting their syrupy introduction. "It wasn't intentional, believe me."

"Then I *am* dead?"

"Everyone here is, I fear," Roger interjected.

Jules shook her head, her red mane rippling as it flowed down across her shoulders. "Not everyone. I've been here before, and I was very much alive at the time. So has Minerva . . . Raven." She turned to him. "Where is our mutual friend?"

She doesn't know I'm in here.

Good. Let's keep it that way.

"She's dead," Raven said simply.

Jules cocked her head slightly and narrowed her eyes. "Well, yes, I know that. But she has to be here somewhere. Wherever the queen is, her lackeys are always in tow. I should know." She giggled, and Scadlock laughed with her, though Raven wasn't sure whether the man knew what he was laughing at. No one else thought it was funny.

"Where is she?" Jules asked again.

Roger spoke up. "She is, in fact, very much dead—even here in the Shire Wood. Look behind you."

Jules turned around. A few yards away, on the ground, lay Minerva's corpse. Even Jules, who was famous for her composure, lost a little of it when she saw it. She turned back toward Raven, looking shaken but still unconvinced.

"That's not her," she said finally, drawing herself up and puffing her chest out. "If it were, you'd be devastated, and you're not. What are you hiding?"

"My pain. From you," he said evenly—his voice, but Minerva's words.

Jules studied him for a moment and appeared to buy it, or at the very least was no longer interested enough to challenge him. Meanwhile, Scadlock had sidled up to her and was gawking at her as though he'd never seen a woman before. The truth was close to it: They called this band the merry *men* for a reason, but it was hard to stay merry for too long without a woman's company. At least it was for someone like Scadlock.

"Might I invite you back to our camp for a drop of ale and a sampling of our hospitality?" he said.

Hospitality in his tent, no doubt, Raven cracked.

Mhmmm, Minerva answered. *But I don't care about that. What I want to know is why she's dead. Something must have happened up there to make her that way.*

And now we're stuck with her.

"Just wait a moment!" Roger said. "What do we know of this lady that we should be so eager to invite her back to our encampment?"

Scadlock raised both eyebrows in an expression that said, "You must be mad," then said in a tone that left no doubt he was stating the obvious, "Because she *is* a lady, Roger. And we are gentlemen. This is what gentlemen do."

I guess there is honor among thieves after all, Raven quipped.

Only when they're hard up.

"No offense . . . what was your name again?" asked Jules.

"William. Or Will if you prefer." Scadlock was trying to be smooth, but he couldn't mask his disappointment and surprise that she'd forgotten his name so quickly, if she had. Jules had a habit of finding and exploiting a person's weaknesses, and Scadlock hadn't exactly been playing hide-and-seek with his.

"Ah, yes, William." She declined to use the more familiar form of his name, as he'd suggested. "Well, William, your offer is most generous. However, it is customary to look a lady directly in the eyes when making such an . . . invitation."

Uh oh.

Yeah.

"May I suggest something?" Raven spoke up hastily, but it was an instant too late. Scadlock had obediently fixed his eyes on Jules, whose own eyes narrowed as she used her gift to hold his gaze.

"So," she said. "You have the gift, as well."

"Yes, Milady."

Oh, crap.

"What is the meaning of this?" Roger demanded, but no one was listening.

"I'm not coming back to your encampment, dear William, but you are coming with me. I think I might find you useful to my purpose."

"Yes, Milady."

"I said, what is the meaning of this!"

Jules kept her eyes fixed on Scadlock as she flipped her wrist in a dismissive backhand toward Roger. "I thought about taking you, as well, but you're too much of a spoilsport. William here is much more my type."

Scadlock's eyes widened, and a silly smile spread across his lips. What was she sending him? Whatever it was, it must have been suggestive.

"Apologies, everyone, but I have to run. Oh, and Raven, my condolences about that poor waif of a girlfriend. Too bad you couldn't bring her back. She always was more . . . talented . . . than you were. Ta-ta!"

She vanished, Scadlock along with her.

Where do you think she went? Minerva asked.

I have a pretty good idea, and I know I can get us there.

Your parents' place?

Yeah, that's where my grandfather was last time, and she'll be looking for him.

"Sorry, Roger," Raven announced, "but I'm afraid we have to be going, too."

Faster than Raven could have imagined possible, Roger had grabbed his bow, wheeled on him, nocked an arrow, and drew a bead directly on his heart. "I will be joining you," he said.

"I'm afraid . . ."

"You should be afraid, good sir. If you move an inch, this arrow will move toward you faster than you can think to remove yourself from this place. You would do well to remember that I have the gift, as well, and that even without it, my arrow will fly faster and truer than any thought your feeble modern mind has ever entertained."

He's bluffing, Raven said. *The gift can't help him if I decide to ditch this place. I don't care how fast he is on the draw.*

Right. But why not take him along?

Seriously? Raven said. *I think I agree with Jules. He's too much trouble. Wait. Did I just agree with Jules?*

You did, but I don't. And if I ever do, you have my permission for an I-told-you-so.

I didn't think I needed permission.

You do, said Minerva. *But the point is, if she's got Scadlock, it might come in handy for us to have Roger.*

Agreed.

"No need for threats, Roger. I assumed you'd want to stay here where you're more comfortable, but if you want to come along, then by all means."

Raven was about to focus on their destination when Minerva interrupted the process.

Aren't you forgetting something?

Raven wasn't sure what she meant until her thoughts guided him to the body she had inhabited before it had been summarily deprived of its head. Raven's killing blow had not only severed head from torso, it had flung the emerald necklace that had hung around her neck into the grass nearby.

I don't want to leave that behind, she told him. *It was a gift from someone special.*

Raven stepped over toward her lifeless body and plucked the necklace up out of the grass. Seeing her body lying there made him wince, but she reminded him that it wasn't really her. She was still right there with him, closer than ever. Wiping the necklace on his shirt sleeve, he draped it around his own neck.

Roger nodded resolutely, satisfied that his threat had worked. "Would you mind telling me exactly where we are going?"

"You'll see," Raven said with a wink. "Hang on. I've got a feeling we're in for one hell of a ride!"

Nice

"How long are we supposed to stay here?"

Paige gazed at him with a half-smile that looked like it belonged on a cherub in a Renaissance painting, a smile that said, "I know something you don't know, but you would know if you'd been paying attention."

"This is it, kiddo," she said at last, when it was clear he wasn't going to stop looking at her with that well-I'm-waiting look on his face. "Like they said on that old game show, this is your life, Eric Daly. You want a future? You're lookin' at it."

"I'm looking at you."

She laughed. "Yeah, you are. And from where your eyes are going, I'd say you like what you see."

Henry looked away reflexively.

Paige laughed again, but there was some sympathy behind it this time. "What did they tell you when they brought you here?"

"Nothing."

She shook her head. "Well, here's what they told me. They said I wasn't going anywhere, so I may as well get used to it because it's a whole lot better than a prison cell. I couldn't argue with that."

"I imagine not."

She sat down on a tan love seat with frayed upholstery. It had to be at least ten years old. Whoever had furnished this place wouldn't have won any awards for extravagance. It was a bare-bones setup. Used furniture. Old, dusty blinds that were broken off at the end in one or two places. A slap-dash paint job that was peeling at the corners, the standard pale cream color chipping away to reveal a sea green undercoat. This was the end of the road for the occupants, who were meant to be deposited and left to fend for themselves. They would either rot or fade into oblivion, it didn't really matter which.

Paige patted the cushion beside her. "Want a drink? Come and sit. I don't bite . . . unless you want me to."

He frowned. "What if I want you to?"

"Who says I don't want to?"

She had a flask of something in her hand. Henry didn't know what it was, but to tell the truth, he didn't care. Henry shook his head and plopped himself down beside her and let her pour some of whatever it was into a shot glass.

"How do you stay so calm about all this?" he asked, taking the shot glass and putting it to his lips.

"Are you sippin' that, Englishman? Don't you know how to down a shot?" She took the glass from him and threw her head back, tossing it down with a satisfied *ahhhhhh!* "Now, *that's* how it's done, kiddo!"

Henry took the flask and shot glass from her and followed her lead. "You didn't answer my question, love. How can you stay so calm?"

She smiled. "Because it's my life. It's always been crazy. It's only since I've been here that I've had any stability at all."

Henry turned and looked at her directly. "What about Mike?"

Paige didn't turn her eyes away from his. "Mike felt sorry for me. That's the best anyone ever did. Before that, they either ignored me or abused me. I mean, look at me? Who would want this?"

Henry shook his head. "There's nothing wrong with you."

Paige threw her head back and laughed long and loud. "Everything's wrong with me. I'm fat. I'm opinionated. I've got cellulite jiggling in my belly and dangling down under my arms like it was tinsel on a Christmas tree. And you say there's nothing wrong with me? I don't need that kind of pity, kiddo. I don't blame you for sayin' it. You're a nice guy and all. I just don't need it. The people who've said it before weren't nearly as nice as you."

"You think I'm nice?"

"And drunk."

"I've only had one shot."

"Then you won't mind if I do this." She leaned forward, put her arms around him, and pressed her lips to his, opening them slightly as she allowed her tongue to escape.

He didn't resist, allowing his own lips to part, tasting her tongue as he felt it dance against his. What surprised him was that he wasn't thinking about

Amber. He was thinking of the woman whose lips were meeting his own. Had he simply grown accustomed to her in the short time he'd been with her? Or did he really find her this desirable? The answer was obvious before he even posed the question.

She pulled back and fixed him with a look that seemed to say, "Yeah, I thought so."

"That was nice," she said.

"You think *I'm* being polite?"

She laughed, and in spite of himself, he laughed along with her.

"The point is, no one's ever pegged me as 'nice' before."

Paige's laughter subsided, and she shook her head. "That's because you don't let people see it. But I'm not people. I'm Paige."

This time, he was the one who leaned forward, curling his arm around her side and up her back as he pulled her lips forward to meet his.

It was even better—and longer—this time.

"Hmmm," she said, licking her lips suggestively as they parted. "Maybe 'nice' ain't the word for it, after all. I'm thinkin' maybe 'hot' fits a little better."

Henry looked at her, trying to read her. Was she just playing around? Was he blushing? The two questions flashed in his mind at once, along with the answers: "I don't think so" and "dammit, man, get control of yourself."

Paige smiled about as big a smile as someone could without showing any teeth. "Now that's the spirit, kiddo," she said. "Like I said, this is our future. You're starting to catch on."

The newfound color drained out of Henry's cheeks and he sank back away from her against a worn sofa cushion. So, that's what this was about? Make the best of it? Love the one you're with? Some sort of mutual, or perhaps even one-sided, case of Stockholm syndrome? He'd always wondered if love were just some sort of self-delusion anyway.

Had he used that L word? He certainly wasn't there. Yet.

He wondered if Raven and Minerva had to deal with any of this. They *had* to stay together for survival's sake. Did they really care about each other, or were they only together because they had to be?

"Bollocks."

Paige's own smile faded, and she turned her body more to face him. The look on her face was one of genuine concern. "Did I say something wrong? Oh, crap. I knew it. I should just keep my damn mouth shut."

Henry's eyes widened a little, and he leaned forward again slightly. "No, I didn't mean that. I just mean . . . I mean, look, love, we're here all by ourselves and we're kind of stuck here."

"Oh."

"No, I don't mean . . . Listen, you've got it wrong. I mean, if you weren't here, you'd be with Mike, and . . ."

"And if you weren't here, you'd be with someone else, too. I get it. No need to spell it out for me, kiddo."

"Wait, no, I . . ."

"Just so you know, I was never in love with Mike. He said he was in love with me, but I think it was just a macho thing, y'know? He needs to feel like he's protecting a woman, and I kinda fell into his lap . . . so to speak . . ." She laughed in spite of herself. "What I mean is, I like you. Yeah, we both gotta be here, but if we didn't, I'd still want to hang with you. A lot. If it ain't the same for you, I get that. Wouldn't be the first time I misread a guy."

She was as insecure as he was. They just tried to hide it in different ways—he with his image as a self-absorbed, dismissive doctor; her behind the tattoos and tough biker-girl exterior.

You didn't misread me. Henry didn't say it, though. Instead, he positioned himself to face Paige, put both arms around her and pulled her to him firmly, tilting his head and opening his mouth slightly as he pressed his lips against hers. He felt her arms run under his shirt and up his back, her nails digging into his skin as she opened her own mouth wider to meet his. He heard her moan slightly and he kissed her harder, but at the same time gently.

But then another sound met his ears, the sound of footsteps just outside. And a hard, insistent banging on the door.

"I know you're in there. Open up!"

Boyfriend

Henry felt like he must have nearly jumped out of his shirt. He'd been so engrossed in Paige and their newfound connection that the last thing he'd expected was a loud and sudden interruption. Especially here, in the middle of nowhere. No one was supposed to even know they were there. From the sound of it, this was no salesman or friendly neighbor dropping by to say hello. This was someone on a mission—and not someone likely to take no for an answer.

"Bloody hell! Who the . . .?"

"Shhhh. Calm down, kiddo." She was trying to keep her voice even and reassuring, but there was a slight quaver to it that told him she was as startled as he was. Maybe more so.

"Open this fucking door right now or I'll break it down!"

Paige got to her feet. She was clearly nervous. "It might be better if you go back to the bedroom, hon. I'll handle this."

"Do you know this person?"

"Yeah. And I know him well enough to know that you don't want to be anywhere around him when he's like this."

"It's Mike, isn't it?" He stood up.

"Yeah."

"But you said . . ."

"Open this goddamn door NOW!"

"No time." She took him by the shoulders and pushed him hard in the direction of the bedroom. He'd wanted to go there with her, but hardly under these circumstances. And it appeared she wouldn't be coming with him.

She wheeled and turned toward the front door, which was being assaulted by a very big fist or a shoe, he couldn't tell which. Henry suddenly felt a wave of panic that Mike was here to take Paige away. If he wasn't there to intervene, he might not ever see her again. For a pragmatic Englishman who strove to maintain his composure, this was an unexpected, and unfamiliar, feeling. There wasn't any time to analyze it, though. Paige had her hand on the doorknob and was starting to turn it. Henry made the split-second decision to be standing at her side when she opened it.

By the time she realized he was there, the door was halfway open and the person on the other side was coming into view. He wasn't tall, but he was big. The beefy kind of big that would have played right tackle on a high school football team, even if he wasn't good enough for a college scholarship.

Henry expected Mike to toss him aside and force his way into the place, but he didn't. He just stood there for a moment, as if he didn't know what was going on.

"Paige?"

"Mike."

"So, this is who they set you up with."

She nodded.

Henry peered past him and saw a half-dozen riders in black leather sitting on Harleys at the end of the front walk. They were watching the three of them closely. Henry had the feeling that they'd be on him like a shot, with a single gesture from Mike. But Mike looked almost frozen, except that he was blinking a little faster than normal. For a moment, the three of them just stood there, all looking at one another, not sure of what to do or say.

Finally, it was Henry who heard himself speak up. "I'm . . . uh . . . Eric." He put his right foot forward and extended his hand, not sure whether the other man would take it or take a swing at him.

Mike reached forward and grasped it firmly.

"Why don't you come in," Henry said. "Paige has told me a lot about you."

Mike nodded, pulled his hand back and glanced over his shoulder, nodding again as Henry moved aside so he could step inside.

"Paige, is it?" Mike said with a chuckle. "You always did like that name, Rosa."

"It *is* my name now, Mike. You want to call me that other name, you can take your ass right back out that door."

"Feisty as ever," he said, chuckling, but it seemed like a forced laugh. Everything about his demeanor seemed forced, like he'd been thrown off his high horse and couldn't remember how to get back on.

They settled in awkwardly at the dining room table, with Henry and Mike on either side of Paige.

"Beer?" Mike said.

"In the fridge," Paige answered. "Get it yourself, Mike. You're welcome to it—if you can stomach piss water."

"Whatever you got." He grabbed a cold, metallic gold can out of the refrigerator and popped it open as he sat back down.

"So," Paige said. "You're out."

"Yeah, since last week. Good behavior." He gave a short laugh. "Been tryin' to track you down since then."

"Mike, I . . ."

Her voice trailed off, replaced by an awkward silence with the two of them just staring out at each other from behind expressions that might have held anything from regret to anger to love.

At least, it was awkward for Henry.

"Just how did you track us down?" he asked finally. "The whole point of being in witness protection is that no one's supposed to be able to find us."

Both of the others turned and glared at him—Mike menacingly and Paige in what looked like annoyance—and Henry realized he'd interrupted something important between the two. But this was important, too. More important than them revisiting their feelings for each other, or whatever it was they were doing with their silent stares. The fact that Henry himself wasn't eager for them to revisit their feelings was beside the point. They were supposed to be safe here, and if Mike's gang could find them . . .

Paige seemed to recognize this, too, because her expression softened. She nodded slightly, then turned back to Mike.

"He's right," she said.

Mike's expression shifted from menacing to where Paige's had been a moment earlier: annoyed. "You know the Condors," he said, as if that explained everything. "But your little boyfriend here is right."

"I'm not her boyfriend," Henry interjected, and Paige shot him another look of annoyance, mixed with something else. Hurt.

"I'm her husband," he added quickly, and the look disappeared.

The inscrutable look left Mike's face and he tossed his head back in laughter. "In your dreams!" he exclaimed.

"This ain't funny, Mike," Paige said. "If you can find us here, someone else could, too. They weren't supposed to be protecting Eric here from you; they were supposed to be protecting him from . . ."

"Duke Malone," Mike finished for her. "Which is part of why I'm here, Paige. This place ain't safe for you. If I could find you, so could he."

Henry shook his head slightly. "Wait a minute," he said. "Part of this doesn't add up."

They both looked at him, and he could see something new in Paige's eyes—concern. Not for him or Mike, but for herself. Henry didn't realize it, but she suspected he was about to ask a question she had hoped he'd never get around to figuring out.

She was right.

"Paige," he said, "your ex is dead. So, who are they trying to protect *you* from?"

Paige swallowed and looked like she wanted to disappear through the back of her chair.

But it was Mike who spoke next. "Me," he said. "Or the Condors. It was her word that put me away. You don't rat out a Condor and get away with it."

"But you *told* her to do that," Henry objected.

"*They* don't know that. If they did, she'd be behind bars, too."

Henry nodded tentatively. That made sense, but there was something more to this. He could see it in Paige's worried expression, and he suspected there was far more than he realized.

Mike drank a swig of beer. "Yeah, piss water," he muttered under his breath. Then he turned his attention back to Paige. "That's why I gotta get you out of here," he said. "If I can find you, Malone's assholes can find you, too. I can't let that happen. You're my girl, and you're coming with me."

Paige put both palms down on the table. "If I go, Eric goes," she said.

Mike took another, longer drink from the beer can. "Are you insane, Rosa?"

"Rosa?"

"Sorry. Paige. He's the one Malone is looking for. If we take him, they'll be after us, too."

Paige leaned forward slightly in challenge. "What's this I hear?" she said in a slightly mocking, sing-song voice. "A Condor scared?"

Mike drained the last of the beer, crushed the can in his fist, and slammed it down on the table. "You know better than that, *Rosa*."

Henry shook his head. This was happening too fast.

"If she goes with you, they'll assume that you kidnapped her and put you right back in prison," Henry said. "Or maybe they'll figure out that you were working together and they'll put *her* in prison. Is that what you want?"

"Who asked you?" Mike thundered, jumping to his feet as he threw the empty beer can across the room.

At the same moment, the front door burst open, and one of the Condors rushed into the room, a thin man whose gaunt physique made him seem taller than he was. A half-grown dirty blond beard grew like wild thistle out of his chin and straggly, greasy hair of the same color drifted down to his shoulders from beneath a throwback World War II biker helmet.

"Trouble, Mike," he said in a voice that was half-mumbled, half-urgent. "There's a car down the block that's been watching us. Another one just pulled up. Some guys got out and started walking this way. Thought you oughta know."

"Deal with them, Chet," Mike growled.

Chet turned and left without another word, and a moment later the sound of a motorcycle starting rumbled through the still-open door. A second engine roared to life a moment later.

"I'm going out there," Mike declared. Paige, without saying anything, was a step behind him. *Was she crazy?*

Henry hesitated just a moment before following. He might be walking out into a firing squad, but it was better than the thought of Mike dragging Paige off to god knows where without him at least *trying* to stop it.

There at the edge of the road stood four men in dark gray suits facing off against half a dozen Condors. In a way, it was comical. The men were clearly overdressed for a god-forsaken desert where temperatures could hit 110. It wasn't quite that hot today, but Henry couldn't help wondering how much they were sweating. He knew he would have been sweating, regardless of what the thermometer said, if he were standing directly across from six members of the Condors. The bikers were all packing, and it would have been a mismatch—except that the men were armed, too . . . with automatic weapons.

"No one has to get hurt here," one of the men in the gray suits was saying. "Give us Marshall and we'll be on our way."

Marshall. These guys were here for him, and they knew his real name. They had to be Duke Malone's errand boys.

Henry was a coward. He'd been a coward all his life, and a very big part of him wanted to run back inside before anyone knew he was there. But a bigger part of him didn't want Paige caught up in any of this. Whatever she might be hiding from him, she didn't deserve this. Henry had no special love for Mike, but he didn't deserve it, either. Not really. None of this had anything to do with him, or any of the Condors.

Henry stepped out away from Paige and Mike before either of them could say anything, raised his hands, and shouted, "I'm over here!" He fully expected those to be his last words, and the moment he uttered them, all four of the men in gray turned their heads in his direction.

That moment was all the Condors needed. Chet gunned the gas and plowed directly into the center of the group, sending two of them either falling or jumping out of the way as they let loose with a volley of bullets that either flew into the air or hit the ground and ricocheted away like high-powered pinballs. One of the bullets struck one of their companions in the knee, and he crumpled to the ground in pain. The other two wheeled back around to face the Condors, only to find the bikers no longer directly in front of them but gunning their own engines as they split off to either side and circled around.

Mike pulled a handgun of his own and started racing toward them. At a dead run, he aimed the gun at one of them and fired.

The man spun around, his shoulder grazed, and dropped to one knee, but sprang up again, firing in Mike's direction.

Mike hit the ground and rolled as a spray of bullets sailed over him, but there was no place to take cover and he remained exposed.

The other graysuit still standing pulled the trigger and sent lead flying in an arc that followed the path of one Condor's Harley. The man, struck repeatedly, flew off the seat as his ride careened sideways and skidded across gravel and rutted pavement, coming to rest with its engine still rumbling nearly all the way across the street. The man lay motionless, blood running from his abdomen, leg, and neck.

As the graysuit turned, a second Condor was bearing down like a rabid hellhound. Before the graysuit could squeeze the trigger, the man was on top of him, sending his weapon hurtling away as the pair rolled over the ground, sharp gravel tearing away pieces of both the Condor's leather jacket and his adversary's once-immaculately pressed gray jacket.

The Condor pinned him for a moment, delivering a powerful blow to the face propelled by a thick longshoreman's forearm, but the other man was just as strong, thrusting his knee upward into his assailant's groin, a blow that sent him tumbling off to the side. In an instant, it was the graysuit who was on top, pummeling the biker with a left hook, followed by a right cross to the temple that left the man shaken and senseless on the pavement.

The graysuit sprang up and retrieved his weapon, quickly unloading a dozen bullets rapid-fire into the fallen man's skull.

Now one of the graysuits who had been tossed aside like a bowling pin in Chet's initial charge was back on his feet, retrieving his own gun and firing at Chet, who somehow avoided being hit and returned fire with his pistol, felling the man with a single shot. He lay on the ground, convulsing, a hole in the center of his chest.

Mike was scurrying along the ground on his belly, desperately trying to reach the mobile home again so he could take cover, but before could get there, the man who'd been shooting at him found his target, slicing off flesh from his left shoulder and biting into the bone underneath. Mike winced and rolled through the dust, but kept going despite the pain.

Two Condors were dead and one man on each side was seriously wounded.

A third Condor fell as the graysuit who had been knocked aside by Chet managed to recover his weapon and fire it a split-second before the biker could pull his own trigger, sending the man's body hurtling backward in what seemed like several directions at once. At the end of this bizarre marionette's dance, he lay lifeless on the ground, his body pierced repeatedly by gunfire.

But the man didn't live long enough to savor his victory. He'd been so intent on the one Condor that he'd failed to notice a second member of the gang had jumped off his bike and come rushing up behind him, depositing a fist to his kidney in the same moment that he wrapped a thick arm around his neck. Before the graysuit could react, the biker grabbed his chin and yanked, snapping the man's spine with a single motion.

"Paige, we have to get out of here!" Henry said, grabbing Paige's hand and pulling her back inside.

"Not without Mike." She pulled free of his grasp.

"You can't go back out there."

"Watch me," she growled, and, running to a small closet, retrieved a sawed-off shotgun from what looked to Henry like a hidden compartment.

"Why didn't you tell me about that?" he asked, incredulous.

"No time to explain, kiddo. Just follow me."

Peeking through the cracked door, they surveyed in the scene: Three Condors dead and Mike severely wounded; one of the graysuits had also breathed his last, and a second was writhing in the middle of the road, his kneecap apparently shattered. Another Condor roared up to him and ended his misery, depositing a bullet in his chest as Paige and Henry watched. That left only two graysuits alive, and one of them was striding up to Mike, gun in hand, intent on finishing him. Mike was trying to crawl, but there was no way he could escape the man who was stalking him.

Like a cat slinking around a corner, Paige opened the door a little wider. She raised the shotgun and braced herself for the backfire.

She aimed.

She fired.

The force of the shot sent Paige reeling backward into Henry, who stumbled and barely caught himself without falling. Outside, the man fell in a heap perhaps ten paces from where Mike lay as the echo from the blast seemed to freeze time.

Then, just as suddenly, everything started again. The only remaining graysuit ran for the car, pursued by one of the three Condors still standing or riding.

He wasn't for long.

Without warning, the fleeing graysuit spun around and unloaded the remainder of his magazine's contents at his pursuer, puncturing both the bike's tires and its fuel tank as another bullet pierced the rider's side. Sparks flew from chrome struck simultaneously by gunfire, igniting the fuel that had begun to escape from the Harley's tank into a fireball that raced across vehicle and rider, consuming them both in a brief but deadly inferno.

The graysuit reached his car before either of the other bikers could stop him, gunned the gas and peeled out, pulling a 180 and disappearing in a cloud of dust and gravel.

Chet and the other Condor who'd managed to survive jumped off their bikes and ran toward Mike, while Paige and Henry rushed out of the house to meet them. Mike's breathing was ragged but, to their relief, still strong. The wound in his shoulder looked a mess, blood still seeping through the caked-on dirt he'd picked up trying to slither across the dusty field that passed as a front yard. He lay on his back, biting his lip to keep from crying out in pain.

"You okay, Mike?" Chet asked.

"Does he look okay, dumbass?" Paige said.

Chet shook his head. "Sorry. Ace, give me a hand here," he said, nodding toward the other Condor. "Help me get him inside."

The pair picked him up, careful to avoid the injured shoulder, and carried him to the double-wide.

Henry looked at Paige as they followed. "What do we do now?"

Mike answered through gritted teeth. "We get the hell out of here. That's what I've been trying to tell you!"

Finders Keepers

They landed smack dab in the middle of the living room this time. Two bodies, three spirits. Raven and Minerva, still bound in Raven's body, and the pre-eminent merry man of the Shire Wood, Roger Godberd.

It was nearly twilight when they arrived. The floor was overlaid in an uneven pattern of long, jagged shadows. A bronze pole lamp crowned by a shade that looked like a crimson-tinged lily bathed one corner in a soft light. Filling out the room were a gold straight-backed chair, a sofa, and a love seat, all framed in lines and swirls of dark wood carved in patterns of leaves and stems.

The room itself was suffused in silence. No one was here.

Where are your parents? Your grandma?

I didn't know, Raven replied.

"What is this place?" Roger asked. He was looking around, his eyes filled with a mixture of wonder and apprehension.

"My parents live here," said Raven. "But I guess they're not home."

Something feels wrong about this, Raven.

I know.

Raven scanned the room more closely, his eyes moving from one corner to the next, across the floor and up to the ceiling. He wasn't sure what he was looking for, but since this place had been created out of his memories to begin with, he was pretty sure he'd notice when something was out of place.

Or someone. Lying behind the sofa, in the shadows. Only visible because a booted leg was sticking out.

Roger's eyes followed Raven's to where the figure lay.

"Scadlock!" he exclaimed, recognizing the boot.

Together, they hurried across the room and pulled the couch aside, kneeling next to the figure of William. He seemed barely conscious. He moaned something neither of them could make out, and he managed to open one eye; just enough to let some light in and make out the faces of the two men poised over him. It seemed as though it had taken all his strength to do that much.

When he saw Roger, he seemed to pull a little more energy from somewhere inside himself. He opened his eyes all the way and managed to push himself up on both elbows.

"Mother of God, am I glad to see you!" he said, his strength returning as he pushed himself up all the way to sit straight in front of them.

He was fading, Minerva observed.

Yeah. He doesn't know this place, and there's no way for him to stay conscious on his own. Jules must have brought him here, then ditched him. If we hadn't found him in the next few minutes, he probably would've been gone altogether.

"What is the meaning of this?" Roger asked, his brow furrowed in a mix of concern and agitation.

Scadlock got to his feet and stumbled a couple of steps before depositing himself on the sofa. His eyes seemed to refocus as he explained that Jules had brought him here, just as Raven had suspected—and had met up with another man, someone named Josef. Scadlock, being a rogue but a jealous sort of rogue, hadn't taken too kindly to this new rival. William suspected this Josef was the real reason Jules had chosen this particular destination. When Scadlock objected, Jules ignored him. The other man dismissed him with a snort, declaring that "the ruffian" was more trouble than he was worth.

Jules had taken a long, hard look at him and smiled. Then she'd walked over to him, draped her arms around his shoulder, and raised her knee sharply, driving it savagely up into his most vulnerable region.

He'd collapsed on the floor, and the man had pulled him, still writhing, behind the sofa.

"I suppose you're right," Jules had said. "He *does* have the gift. I just thought he might be some use to us."

"Too much trouble," the man scoffed again, and the two of them left. The last thing Scadlock said he remembered was the sound of a door closing behind them.

But where are your parents? And your grandmother? Minerva asked Raven. *They should be here.*

Raven was asking the same questions. He didn't have an answer. He searched the room again, trying to get a sense of where they might have gone. There was no sign of them. Everything was just as it should have been, except, they weren't there. The room was quiet, nothing was moving, save the shadows, ever so gradually, as the Between sun continued its gradual descent. But even though they'd discovered Scadlock and brought him back to his senses, he couldn't shake the feeling that something was wrong.

"Looking for someone?"

The sound of the voice abruptly breaking the silence nearly caused Minerva to jump out of Raven's skin. The door to the kitchen opened and out stepped Jules, with Josef a step behind.

"You didn't think we'd abandon you, now did you?" she said teasingly.

They hadn't left at all. Maybe the sound of the door Scadlock had heard had been the kitchen door, not the front door. Or maybe . . .

Raven felt a hand at the back of his neck and, almost simultaneously, a sudden, cutting pressure at the front of it. He felt like he was choking. Then, a second later, the pressure released and he heard something snap.

The emerald necklace.

"Never turn your back on a thief, my friend," Scadlock laughed, stepping backward and holding the necklace up triumphantly in his right hand, a mischievous smile dancing across his face.

Raven lunged at him, but he was too quick, stepping aside gleefully like some nimble-footed sprite. Almost in the same motion, he brought his other hand up in a fist and slammed it into Raven's right temple, sending him reeling backward and onto the love seat. The next moment, Roger stepped between the two of them, separating the men and glowering at his fellow bandit.

Apparently, Scadlock hadn't been fading at all. He'd pretended to be out cold so he could snatch the emerald necklace while Raven was distracted. All that business about them abandoning him had been a bunch of bull.

"What is that thing?" Roger demanded, nodding toward the necklace, as Scadlock stuffed it into a pouch he wore around his waist.

But it was Josef who answered. "That *thing*, as you so eloquently describe it, is a fragment of the emerald tablet of Thoth, the Egyptian deity also known as Enoch, from the Bible."

Roger looked at him, puzzled.

"Of course, you wouldn't know about it," Josef said dismissively. "Let me educate you: According to legend, the patriarch Enoch buried all the secrets of the antediluvian world in an unknown location. These secrets were thought to contain all the wisdom and power God had imparted to the race of man before the flood."

"What you speak of is the devil's work," Roger said, his voice rising as he made the sign of the cross. "For the love of the Holy Mother, do not say that you believe in the dark arts."

Josef's eyes narrowed, but he wasn't looking at Roger. His eyes were fixed on Raven, studying him. Raven knew enough to keep from meeting his grandfather's gaze. He was well aware of what would happen.

"I believe in power," Josef said flatly. "If it works, I don't question it. I use it. And I intend to use the emerald . . . or as we who are enlightened call it, the Philosopher's Stone."

"To what end?" Roger asked.

"To preserve memory. That's its ultimate purpose. It acts like someone with the gift—it has the power to restore the dead to the world of the living. It was the basis of my work for the Führer and, later, for my own purposes. In the service of misplaced affection, I offered it to your grandmother in the hopes that we might reconcile. She took *it* but rejected *me*. I've been trying to get it back ever since."

Jules tried to disguise her jealousy as she glared at him sidelong, but she wasn't doing a very good job. She had been the rival to Raven's grandmother for Josef's affections, and it still stung that—even now—she wound up on the losing end of that competition.

Do you know what this means? It was Minerva's voice, inside Raven's head.

Yeah, it means that emerald can revive my grandfather. And Jules, too.

Josef took a step toward Scadlock, his hand outstretched. "Now, if you don't mind handing it over, the four of us can be on our way back to the land of the living."

Scadlock raised his eyebrows. "The four of us?" he said mockingly. "Where I come from, we have a couple of sayings: Finders are the best of keepers, and when opportunity comes knocking, you don't let someone else answer the door. Come now, Robin, let's see what's out there."

He reached forward abruptly, grasped Robin's forearm, and shut his eyes tight. In a flash, the two of them were gone.

⌒

"You trusted a *thief*?" Jules was staring at Josef, incredulous.

"I don't recall hearing any objections from you."

She sighed. "Do I have to clean up all your messes?"

"This is why we are no longer together."

"It looks to me as if we are. Even death couldn't keep us apart, *sweetheart*."

Looks like the happy couple isn't so happy, Minerva observed.

I don't care about them. It looks like that emerald was our ticket out of here, and we didn't even know it. Now it's gone.

Raven was right. But even if they could get back, returning to the world of the living would have put them right back where they started: getting progressively weaker until they both faded right out of existence. What would happen then? To them? To Amber.

Amber. I'd forgotten all about . . .

Forgotten? Oh, hell. You don't mean . . .

The panic he felt from Minerva was all the answer he needed. She never forgot anything, but if her mind had been off of Amber too long, there was only one possible outcome.

If Minerva could have shaken him by his shoulders, she would have, but she didn't need to. Raven knew exactly what was at stake.

We have to find a way back.

Hamptons

Phantom didn't like waiting. He hadn't heard anything since the kidnapper had made his demands, and his efforts in finding Rudy had all run into dead ends. He had heard something interesting: Henry Marshall's location had been compromised. He disappeared after a shoot-out between a biker gang and another group of men.

He didn't need any intelligence agents to tell him. It was all over the internet. The reports said the residents of the home had disappeared. The address matched the safe house the agency set up for Marshall.

Phantom was sure one of the groups had been sent by Rudy's kidnapper, and they'd found Marshall based on the info he'd given them. Which group, he wasn't sure, but it seemed unlikely that a bunch of bikers would care about any of this. How they'd gotten involved was anybody's guess. He'd have to put some people on it.

Phantom answered the phone when it rang, but it wasn't about Rudy or Henry Marshall or any of that. It was about Amber Hardin-Torres, the woman they'd captured along with Minerva Rus and Raven Corbet. All three of them were lying unconscious at a secure location, but now, something was wrong.

Phantom ended the call and grabbed his coat as he dashed out the door. Bypassing the elevator, he hurried down five flights of stairs to the street below. Cars, taxis, and delivery trucks lurched by in heavy traffic; an occasional horn blared as an impatient driver tried to change lanes, and a deep bass pounded from an amplified woofer to rise above the other sounds of the city.

Phantom clicked a button on his key chain and the lights on a navy-blue Mercedes AMG S winked at him. He opened the door and tossed his coat onto the passenger seat.

To anyone else on Wall Street, he looked like just another stockbroker in a hurry to get to the trading floor. But someone watching, three cars back, knew better. After Phantom pulled away from the curb, the observer pulled out to follow the man he recognized as Neil Vincent. It hadn't been easy, but the man watching was a trained tracker. He had a talent for recognizing faces, even if Vincent had shaved his once-trademark beard and looked to have had some work done on his nose.

The man knew enough to remain inconspicuous. He'd attached a tracking device to Vincent's car, so he wouldn't lose him. He drummed his fingers methodically on the steering wheel to Fleetwood Mac's *Go Your Own Way*, as he sat in the gridlock of New York traffic, waiting for the light to change. He had patience. It had been a part of him for years, out of necessity. Like a snake on the hunt, he had to wait for just the right moment to strike—when his prey was in range, preoccupied and unsuspecting. If that prey happened to lead him to an even tastier piece of meat, so much the better. He needed to see where Vincent was going; if he was right, the man would lead him to the quarry he'd been seeking.

Traffic finally started moving again, funneling him onto the FDR Parkway and past the Brooklyn Bridge. Vincent didn't turn there. He kept on going, northbound, until he hit the Long Island Expressway, then veered right across the East River and away from Manhattan. Traffic lightened a bit as the road whisked him eastbound toward the Hamptons. He turned south on the William Floyd Parkway and then east again on the Sunrise Highway over land that extended like a beckoning finger out into the Atlantic.

After a time, the man following risked pulling within visual range, which wasn't easy. Once traffic cleared, Vincent had started barreling ahead at speeds well over the limit, even once he turned off the highway. Vincent hadn't noticed him, which was fortunate. Someone with his training should have been aware of everything around him. From the ten-year-old towhead riding his skateboard to the warblers chirping in the branches overhead.

Vincent was clearly distracted. That was dangerous. Not just to him, but also to the gray-haired man in the golf shirt who had parked his Mercedes at the side of the road and opened the door just as Vincent came along. Going twenty miles over the speed limit, Vincent swerved slightly into the oncoming lane. The gray-haired man shouted an obscenity as he passed. Vincent either didn't care or didn't notice.

Vincent's tail eased off the accelerator, dropping back out of sight, relying once more on his GPS. He couldn't risk drawing attention by speeding through the streets of East Hampton like this. No matter how distracted Vincent was, he was bound to notice someone trying to match his speed.

A few moments later, the blinking dot on the grid indicated Vincent's position had come to a stop a few hundred yards ahead. Vincent's pursuer eased off onto the shoulder, cut the engine, and began walking the rest of the way, staying close among the maple trees, cedars, and undergrowth, to shield himself from view. He arrived at his destination just in time to see Vincent disappear into an expansive Tudor-style home, its red-brick ground floor supporting a gabled second story with dark wood timbering set against lighter, cream-colored paneling.

It was anything but small, so it might take some time to sniff out exactly where Vincent was inside . . . if he got past security. There was bound to be security, and plenty of it—not just the human variety, but the electronic sort, as well. Fortunately, he was adept at disabling both. His training told him to bide his time, wait for something to happen, and then take advantage of his quarry's distraction to make his move. But his instincts told him something else: Time was of the essence.

"No time like the present," he whispered under his breath. He moved silently through the trees toward the estate.

Translucence

Phantom threw his coat at the wooden rack in the foyer, sending it clattering to the floor. He didn't give it a second thought, racing down the hall past a pair of guards and turning the corner into the study. The two men didn't try to stop him; they knew him by sight and by demeanor.

The ceiling of the study was twice as high as in most rooms, dark mahogany accenting lighter wall panels, giving the inside a feel much like the home's exterior. It was darker, though. The windowless room was lit only by antique lamps whose light was softened by opaque, gold-tinted glass. A skylight overhead provided scant illumination, thanks to an overcast sky. The mahogany accents were thick in places, drawing themselves up to curled, almost claw-like leaves at their apex near the ceiling. Built-in bookshelves took up the lower section of two walls entirely.

Phantom stepped across the room to a small writing table and kicked one of the legs lightly. The table didn't move, but something else did: One of the bookshelves receded slowly into the wall, then swiveled, sending copies of *War and Peace*, *The Grapes of Wrath*, and two volumes of *The Decline and Fall of the Roman Empire* tumbling to the floor. It was a nuisance, but far better camouflage using real books.

Phantom had neither the time nor the patience to retrieve the fallen volumes; he had no reason to suspect that anyone would access the room, especially with the electronic security covering the grounds and guards at every entrance. He rushed forward into darkness that gave way to a dim, white light as he triggered the motion sensors aimed at the entrance.

The corridor ran several hundred feet, the lights blinking out as he passed. He had gone too far, missing the trip for the hidden side chamber.

He worked his way back along the right wall, feeling with both hands until he detected a barely perceptible crease. His fingers moved down the crease until they found the tiny notch harboring a button. Pressing it, he watched as a panel slid aside, allowing him access to a small room with a security panel at the opposite wall. There was no guard; just a fingerprint scanner and a touchscreen that blinked at random intervals, cycling images of a keypad, a cartoon Uncle Sam, a drawing of a chessboard, and an image of dynamite.

In reality, the intervals *weren't* random. If you knew the pattern, you could access the keypad by pressing the images in just the right order.

Phantom touched the chessboard, the Uncle Sam, the keypad, then the dynamite. The keypad became steady. He entered his code and pressed his thumb to the scanner.

The door popped open with an audible click.

"What's going on?" he demanded as he rushed into the room, taking inventory of who was there.

The figures of three people, a man and two women, lay in parallel hospital beds. There were no monitors, IV lines, or waste-disposal bags. All three were dead, though two of them looked, to all appearances, alive and healthy.

The third was a different matter: Her skin was pale, beyond the point of looking sickly; it was becoming translucent. Her *whole body* was becoming translucent.

"Sir . . ." A short woman with a dome cut of auburn hair, draped in a medical gown, took a step toward him. It was Marina Escobar, the nurse practitioner who had been with him when he'd tried to revive Jules.

Phantom brushed past her to the bedside of the woman who seemed to be disappearing before his eyes.

"What's happening to her?" he demanded.

The woman's face seemed to glow like a dim star in the night sky, flickering like a faint current traveling over a frayed wire.

"I don't know," Escobar stammered. "She's been like that for a while. And getting worse."

As they watched, the woman's chest jerked upward as though yanked by an invisible rope.

"Prepare a shot of adrenaline," Phantom ordered.

"But, sir, you know what happened with . . ."

"Do it!"

Phantom didn't have time to argue. He wasn't a doctor. He knew full well what had happened with Jules, but he didn't know of anything else that might stop what was happening. He had no idea if adrenaline would even work on a dead person. Could it? It didn't make sense. But none of it had made sense from the very beginning. And he had to try *something*. If it was happening to one, it could happen to the others. He couldn't allow that. He had to take the chance.

Flustered, Escobar rushed to a cabinet on the other side of the room and removed a vial. Pulling a syringe from one of the drawers below, she plunged it into the vial, drew the liquid into it. She moved to the body, and thrust the needle into her heart.

But the woman wasn't there.

All that could be seen was the faint outline of her body, shimmering like a reflection on a pond. The nurses hand plunged through the apparition, the needle emptying the contents of the syringe into the mattress.

"What?"

Escobar pulled the syringe out of the bedding and held it up in front of her, staring at it.

The image of the woman continued to fade.

"Never mind her," Phantom nearly screamed. "Get the others!"

Escobar tossed the empty syringe toward a plastic-lined metal trash bin and scurried across the room, retrieving two more vials and syringes. Hurriedly preparing the first, she plunged it into the chest of the man. This time, she felt resistance. Slowly, she squeezed the syringe until all the liquid was injected into his chest.

Then she waited.

The figures on a digital wall clock advanced methodically.

Nothing happened.

"Her! Try her!" Phantom demanded, and Escobar dutifully stepped to the center bed, repeating the process. She plunged the long, sharp needle into the third figure's chest.

The woman gasped. Her eyelids flew open like a boarded-up window blown open by a hurricane.

She sat bolt upright, her head jerking back and forth.

Blinking a few times, she focused on the scene in front of her.

Where the hell are we?

Roused

Raven? Pay attention. I said, where the hell are we?

But Raven didn't answer. He was gone.

Minerva looked down in front of her and saw her own hands, her body. She was no longer trapped inside Raven. She must have somehow escaped the Between and returned to her own revived body. The first thing she noticed was the syringe still poking out of her chest. She closed her fingers around it, slowly removing it from her chest.

The second thing was that she wasn't tired at all.

It no longer felt like she was on the verge of fading.

Whatever had been in the syringe shouldn't have affected her at all. She was still dead—at least as far as she knew.

Yet here she was.

Minerva scanned the room. A woman and a man stood staring at her.

"Why did it work on her and not on him?" The woman asked, a look of confusion on her face.

The man didn't answer, rushing forward to restrain Minerva.

She was too quick. She leapt back, putting the bed between herself and the middle-aged man.

Her energy had returned, all right.

"There's nowhere for you to run," Phantom said, working to stay calm as he fixed her with his best authoritative gaze.

Big mistake.

Phantom froze. Where had that voice come from—that voice inside his head?

It was her. He knew it the second he asked himself the question.

He'd been warned not to look her in the eye. It had been near the top of every briefing he'd received on Minerva Rus.

But old habits die hard, especially for someone from a military background who's used to sending a message with a withering look as effectively as with a spoken command.

The memory she sent into him wasn't the worst she'd ever experienced, but it was effective. The memory of Dr. Fitzgerald's goons and the lab where Carson tried to make her forget Raven—or convince her that she was crazy for having seen him.

Phantom couldn't move.

He wasn't paralyzed. He could feel his limbs, he just couldn't get them to so much as twitch.

Minerva decided to try something. Focusing her memory, she visualized herself tying it off like a bow on a Christmas present, only tighter. If she was right, she'd be able to hold the memory in place at the edge of her own consciousness, at least as long as she needed to while she focused on other matters.

Like Raven.

She turned away from the man, looking tentatively once over her shoulder—*good, he was still frozen in place*—and hurried to Raven's bedside. His eyes were closed and he wasn't moving, but he didn't appear to be fading.

"Raven!" she said sharply, hoping to snap him out of it.

He didn't respond.

She reached down and pulled back his eyelids, staring into them in the hope that she might reach him that way. Although his pupils constricted at the light, there was no sign he was aware of her, or anything else.

She wheeled around and glared at Phantom again.

"Whatever you did to me, do it to him!"

"I did," said the auburn-haired woman. "I did it before I did it to you. It didn't work."

"Why?" Minerva demanded.

"Probably because he's dead," Phantom offered.

"Revived," Minerva corrected.

Phantom was in no position to argue. "Revived," he repeated, unable to fully mask the resentment he felt at being corrected and ordered around by a woman in her early twenties.

"I'm revived, too, in case you hadn't noticed," Minerva retorted. *So that doesn't explain it.*

She'd gotten so used to speaking with Raven mentally that it was jarring when he didn't answer her thoughts. Why had the adrenaline worked on her, but not on him? *Memory. It must have something to do with memory.*

Then it hit her: Amber had used a shot of adrenaline to pull her out of a dream world where Jules had trapped her—and almost killed her before she had died in a hail of gunfire on her way to rescuing Raven. It looked like she'd have to save him again . . . but he was definitely worth the trouble. The point was, she had the memory of being brought back to consciousness by a shot of adrenaline. That *memory* had triggered something when the needle penetrated her chest. It had brought her back, just the way it did before.

Raven didn't have the experience. Of course, it wouldn't work on him.

But that didn't explain why she felt revitalized, as strong as ever. No longer in danger of fading.

What did explain it . . .

"Where's Amber?" All her confidence and control drained out of her, replaced by a tremor in her voice that made her sound like a scared little child.

The man and the woman looked at each other.

"I said, where's Amber?" A mixture of anger and panic replaced Minerva's initial fear.

"She's . . . gone," the auburn-haired woman said finally.

"What do you mean, 'gone'?"

"She was there," she said. "Then she simply disappeared. Gradually. As though she had just faded out of existence. Or like she'd never been there."

Minerva realized why she was feeling better: It had nothing to do with the adrenaline. She'd been on the verge of fading because she'd been trying to sustain the memories of two different people simultaneously.

Raven had started to fade because of her divided energies, and then Amber.

Minerva had acted impulsively in reviving Amber. Now, despite all her good intentions, Amber was gone and she was separated from Raven.

Again.

"Noooooooooo!"

The force of Minerva's cry would have caused Phantom to take a step back had he not been rooted in place. It did make the auburn-haired woman retreat—not one step, but three.

Minerva closed her eyes against the reality of what she feared. She focused, remembering everything about Amber. Her height, her voice, her face, her hair, the memories the friend who called her "Sis" had given her just before she died, and those they had shared since. The memories were still there, all perfectly formed. But the process of retrieving them again was draining.

She was vaguely aware that the mental knot she'd tied around her captor was loosening.

She had to try harder. She owed her that much. Minerva squinted, willing herself to reassemble a perfect memory of Amber and revive her a second time. When she was satisfied she'd done all she could, she opened her eyes and sent her gaze across the room . . . to an empty bed.

Amber was truly dead. Lost forever.

The truth washed over her. She sank to her knees, oblivious to the hard tile floor, weeping uncontrollably.

The knot she had tied around Phantom slipped off and disappeared.

Neil Vincent stepped forward and draped his arms around her in cold comfort.

He had her again.

Disconnect

Raven felt his knees buckle, and it was only with a great deal of effort that he managed to stay upright.

Minerva was gone.

He felt like someone had opened a vacuum-sealed portal between his soul and the outside world. All the air had suddenly rushed out.

But it wasn't air. It was Minerva. He couldn't feel her, couldn't touch her with his mind. She was just not there.

"What's happening to him?" he heard Josef say.

The others could see what was going on, he realized. He struggled to steady himself against the feeling of utter loss, the feeling that some part of him had been violently ripped away. Where *was* she?

He closed his eyes and tried to focus.

"I don't know," he heard Jules say, in answer to his grandfather's question. "Looks like he's been hit by a truck."

There was no way they could have known what had just happened.

"Where's Minerva?" Josef asked, as if on cue.

Raven opened his eyes.

"Dead," said Jules. "I mean, dead for good, back where I came from, before this. Sherwood Forest. I saw the body."

Josef raised an eyebrow and pursed his lips. "This is the Between," he muttered, as much to himself as to Jules. "If there's anything I've learned about this place . . . things are seldom what they seem. We should take nothing for granted."

Jules nodded. From the expression on her face, she seemed to be reconsidering. "You could have a point," she said. "Come to think of it, there was a moment before, back in the forest, when our friend Raven seemed almost unaffected by Minerva's death. He took it *too* well."

"Which means . . ."

"Maybe she's not gone, altogether, after all."

Raven could feel clarity gradually returning. Normally, it would have worried him that Jules was on the verge of seeing through his deception. But he had bigger concerns, like where Minerva was *now*. Even if he couldn't feel her inside him, the fact that he was thinking about her should be enough to keep her going—he hoped. He'd cut off her head back in Sherwood. Did that mean she had no body to go back to? Was she floating around in some disembodied state? Or had she, somehow, found her way back to her revived body? They were questions he couldn't answer. The best he could do was to guard her with his memories.

And hope.

If she had, somehow, found a way back to the world of the living, that meant it was possible to get there. She hadn't left by choice—he was sure of that much. She would have taken him with her, or at least let him know what she was up to. If she was there, something or someone on the other end must have yanked her back.

Jules and Josef seemed to have shifted focus away from him and onto each other.

"None of it matters at this point," Josef groused. "We'll never get back to the real world without the emerald."

Jules turned up one corner of her mouth; Raven couldn't tell if it was a smirk or a grimace. "You really think you know everything, don't you?"

"What's that supposed to mean?"

"It means that if you don't have an answer, you assume no one else does. You always did think way too much of yourself."

Raven had to admit he took some guilty pleasure in watching them bicker. It was like watching a bad family sitcom about a failed marriage. They'd loved each other once, resented the hell out of each other now, but still needed each other in spite of it all. Unfortunately, he might need them, too. At least for now. His guilty pleasure vanished abruptly.

Josef arched his back and puffed out his chest. She was right: He did think a lot of himself. "My research is the only reason you stayed alive as long as you did. My memories are what is keeping you alive," he barked.

"But you can't get us out of here, can you? Fat lot of good your research does us if we're stuck here for the rest of eternity."

Josef's arms stiffened, he balled his hands into fists. "And I suppose you can? Get us out of here, I mean."

She raised both eyebrows, then lowered them into a glare. She waited a few seconds before answering. Raven could tell she was taking some satisfaction in having the upper hand. "Maybe," she said finally. "You'll have to wait and see."

Faire

"Huzzah! Good morrow, milord! What fine raiment you have attired yourself with this day!" The squat, greasy-faced man with a wiry red beard and substantial potbelly wore a coat of flimsy chain mail and a phony-looking silvery helmet. Complete with a pair of curved horns sticking out of the top. He was supposed to be a Viking raider, but he looked more like a poorly made mannequin brought to life. He reached out and pinched a bit of the visitor's garment between a greasy thumb and forefinger. "Quite fine indeed," he declared.

The wearer of the garment swatted the hand away forcefully. "Hey! What the hell?" His forced British accent, which didn't fit with the faux Viking persona, vanished, replaced by a dialect that betrayed his true ancestral homeland. Somewhere in the United States of America, circa late twentieth century. He looked at his hand and seemed genuinely distressed. "Dammit, now I'll have a bruise there!"

The visitor and his companion ignored the man and pushed ahead.

"Wait!" he called after them. "I need your tickets!"

They ignored him.

"Security!"

Baroque music swirled around them. A seemingly endless row of merchant stands lined the dirt path on either side of the visitors, their owners hawking everything from crystal trinkets to leather satchels. Colorful flags displaying St. George's Cross for England, the red dragon of Wales, and the red lion rampant of the English royal family, fluttered in a light breeze atop high poles that pierced a partly cloudy sky.

"I've never witnessed a market such as this," the visitor told his companion, who merely nodded, distracted by the sight of a dark-haired woman whose bodice elevated her bosom to such an extent that it appeared about three times its normal size.

"A coarse mind bringeth a sinful heart," the first man chastened.

"And a ticket bringeth admission to our good faire," came another voice. "Without one, I'm afraid you're SOL."

The two men found their path blocked by four others, all significantly larger than the faux Norseman at the gates had been, although two of them were dressed in similarly bad chain mail and poorly made armor. A third looked like a heavily muscled Moor, decked out in a flowing green and gold robe and a purple headdress with a feather protruding from the back. The fourth looked entirely different: He wore a dark blue shirt emblazoned with the letters "Faire Winds Renaissance Faire" in an arc of white Old English lettering; in one hand was a piece of parchment affixed to a thin wooden board with a metal clasp of some sort.

Roger Godberd bowed slightly. "Kindly allow us to pass, and we'll be on our way," he said, his tone impatient beneath the strained civility.

"Not without a ticket," said the man in the blue shirt. "Do you have one?"

Roger didn't say anything. He didn't know what the man was talking about.

Scadlock stepped forward and bowed a little more deeply. "I fear there has been a . . . misunderstanding," he began, but the Moor stepped forward and cut him off. "No misunderstanding. We charge admission. Pay up or get out."

Roger bent close to Scadlock and whispered, "Highwaymen."

Scadlock nodded and whispered back, "I do fear they are unaware of whom it is they're crossing."

"I fear you're right."

"What are you two saying?" the man in blue demanded. "Look, we don't want to evict you. We'll just escort you back to the ticket booth. You can pay and come back in. They can even stamp your hand."

"Stomp on my hand?" Godberd said, mystified, and at the same moment the Moor and one of the Vikings stepped forward to take hold of him, one at either arm. The second Viking—the larger of the two—took Scadlock by the shoulders . . . or tried to. At the last second, he slipped underneath the man's intended grasp, somersaulted deftly backward and stood in a fighting posture. Roger, meanwhile, twisted his body to dislodge the other two men's grip. In almost the same motion, he kicked out one leg that sent the Moor tumbling. Spinning quickly, he turned to face the Viking.

The man with the clipboard took a step backward.

"What's going on here?"

A petite woman dressed in what appeared to be leather armor appeared from the other side of the blacksmith stall. Her dark brown braid swished this way and that as she strode toward them.

The man in blue turned toward her as the Moor got to his feet and dusted himself off. The other four men seemed taken by surprise. Godberd and Scadlock kept their eyes fixed on the two Vikings, neither of whom seemed eager to engage them further.

"Nothing of consequence," the man in blue said, unconvincingly. "These two men haven't bought tickets. We were in the process of escorting them to the front gate."

The woman's laugh took him by surprise. "Who's escorting who, Chad? It looks like your men have their hands full. Should I call in the sheriff?"

Scadlock laughed involuntarily.

The woman pivoted toward him. "Do you find that funny?"

"Yes, milady. But he wouldn't. The shire-reeve, that is."

The woman put her hands on her hips and glared at them. She seemed to be considering something, taking stock of the two men. "Your accents—they're too good . . . for visitors, I mean. And your garb, well, it's not quite 'period . . .'"

"Period?" said Godberd.

"It's a few hundred years too early to be Elizabethan, but it still looks a lot more authentic than the stuff they sell around here." She caught herself. "No offense to our fine merchants, of course."

"What are you saying, Terri?" the man in the blue shirt asked.

"What I'm saying is these two are obviously paid performers. *That's* why they don't have tickets."

"They never said . . ."

But the woman in leather ignored him and turned to the two visitors. "What is it you *do*? Are you jugglers? Dancers? Woodworkers? Archers?"

"Archers," Scadlock piped up. "You have found us out, milady. Well, in truth, my companion here is the expert bowman; I am but his humble student."

The woman stepped forward and clapped Scadlock on the shoulder. "Good man, then. We'll let you stay and earn your keep today in the arena. Just so happens our joust got canceled. One of the knights went AWOL—

you know how it is. An archery show would be a nice change of pace. You can even come to the after-party and get drunk with the rest of us."

"You shall supply the ale?"

"As much as you want. There's just one thing: You'll have to prove to me you are what you say. If you're as good as you claim, we might even invite you back in the future to play Robin Hood or something."

Roger winced but kept his mouth shut.

"Follow me," the woman said. "I'll show you our archery booth, and *you* can show *me* how good you are."

Scadlock whispered into Roger's ear, "Does that mean what I think it means?"

The woman overheard the question. She glanced back over her shoulder without stopping and said in a flat tone, "It doesn't. What it means is that if you two are full of it and you really suck at archery, I *will* call the sheriff and you'll be spending the night in jail. Any questions?"

Scadlock thought it best not to say anything more. Roger stayed silent as well. He'd let his longbow do the talking.

Request

Phantom was surprised she didn't resist. He was bigger, physically, but he hadn't expected her to stand there and let him blindfold her and bind her hands behind her.

He couldn't leave her here—not with Raven. It was too big a risk. He might seem unconscious, but what if he came to? What if the two of them managed to connect? The room would not contain them. He needed to keep them separate, move her to someplace more secure.

He was relieved that, for the moment anyway, she didn't seem to be resisting; her body was trembling and her voice mute.

In her mind, Minerva was screaming. Desperate. *Raven, where are you?* she cried, knowing that he lay there just a few feet away.

There was no answer.

Amber's gone. Do you hear me? And it's all my fault. It's like I killed her. What if I forget you, too? I can't do this anymore.

Nothing. She felt her body shaking—her body, not Raven's. What once seemed natural now felt surreal. It was like she'd become a stranger in her own skin.

Goddammit, Raven, answer me!

The touch of the man felt suffocating, parasitic, filthy. She recoiled against it, and her body shook that much harder, but she couldn't bring herself to fight. She had neither the will nor the energy. What did any of it matter with Amber gone and Raven lost? She might as well be back in her bedroom, lying there paralyzed, the way she had been before Raven had helped her discover her gift. That would be better than this—better than having found love, friendship, and meaning, only to have it all ripped away because of who she had become. Because of the choices she had made.

She heard a woman's voice: "I'll contact you if anything changes with him." The woman's voice was still shaking from what she'd seen.

"Immediately," the man said firmly.

"Of course."

Then the voice whispered in her ear. "Don't be scared. Don't fight. I won't hurt you. I'm taking you to someplace safe."

It sounded sincere, but Minerva had learned that sincerity was usually a cover for something else—especially when the speaker had just finished tying you up. But even that didn't really matter. She wasn't scared. She'd already lost the only people she really cared about. She couldn't fight. She had no stomach for it. And she couldn't be hurt any more than she already had been. She was numb. Someplace safe? There was no such place in this world, probably not for anyone. Certainly not for her. Yesterday, she would have fought to the death for her freedom. Today, freedom was an illusion and fighting a waste of time.

Quit being so melodramatic. That's what Raven would have said. Imagining his voice only made things worse. She tried to shut it off . . . without forgetting him. She would never forget.

The man led her forward, keeping a tight grip on both her shoulders. A moment later, she heard more footfalls and realized that others—guards, she guessed—had joined them. The darkness behind her blindfold was complete, but after a few minutes she became aware that the shadows had lightened. It was either the sun or artificial light from a lamp; she couldn't tell which.

The other footsteps faded away, and her captor loosened his grip slightly. They stopped, and he gently turned her. She felt his touch against her wrists. A moment later, the rope binding her was loosened and removed.

"Sit down. Please." The voice was softer, surprisingly so.

Minerva reached behind her and found what seemed to be an over-stuffed chair, covered in leather. Cautiously, she lowered herself onto a soft, deep seat cushion.

"I need your help." The words surprised her.

Minerva didn't say anything. But somewhere in the back of her mind, her own internal voice responded: *You need my help? Go to hell.*

"I know you don't have any reason to trust me, but I don't know who else to ask." His tone was troubled; this wasn't an interrogation. If it was, he was very good at faking his emotions.

Her captor's voice cracked slightly, almost quivering, but it wasn't from nervousness. She felt he didn't really want to confide in her, but he had no other choice. This was the sound of someone who was used to being in control, but had lost it. He was grasping at straws, hoping for some way to regain it.

He paused.

"My son's been kidnapped," he finally said.

The statement jarred Minerva out of her numbness, a little. Some of her old sarcastic self broke through in the back of her mind. *Oh? Like what you did to me? Ironic much?* She was still hoping Raven might pick up on her thoughts.

"His name's Rudy."

Minerva stayed silent. It wasn't her problem. Who did this guy think he was, anyway? She didn't want to talk to him and, despite her intuition, she wouldn't allow herself to believe he was on the level. The best way to find out was to let him keep talking.

"He's thirteen. A freshman in high school. His mother . . . she's not around anymore. I've been raising him since he was five. They're holding him hostage to make sure I do what they want."

Minerva's curiosity got the best of her. "Who is?"

"A . . . business associate. Or someone who wants me to think that's who it is. I'm not sure. That's why . . ."

"A business associate? You mean a kidnapper like you? Maybe that's where he learned how to do it." Her words were hard, but she was trying to keep herself from bursting into tears. She shouldn't care about this guy's son. She cared about Raven. And Amber . . . she felt her shoulders shaking as she fought back a surge of sobs.

He didn't say anything.

Finally, she heard him inhale. He'd found the courage to say whatever it was he needed to.

"We're alone here," he said. "I sent the guards back to where we were before."

"Okay . . ." What was he trying to say?

"Your hands are free. You can take the blindfold off. I won't stop you. Please."

Minerva had been so rattled, she hadn't even considered removing the blindfold. "Do you know what you're doing?" She hadn't realized she'd said it aloud until it was out of her mouth. *Dammit, that was stupid. Just blow*

*your biggest advantage by warning him ahead of time. I don't care if his son
did get kidnapped. That doesn't give him the right to do what he's done to me.*

Except, in spite of all that, she did care. She sensed that he was telling the
truth. *What was his name? Rudy?*

She reached behind her head and untied the cloth that covered her eyes,
blinking at the sunlight leaking through a skylight overhead.

The room looked like an expansive parlor or living room. It was sparsely
furnished, with cobwebs in some of the corners and a layer of dust on the
dark mahogany end table beside her. The ceiling was dominated by the
skylight and accented by dark wood crossbeams. The panel had been transparent once. Now, a thin film of water spots, dust, and pollen had settled in
on the panes, all but obscuring the sky above.

As Minerva's eyes focused, she allowed them to settle on the man who sat
across from her. The tall, wiry form leaned forward, elbows on his knees,
forearms extending upward to meet in clasped hands just under his chin.
A deeply furrowed brow supported his almost entirely receded hairline.
He stared at her with dull gray eyes. The eyes seemed covered by a film of
sorrow and weariness that failed to mask his intensity.

He stared directly at her.

Did he know what he was doing in meeting her gaze? Did he realize that
she could, with a single, thought, steer him to agony or madness, or both?

Apparently, he did.

"Yes, I know what you can do with your memories," he said in answer
to her unspoken question. "Why do you think I brought you here in the
first place? You're very valuable to our government, either as a weapon or
a means of intimidation. I hadn't decided which way we ought to use you,
but that was before my son was kidnapped.

"Now, I suppose, those orders are on hold."

Minerva held herself in check. Her curiosity, and the nagging feeling that
the man in front of her really *did* need her help, kept her from lashing out.

Besides, he was a distraction, and she badly needed a distraction.
Somewhere away from the abyss that threatened to drown her in loss.
"Orders? Are you a soldier?"

"Air Force. Retired. Officially. Unofficially, I do this . . . about which, I
can't really say more without compromising state secrets."

"Seems like you might have done that already."

He nodded. "Yes," he conceded. "Sometimes you have to make a difficult choice. My responsibility to my country is to follow orders, but my responsibility to my son is to make sure he's safe. He comes first."

"I don't see how I can help . . ."

"By using your gift," he said. "I'm too close to this; it's hit me too hard. When you've lost someone, you can't think objectively. You can't see and properly analyze every possible course of action to make the right choice."

I know how you feel. You're afraid of making the wrong choice. If you do, someone you love might die. Trust me, I can relate.

"I need you to look inside my mind, to see everything that I've seen and tell me what I might be missing. I need to find out who's holding my son and how to get to him."

Minerva shook her head. "I might not be able to tell you."

"You have to try."

She paused a moment, considering. "If I do this, you'll let me go?"

"I can't promise that."

Whatever else he might have been lying about, at least he was wasn't BSing about that.

"You have to understand," he said, "if I were to let you go, I'd be responsible for losing what some people—the few who know about you—think is our nation's most valuable asset. I operate independently, for the most part, but the people who know about what I'm doing would not be very forgiving. I could be court-martialed or, more likely, given the nature of my position, outed to the enemy.

"I wouldn't be able to protect Rudy. I'd be dead."

The enemy? Who's the enemy? I've seen a lot of them lately, and you're one of them. Why should I . . . ?

Then something occurred to her.

"Okay, I'll do it."

The man sat up straight. It was clear he hadn't expected her to agree so easily. He sat silently for a moment, then nodded once.

"Let's do this then," he said.

"Yeah, let's do this."

Family

Henry was decidedly out of his element. Holed up in a rickety old barn somewhere in Imperial County, he sat on a partially unbound bale of hay and watched as the Lost Mountain Condors went about their business.

It seemed the Condors' "business" mostly consisted of drinking beer and regaling one another with tales of past glories they'd already told a hundred times. The talked about their buddies who had been gunned down in the street battle with the graysuits. Their tone was reverent but matter-of-fact: They expected this kind of thing; it came with the territory. Revenge would come, but that was for another time, another day. The fallen riders wouldn't have wanted them to sit around in the meantime. They would have wanted them to drink a beer or three and share a laugh in their honor.

The surviving Condors were in their element. They didn't seem to mind sitting here in this sweltering barn teeming with flies and gnats that buzzed in and out on invisible tides of superheated desert air. Even the beer was warm. They didn't seem to care about that, either. They'd picked up a few six-packs from a guy named Davonte Jameson, who ran a small biker club called the Sand Dukes out of Brawley. Jameson had let them have the beer in exchange for letting him ride along, saying he was due for some "action." Whatever that meant. There wasn't any action. Just a bunch of guys sitting around, waiting for something to happen.

These bikers lived to ride, first and foremost, but proving their manhood seemed to rank a close second.

Which meant finding—or making—some excuse to start a fight.

Davonte had started one over who'd get the first beer. Chet had gotten the worst of it. He had given as good as he got at first, but Davonte ended it with a vicious right cross that sent one of Chet's teeth flying across the barn and left him sprawled on a bed of itchy straw.

Everyone laughed except Davonte. He merely curled one corner of his mouth upward and walked over to pick up his trophy. He popped the beer open and sat down to enjoy the spoils of his victory. Chet sat up, rubbing his jaw. He stood and walked over to Davonte, extending his forearm, which was accepted in a tight mutual grip.

All of this seemed perfectly normal. To everyone but Henry. Even Paige seemed right at home, her voice rising in laughter as she listened to Mike recall the time one of the fallen Condors had tricked a Highway Patrolman into letting him off with a warning. The biker told the officer he was rushing to the hospital because his wife had called him to say she was about deliver their baby—never mind he wasn't married and the hospital was in the opposite direction. Mike said he'd seen it on a sitcom. "It worked even better in real life!"

Mike put his arm around Paige and pulled her close, then suddenly released her and bumped her playfully with his side so she nearly fell over.

They laughed some more.

What was wrong with these people? This place was miserable, and they were behaving like there was nowhere else they'd rather be.

Henry watched Paige and Mike closely. Maybe he had imagined the chemistry he felt with Paige. Now that Mike was back, she seemed to have forgotten all about him. He wasn't one to mope, especially over a woman. He usually had no problem with women, always making himself the center of attention. But here, he felt completely out of place. He couldn't even manage get the attention of the one woman he had started to care for.

He stood up, brushed the dust and straw off his pants, and declared, "I'm leaving."

They all looked at him like he was crazy.

Davonte just shrugged. "Fine with me," he said. "Ain't worth my time to worry about."

"Like hell." Paige stood up and glared at him. At least he had her attention.

"Yeah," said Mike. "Like hell. We bust our butts to get your ass out of some deep shit, and now you just walk away like it's all good? Well, it's *not* good, gringo. We're all out here in this hellhole because of *you*. Because some SOBs came looking for *you*. Three of my brothers are goddamn *dead* because of *you*, and you want to just walk away and get yourself fucked over just like them?"

"Hey, it's my life," Henry protested.

"You're not listening, gringo. Your life belongs to us now—three times over. You're not going anywhere."

Paige was walking toward him, her eyes fixed like no one else was even there. "So, what happened between us meant *nothing*?" she demanded. Striding up to him, she put both hands on his shoulders and shoved him.

Shoved him!

No woman had ever done anything like that to him.

Henry lost his balance and stumbled backward over the hay bale he'd been sitting on. In almost the same moment, she was standing over him, extending her hand.

After a moment's hesitation, he took it and she pulled him to his feet. Their eyes were level with each other. Just beyond the steel in her eyes, he could see what looked like moisture. "I asked you a fucking question." Her voice was abruptly lower, less forceful, more unsure.

"Yes," Henry said. "The answer is yes. But I think Mike has his own ideas. I can bloody well see he wants to pick up right where he left off." A part of Henry was worried that Mike would walk over and kick his ass for that. Probably worse. A sidelong glance in his direction, revealed Mike hadn't moved an inch. His expression told Henry the big biker would be in his face like a shot, if he said the wrong thing.

He didn't care.

"We've been over this before, idiot," Paige said, her voice hardening again. "There's nothing between me and Mike. He's my *brother*. Like all these guys. We're family. And if you don't like my family, well that's just too damn bad. But you ain't leavin'. Even if you don't give a rat's ass about me, you ain't leavin' after what these men went through for you. Mike's right. You don't owe me anything, but you owe them big time."

"Look, Paige," he said, putting his hands on her shoulders.

She reached up and brushed them away.

"Don't 'look, Paige' me!" she said.

"I don't belong here."

"With me? Is that what you mean? With me?"

"No, I didn't say . . ."

"I know I'm not the best-looking gal in the world, but you don't treat people like this, Henry. You just don't." He could see the wetness returning to her eyes, despite her best efforts to hold it back.

"You don't understand," he said. "I'm just tired of all this buggery. Not you . . . This . . . I love you. I mean . . ." Had he really said that? He'd spent most of his adult life making sure he never said those words, no matter who he was with. It was like a code for him, and he'd never had any trouble keeping to it until now. This woman who stood in front of him, who he'd never actually *been* with. What was wrong with him?

Paige stopped and blinked. "You . . . what?"

Yep, she heard him, all right. There was no taking it back. Despite his code, he didn't want to.

"He said he loves you, Paigey," Chet piped up chuckling.

"Yeah," said Davonte. "You deaf, woman?"

Paige seemed to come back to herself and nodded. "Good," she said. "Me too, kiddo. But you knew that, right? So why the hell are you trying to run out on me?"

"I'm not," Henry protested. "I just thought . . ."

"You do way too much of that," she said, taking a step forward so there was virtually no space between them.

Henry felt her breath on his face.

"Need some convincing?" she said.

Before he could open his mouth, she had wrapped her arms around him and pressed her lips hard to his. He met her kiss with equal enthusiasm, suddenly not caring about Mike or Chet or Davonte or any of it.

"Whoa yeah!" one of the Condors shouted.

"There it is!"

"That's what I'm talkin' about."

After their lips parted, Henry shot a quick glance at Mike, who hadn't moved from where he had been seated. His expression hadn't changed, his eyes still fixed on the two of them. Finally, he stood and strode over to them. He grabbed Henry by the forearm and pulled him close enough to whisper, "She's right, gringo. We're family here. I should have killed you for disrespecting my brothers who died there. *She's* the only reason I didn't. Remember that, asshole. Because if you hurt her again, you're dead."

Bargain

Josef stared at Jules. So did Raven. Neither had the slightest idea what she was talking about. Both were equally intrigued and suspicious of what lay behind her words.

"She's not dead."

"Who?" Josef asked.

"That one's precious little whore." She nodded toward Raven.

"Of course, she's dead. We're all dead," Josef said.

"I mean she's not dead for good. She's not here . . . which means she has to be somewhere else. Like back in the waking world."

"That's ridiculous," Raven interjected. "You saw her body."

"That's right, lover boy. I did. But I've been thinking, and you know, you didn't seem all that upset about seeing her lying there. I've spent some time with you, remember?" She purred that last bit. If a purr could be condescending, this was it. "Something seemed strange about it at the time, but I didn't think too much about it, until now. It doesn't add up. She's not dead and she's not here, which means she's either somewhere else in the Between or she's back in the real world."

"You're wrong," Raven said flatly.

"I don't think so," Jules said, shaking her head slowly. "And I don't think she's here in the Between. You're not sad enough. That's the problem. That's the giveaway, lover boy."

"Your point?" Josef said, impatient.

"My point is that she's our ticket back—or he is." She nodded toward Raven. "All she has to do is remember him. She can bring him back. Then, he can bring us back. I think he knows the two of us . . . intimately. He can do us that little favor. What do you think, lover boy?"

Raven stared at her. Was she nuts? If Minerva were in the real world, wouldn't she have brought him back already?

The thought snagged in his mind like a kite caught on a tree branch. He hadn't considered it. Jules was right.

Something *was* wrong. He couldn't hide the worried look that suddenly washed over his face.

"Oh, don't try that now," Jules chastened him. "It's too late to fake looking all weepy. I know what you're doing. You're not getting any Academy Awards from me."

Raven steadied himself. He didn't feel like he was fading. Someone's memory was keeping him here? Jules? He doubted it. Josef? No. It had to be Minerva. She hadn't brought him back, but she hadn't forgotten about him, either, which meant she was still out there somewhere—wherever "there" was.

"Look, whether you believe me or not . . ."

"I don't. That's the point."

"Like I was saying, whether you believe me or not, what makes you think I'd bring you back to the real world? I'd rather forget either of you ever existed."

"Oh, I think you will. Josef, we *do* still have our dear Raven's parents here, don't we?"

"Indeed."

"And we'll keep them safe and sound for you. A little insurance that you'll bring us back to the waking world."

"You can't hold my parents here," he announced. "I'll just use my own memory to revive them—if I ever get out of here."

"Poor baby, he doesn't understand," Jules said in mock sympathy.

"No, he obviously doesn't."

Raven looked at them blankly. What kind of game were they playing now?

"I guess we'll just have to explain it," Jules said to Josef, then turned back to Raven. "You can't just bring *anyone* back, dear.

"They have to *want* to go back. Your parents obviously don't. A lot of people don't . . . actually. They've lived their lives and they're ready for a good, long coffee break. Either here in the Between or, if no one remembers them, in oblivion.

"Life is hard and then you die, right? Sometimes dying's better. It's only people who have unfinished business who want to go back. People like you. And us.

"If you don't bring us back, we'll make sure your parents' afterlife is anything but restful."

"On the other hand," Josef mused, "we could offer them an incentive to return—if you cooperate, that is. You help us, we help you. All very equitable."

"Easy-peasy," Jules chimed in.

Raven shook his head, trying to make sense of it. It was possible the two of them were making all this up, but it made too much sense. He'd thought of his parents after Minerva brought him back, he'd remembered them well enough to have brought them back . . . if they'd wanted to come. He shouldn't have needed Jules' help at all.

But, that was all in the past. The fact was, she and his grandfather had his parents trapped here somewhere in the Between, in the now. He was sure they'd keep their promise to make their afterlife miserable.

Raven was in no position to bargain. At this point, he didn't know whether he'd ever get back to the real world. Or if he'd ever see Minerva again.

If Minerva was lost to him, nothing mattered. He'd fade into nothingness. There would be no way to protect his parents. As to whatever Jules and Josef decided to do back in the real world, was that really his problem anyway? Carson could deal with it. That was *his* job, right?

"Do we have a deal?" Jules prompted, extending her hand.

"No matter what you think, Minerva's gone," Raven persisted, ignoring her gesture.

She returned her hand to her side.

"All right then," she said, half-sighing. "Have it your way. If and when you disappear, we'll give you twenty-four hours to revive us. If you don't, your parents . . . well, let's just say we'll spend the rest of eternity making this purgatory hell for them."

Skylight

Minerva fixed her eyes on the man in front of her and allowed her thoughts to be drawn into his soul. It was like entering a whirlpool. She was sucked in through a labyrinth of twisting, turning memories—fragments of thought, vivid images of fears unrealized, hopes crushed. She'd been in a Halloween fun house once as a child; it was a little like that. Mirror images flashing back at her from all sides, a spinning kaleidoscope of colors mingling with blurred and muted visions. These were memories nearly lost through disuse, atrophied like muscles neglected, relegated like old knickknacks to the attic of the subconscious.

She passed an old baseball uniform, a glass case filled with trophies, diplomas. A street sign that read "Lafayette," a string of rosary beads, and a newspaper clipping of the attack on the World Trade Center.

She felt waves of emotion, too. Very much like when she'd explored Amber's mind. Except there was less pain . . . less physical pain, anyway. The pain she found was of a different sort. The pain of his wife leaving him; the loss his son. That was the most acute. Other memories were sealed behind doors he had created to guard his secrets. Secrets, he'd been told, could never be revealed. Military secrets, cryptic words, phrases having to do with national security. She broke down all those doors and peered into the little chambers. She needed to, if she was going to help him. Beyond that, she had every intention of helping herself.

Helping herself might enable her to help . . . who? She had only hurt Amber. She'd lost Raven. Who else mattered? Her kid brother Archer? Would she screw his life up, too?

Stop it! she told herself.

She had to focus or she'd fall out the other side of his mind without helping anyone. At least she could try to help *him*. Not because of who he was. She didn't even care. She would try for the sake of his son. She had to help *someone*. She had to feel like there was a reason to keep going. If this was all she had, she would fight for it.

If nothing else, she was a survivor.

She stopped at one of his mental doors, which he'd sealed particularly well. It was like the thick steel door to a bank vault, complete with one of those bulky, circular handles that looked a little like the wheel on a pirate ship.

Come on, Neil. If you want me to help, you've gotta trust me.

The door held fast, but she didn't need his permission. She was already inside his mind. Once she was there, the force of her will was stronger than any resistance he could offer. Her will was guided, at this moment, by the drive of her curiosity. No one guarded a secret so tightly if it wasn't important. For all she knew, it might be the kind of secret that would show her how to bring Amber back.

That was too much to hope for. But still . . .

She focused on the door. It gave way, leading to what looked like the inside of—surprise—a bank vault.

Several safe-deposit boxes lined one wall; most didn't have keyholes or handles. Minerva approached one that did and willed it open—no key necessary.

Inside was an emerald on a chain that looked like the necklace Raven had given her, along with a typed note that read: "This is what you're looking for. Whatever you do, do *not* let it fall into the wrong hands."

Minerva put it back where she had found it and moved to the next box.

This one held nothing that seemed of any interest: a stuffed blue bunny that was missing an eye, either a toy from Neil's own past or something that belonged to his son. She put it back where she had found it.

The third box contained another note. This one hurriedly written in longhand. It wasn't in English, just a long series of letters, numbers, and symbols from a computer keyboard. A code of some sort? A password. If it was the latter, it was the longest she'd ever seen. She counted thirty-seven characters. Minerva had been told once that the average person could memorize seven or eight numbers or letters in sequence. She'd taken that as a challenge. She'd figured out on her own that she could memorize how to spell words that were longer than that—like immunosuppression, seventeen letters, and even electroencephalogram, twenty—by grouping them into chunks and recognizing patterns. Her mother, who didn't know the difference between "there" and "their," once told her she could win the school spelling bee "if you'd just get up off your lazy ass and study."

Thanks, Mom. You know just how to make a kid feel appreciated.

She hadn't been lazy, just unmotivated. That was different. Here, she had plenty of motivation, but a much harder task. There was no discernible pattern to the characters. It was like pi, which she'd memorized to the sixteenth decimal place. This was more challenging because it contained hashtags, letters, ampersands, and assorted other figures scrambled among the numbers.

She was sure she could do it if she just had a little time. She searched for any pattern. Finding none, she tried to make each letter character stand for something. "3nvs4$+14^r&#b28@*" became "three nice vampires searching for dollars and fourteen-karat rings and hash browns to eat at Starbucks." That was eighteen. Almost halfway there, and her sentence almost made sense, although vampires didn't eat hash browns and Starbucks didn't serve them.

Something threatened to distract her. She sensed she had to finish quickly, but she had to be sure of what she was seeing. If she could create any sort of sensible pattern, she'd be set. She didn't forget things. Ever. Except for the woman who had become like a sister to her . . .

Stop with the guilt and focus!

". . .w9({ . . ." It was getting harder. ". . . with nine . . ." What could she make out of parentheses? Maybe shorten it. Par? Pair. What came next? She forgot what they called that . . . wait. Braces. ". . . with nine pairs of braces . . ." That worked. Sort of.

What the . . . ?

There was a loud bang. Minerva's eyes flew open. It felt as if she'd been thrown from a car doing eighty on the interstate. In the same instant, she was no longer in the bank vault of Neil Vincent's mind.

The bang was followed by the sound of glass shattering overhead. Instinctively, Minerva looked up, then dove to the floor, raising her arm protectively over her head, her back facing upward like a turtle's shell.

Same principle—not nearly as effective.

Shards of glass rained down, most bouncing off harmlessly, but some slicing through the fabric of the hospital gown to her skin. She grimaced in pain and screamed involuntarily, cursing herself as she did. Remembering what Carson and Amber had taught her, she tucked and rolled, then sprang to her feet as the last of the skylight came crashing down, along with a figure clad in dark, tight-fitting garments. His face was obscured, except for his eyes, with a black cloth tied back over his face. He had thrown a rope down from the ceiling and was almost skittering down it, using one hand and both feet. Looking like a ninja warrior without the teenage, the turtle, or the mutant parts. In his free hand, he held a pistol that was trained not on her, but on Neil, whose blank stare took in the place where she had been sitting, not moving, not even blinking.

Was he . . .?

Maybe having her jerked from his mind had been too much.

No time to worry about that now. Minerva wheeled away from him to face the intruder, who was paying very little attention to her.

"Hey!" she shouted.

"Shut up! The guards will be here any minute."

This time, it was Minerva who froze. She recognized the voice. "Carson?"

"You were expecting Adam West?"

"Who's Adam—?"

"Never mind. We've got to get out of here." He grabbed her by the arm, but she pulled away.

"We can't leave Neil here."

Carson paused briefly and looked at the man, who seemed oblivious to everything going on around him. "Yes, Neil Vincent," he said. "Former Air Force colonel. He used to be with the NRC. He's FIN."

"Not just FIN, he's the top guy," Minerva said.

Carson nodded. He wasn't supposed to know that, but the data dump Sutcliffe had sent him had said a lot—that was how he'd found Vincent and managed to follow him here.

Footsteps echoed down the hall, approaching rapidly.

"C'mon!" Carson urged.

"We can't just leave him here!"

"You're right," Carson said, and drawing his pistol like a flash, before Minerva could object, he aimed at the man's forehead and put a bullet into it with a *thwick*. "Glad I left the silencer on," he muttered to himself.

Vincent fell to the side.

"What the—?"

"Come *on!*"

This time he grabbed her arm and didn't let go, pulling her along beside him as he ran for the door. She had no choice but to match his stride as they raced through the house. The footsteps stopped just as they reached the front door. The guards had Vincent. It wouldn't distract them for long, but it gave the two escapees a precious few extra seconds. They burst through the front door and onto the porch, then the lawn of the estate, running as fast as they could.

No one tried to stop them: Carson had executed three members of the estate's external security team on his way in. However, a very loud alarm that sounded like a manic railroad crossing was going off. Even if the guards from the house were too far behind, the place would be a magnet for police within minutes.

They ducked behind a hedge, out of sight, just before the pursuing security force stumbled through the front door. There were four of them. Unsure where their quarry had fled, they scattered to the four points of the compass. Fortunately, Minerva and Carson hadn't gone in any of those directions: They'd climbed a sturdy white oak that looked like it had been here since the time of the Revolution. Its branches and leaves were dense enough to obscure them, unless someone knew to look.

The guards didn't.

"Why the hell did you kill him?" Minerva whispered.

Carson pulled the black cloth off his head and stuffed it in his belt. "He knew too much. If I hadn't killed him, his fail-safe in FIN would have—as soon as he finished extracting whatever information about you he could get."

"His fail-safe?"

"The one agent who knows for sure who he is. His chosen successor."

"But his son . . ."

"They're holding him hostage, aren't they?"

Minerva nodded. Carson had expected as much based on the hacked intel Sutcliffe had sent him. It had included information about Vincent's family, which consisted of a wife, who'd abandoned him several years before, and a son named Rudy. The boy would have been their target.

"Not our problem," Carson said matter-of-factly.

PARALUCIDITY

Did he have the ability to compartmentalize everything? To seal off any shred of empathy because it might interfere with the task at hand? Apparently so. He'd shot Raven's grandmother in cold blood, hadn't he?

"Raven," she said. "He's still back there. We can't leave."

Carson shook his head decisively. "We can't go back. Not now. He knows how to take care of himself."

"You don't get it. He's still unconscious. He can't take care of *anything.*"

Sirens wailed in the distance, layered one on top of the other, rising toward a crescendo as they approached.

"Well, we can't help him if we get caught, which is what'll happen if we go back."

Minerva felt both her hands balling into fists. "Do you care about *anyone*?" she seethed in a low whisper.

"I care about keeping us all alive."

"Well guess what, Mister Big Shot, you failed. Amber's gone."

161

Up a Tree

The moment Minerva said it, she wanted to take it back. It wasn't Carson's fault. It was hers. She'd just put it off onto him because he was being so stubborn. So unfeeling.

His reaction wasn't what she'd expected. The blood seemed to drain from his face, and the muscles in his perpetually tense expression went slack.

He tried to shake it off, groping to recover that look of intense determination. "If she's gone," he said, "then we'll have to get her back. That'll give us something to focus on while things die down. Then we can come back and get Raven and . . ."

Minerva looked down, then forced herself to look back up at him. She could tell by the slight quaver in his voice, from the look on his face, that he'd understood her the first time. He just didn't want to accept it. "Carson, Amber's gone for good," she said softly. "She's dead. And this time, I can't bring her back."

Carson stared at her, blinking more than usual, trying to keep his face from twitching, then he looked away. The man's entire life was bound up in doing what was expected of him, but, more to the point, what he expected of himself. He was very good at what he did for one simple reason: He could not tolerate weakness, worse yet, failure, in himself. So, he didn't let it happen—at least not if he could help it. When things didn't go the way he'd planned, he was devastated.

Minerva had recognized that a long time ago, but she had a feeling it was something more than his typical self-reproach.

He avoided her eyes.

Had he been . . .?

No, he couldn't have been, but then . . . yes, that had to be it. He had cared for her. He'd never shown much indication, beyond a barely perceptible softening of the voice or an occasional smile, but he never showed much indication that he felt *anything*. That's why he could be so frustrating. Come to think of it, Amber had been the same. She'd never really let on she had feelings for anyone, doing her best to hide them behind good-natured banter and a constant flurry of activity and achievement. Who had time for a relationship when you were busy being a doctor, skydiving, learning martial arts, and doing whatever else she'd done in her impossibly busy life? She certainly had never given Henry the time of day, even though he'd made it obvious that he was interested. Maybe that hadn't been just because she wasn't eager to get involved with anyone. Maybe she'd been interested in someone else.

Minerva had no idea whether Amber had shared Carson's feelings, but the hurt on Carson's face was clear, no matter how much he tried to hide behind a mask of indifference.

"I'm sorry," Minerva ventured. "I didn't mean to tell you like that. I didn't know . . ."

"Forget it," Carson said, putting both hands up in a gesture that was meant as much to deflect her attention from his face as to feign detachment. "I know you loved her, too." His voice halted briefly, realizing what he'd said. "We all did," he added hurriedly

That part, though true, was unconvincing.

Minerva knew there was no point in pressing the issue. What would it accomplish? Minerva herself hurt too much to pursue it, even if she had wanted to, but it was oddly comforting to know that, underneath his stoic exterior, Carson *did* have feelings. He really *did* care. She'd come a long way toward trusting him since he'd kidnapped her and he'd proven himself—mostly—since then. Raven would never trust him because of what he'd done to his grandmother, but Minerva's own concerns were less personal. The biggest reason she remained wary was that she hadn't been able to get a read on him.

Carson was so adept at walling off his feelings, it was impossible to know where you stood with him, except through his actions. Was he a cold-blooded assassin? A nemesis? A mentor? A savior? Yes. He'd been all these things to her at various times, but he'd never let her see inside. To find out what made him act the way he did. She'd assumed everything he did was driven by tactical rather than ethical considerations, she still suspected that was the case. Most of the time.

But not all the time. Not with Amber. If the bond they'd shared had been based on the rigid masks they both hid behind, it had been a bond, nonetheless. Their determination to remain unemotional undermined that very intention.

Ironic. And, to Minerva, reassuring at the same time.

She stretched out her hand and put it on Carson's. To her surprise, he took it and squeezed back. There was someone in there after all, no matter how much he tried to hide it.

The sirens passed them by, attached to one, two, three police vehicles that pulled into the semicircular driveway of the estate. She hoped they couldn't see her, and she took some comfort in the fact that they were preoccupied by taking statements from the security guards. She wondered how much people from a top-secret organization like FIN would tell the police that would be useful.

"What's the point of calling the cops?" she asked.

Carson seemed relieved that she'd turned the conversation away from Amber.

"It's a way to scare people off," he said. "The cops come, and anyone who might be nosing around takes off. Then they feed the police some B.S. story about the alarm malfunctioning or being triggered by a raccoon sniffing around for food. Something like that. By the time the cops get there, the people who set off the alarm are long gone. If the alarm doesn't scare them off, sirens do."

"So, we just wait up here till they leave? My butt's getting sore."

"It won't be long. Your butt'll survive."

Was that some feeble excuse for a joke? From him, she'd take it. She forced herself to laugh, figuring it was worth it if it would get him to lighten up. "And I suppose secret agents like you have butts of steel." Her attempt at humor wasn't much better than his, but at least it was a joke—even if it was a bad one.

"Call me Clark Kent," he deadpanned. Now that *was* a joke, still a bad one, but it was progress, of a sort.

I guess a woman was your kryptonite, Minerva said to herself, *just like a man is mine.*

Dreamtime

Minerva went over and over it in her mind. She hadn't forgotten Raven; he'd been the first thing she thought of when she had woken up again, but for some reason, he hadn't come back.

After about an hour and a half, they were able to climb down from the tree, find their way back to his car. From there, they made their way to a small, nondescript motel just outside Scranton, Pennsylvania. It had an antique looking TV, a Gideon's Bible in the nightstand, and a rotary-dial phone, but not much else beyond the requisite tear-open packs of shampoo/conditioner and body wash. Not even a continental breakfast.

Minerva sat on her double bed, which sagged a bit and was situated away from the window. Carson insisted on taking the bed nearest the door. At least he was protective. Not that she needed it, but it was still nice to find in a man. It reminded her of Raven, which started her focusing on him again, racking her brain about why she hadn't been able to bring him back.

Carson, lying on his bed, fully clothed, clicked the remote and the screen lit up, flickered, then held steady on the Home Shopping Network. He surfed absently through the channels. Basic cable and nothing much on. He settled on a news channel, a panel of so-called experts were bickering about the upcoming presidential election, talking over one another to insist that one candidate was a con artist and the other just wanted to make a name for himself so he could sell books and make tons of money giving speeches.

"Boring," Minerva remarked.

He moved one channel up and settled on a channel showing *Groundhog Day*, a movie about a guy who kept living the same day of his life over and over.

"Even more boring," she said.

He switched it again, another movie channel. This one was showing *50 First Dates*. The male lead had fallen in love with a woman who had this weird kind of amnesia that caused her to forget whatever had happened the day before. So, the guy kept meeting the woman and trying to sweep her off her feet, setting up a date for the next day, only to have it start all over again when she forgot she'd ever met him.

Carson looked at her. "I'm sensing a theme here," he said. "Want me to change it?"

"No," Minerva said. "Wait."

She'd seen this one before. She remembered that nothing had cured the woman's condition, but they did end up getting married. He made a videotape of their wedding to show her every morning. At some point, she'd become an art teacher. Even with her short-term memory loss, she dreamed of the guy every night and painted pictures of him when she was awake.

"That's it."

"What?"

"The first time I brought Raven back, I brought him into my dreams."

"So?"

"I've been trying so hard to bring him back, I've stopped actually using the gift. Maybe part of me is scared because of what happened to Amber. I don't know, but—"

"You think that if you dream about him again . . ."

"I might be able to bring him back."

Maybe Amber, too. She wasn't going to voice that last part; no sense getting Carson's hopes up.

Raven was still in a revived state; he just was stuck in the Between. Amber, on the other hand, was gone. But Raven had been gone the first time, too. Maybe . . . She caught herself. She didn't want to get her own hopes up, either. If she'd been hindering herself by trying too hard, the last thing she needed to do was to work herself up into a frenzy of what-ifs and maybes.

"Turn off the TV," she said. "I need to go to sleep."

Carson clicked the red button at the top of the remote. The TV flashed and flickered off. "Need anything else."

"I don't know. I'm nervous. I need to be calm, but I'm afraid it might not work. And I'm excited it might."

"Ever try counting sheep?"

"Very funny."

"Sorry, I've got nothing," he said. "I've trained myself to be a light sleeper just in case something happens." He nodded his head toward the window. "I don't know how to relax."

Minerva reached and pulled the braided brass cord on the light beside her bed. The room went dark, or almost dark. A neon glow from the sign outside and white light from the highway crept underneath the heavy curtains and crawled around either side, as if drawn in by the sound of the heater whirring under the window. The warm air blew upward, causing the curtain to rise and fall, creating an ebb and flow to the light that seemed almost hypnotic. Minerva closed her eyes and tried to imagine that the light was the flickering of her candle back in her bedroom the night she'd first dreamed of Raven.

Hopefully, she could dream of him again—and Amber, too. She settled her mind, breathing deeply, in and out. Rhythmically, matching the pulse of the heater.

It clicked, the fan switching off as the thermostat reached its preset temperature, and the air went still.

Minerva kept breathing in cadence. Staring through closed eyelids at the slivers of light that still found their way into the room, imagining the candle flickering, shadows dancing. Thinking of Raven and the first time he'd come to her. Remembering . . .

She drifted off—she *was* back in her old bedroom. It must have been very late, the house was silent. She couldn't hear Archer playing video games, as he so often did through all hours of the night. She couldn't hear Jessica, either; she'd probably drunk herself to sleep.

And she couldn't feel her legs.

That was normal. She'd been paralyzed since the accident. But wait, she wasn't paralyzed anymore, was she? Past and present wove themselves together, indistinguishable except where they contradicted one another.

She didn't know what to believe. She accepted it as reality, though somewhere in the back of her mind she suspected it was a dream. A car horn sounded somewhere outside, then silence.

"Hello, beautiful."

Startled, she used her arms to pull herself upright. "Raven."

"You were expecting maybe Chris Hemsworth?"

"Uh, no. Not my type."

He chuckled easily. "More into mutants than Norse gods, I see."

"Ghosts, actually."

He put his hands up and waved his fingers in the air. "Oooh. Spooky!" he teased.

She looked him over carefully. Was he really here?

He seemed so at ease. It has been a long time since she'd seen him that way; everything had gotten so crazy, so demanding, so dangerous—always dangerous. She'd almost forgotten how natural everything had seemed when he'd first come to her.

"You're still thinking too hard," he said. "You have to let it go and just be here with me."

"I need you to come back."

"I'm right here."

"But I need you to come back and be with me."

"Yes."

He came over to the bed and sat down beside her. It felt so familiar. He took her hand, but when she opened her mouth to speak, he shook his head slightly and leaned forward, allowing his lips to meet hers. Wrapping his arms around her, he pulled her to him and kissed her deeply. When their lips finally parted, she let her head rest on his shoulder, the sound of his breathing soft in her ears.

"I've missed this," she said.

"Me too."

"Please don't leave me." It was he who spoke the words. "I can't exist without you."

He wasn't just blurting it out or making some grand pronouncement. What he said was true, and they both knew it. She couldn't exist without him, either. They'd been together in every way, as children, in dreams, as lovers, beyond the realm of the living, even together in the same mind.

"I didn't mean to," she said.

"I know. Just relax. We're together now. It's going to be okay." He seemed so sure. It was easy to be sure in each other's arms, away from everything that threatened them. It was like they were together in a bubble where nothing else mattered.

The candle flickered at her bedside; she heard another car horn.

She held him tighter, dimly aware that something outside her was fighting to tear them apart. Where it was, she didn't know—it was just "out there."

She wanted to stay in here, with him.

He pushed her back gently and rubbed her shoulders, smiling a smile that only made her want to hold him again. "Raven . . ."

He kissed her softly again. She swallowed the rest of what she had meant to say, allowing their lips to move together, their tongues to mingle and venture inside. To taste.

No matter how much she wanted to lose herself in the moment, to make it stretch into eternity, the question still tickled at the back of her brain.

"Are you really here?"

He looked at her with softness that could have been sorrow, concern, or contentment. She wasn't sure.

He opened his mouth to answer and something shook her. She fought it, turning away, but it wouldn't stop. She felt a hand on her shoulder. It wasn't Raven's. She panicked.

Her eyes flew open. Sunlight, not the artificial glow of streetlights and neon, was pushing from behind the closed drapes. Carson was standing over her.

"Wake up, princess," he said. "We have to go."

Darkness

"You're awake."

Raven tried to reach up to clear his blurred vision, but his arms wouldn't move. They were bound at his sides, held down by plastic restraints.

"Where?" He mumbled, hearing his voice come out distorted. It had been a long time since he'd used it.

The woman walked over to a sink and filled a small, plastic cup from the tap.

"Let me help you," she said, pressing a button at his bedside that raised his torso up at an angle. She put the cup to his lips, but he turned his head away.

"Don't worry," the woman said. "It's just water. I thought you might want . . ." She stopped herself. "Oh, of course. Silly me. Your kind doesn't need to bother with such trivial things. I guess you don't get dehydrated, do you?" She laughed a little, nervous laugh and put the cup aside.

She knew he wasn't alive—at least not in the normal sense.

Raven stayed quiet and studied the woman. Hair somewhere between brown and dark red framed her face in a bowl cut, making it look rounder than it was. A few wrinkles stretched from the corners of her eyes. He wondered if she colored her hair. Not that it mattered.

He needed to get to Minerva, and this woman had him here—wherever here was—against his will. He didn't care for being tied down.

He tried again: "Where am I?"

"Safe," she said in a tone that was decisive yet hardly convincing. It was clear she had no intention of getting more specific.

"How long do you plan to keep me here?"

"As long as necessary."

This was getting him nowhere. He'd need to take a different approach. "You're a doctor, aren't you?"

"Actually, a nurse practitioner. You can call me Marina."

"And you've dealt with memortals before?" He was shaking off the effects of being caught in the Between for so long.

"Just the three of you—" She caught herself. She wasn't supposed to tell him anything; her superior had been clear.

Raven glanced around. He and Marina, as she'd introduced herself, were the only two people in the room. There were two other beds, but both were empty. Minerva and Amber. "What happened to the other two?"

"That's none of your concern, dear. Just try to relax and make yourself comfortable."

Tied down in a hospital bed? Fat chance.

He stayed quiet for a moment, then said, "I need your help."

"If I can."

"Something's wrong with my vision. I can't see colors, weird lights are dancing around. I think I might be fading. You say you've worked with people like me. You know what that is, right?"

She frowned. "Yes, I . . ." But she caught herself this time, before she said anything about Amber. "I know what you're talking about."

He furrowed his brow and bit his lower lip, trying to look worried without overdoing it. "I don't want to die again. Is there anything you can do to stop it?" He was counting on her not knowing much about memortals.

"Let me have a look at you," she said, trying to sound reassuring. "*We* don't want you fading, either."

She took hold of his arm and squeezed it. "You seem solid enough to me."

"But that's not how I *feel*," he said. "It's my eyes, mostly."

The woman frowned and turned away from him, walking over to a white, wheeled cabinet a few feet away. She opened the top drawer and rummaged around until she found what she was looking for: a small, pen-sized flashlight.

Yes. That's it.

She moved over to his bedside and turned the light on. "Now look at me, dear."

He did.

When Raven was very young, he'd been afraid of the dark. His parents had lived in a rural area without any streetlights, so his room would get pitch black on moonless nights. Stormy winter nights had been just as bad, with the clouds blotting out the moonlight and the darkness spreading in what seemed like inky black syrup. He'd imagined it forming into invisible shapes of slime monsters with tentacles reaching out to grab him and pull him into their gaping, bottomless maw. He shivered even now thinking about it. He'd tried to hide the fear from his parents, but they'd found out when he woke up screaming one night. After that, they'd bought him a ceramic night-light shaped like a little cottage with a family of rabbits. Everything had gotten better.

He didn't want it to be better now. He forced himself to remember the terror of the utter blackness, allowed his imagination to remember what he'd once thought might be lurking there. Fixing his eyes on those of the woman, he poured the images, and the terror they had produced, directly into her mind.

The woman dropped the penlight as she stumbled back, arms flailing desperately against some phantom menace. "I can't see!" she screamed. "Make it stop! Get it away!"

Raven winced. He didn't know this woman and felt more than a little guilty for inflicting this kind of horror, but he didn't know of any other way to do what needed to be done.

"Please! Make it *stop!*" she yelled again, whimpering like a lost puppy. She reached to her eyes and started rubbing, then pawing at them desperately. If she didn't stop, she really *was* going to blind herself.

"I can help you," he said evenly, trying to disguise his own horror at what he was doing to her. "But you have to help me."

"Anything! Just make it go away. Please! *Make it go away!*"

"You have to release me," he said.

"I can't!" she wailed. "I don't know what they'll do to me."

"But you know what *I'll* do to you if you don't." He didn't know if he could keep this up much longer without damning his own conscience to some sort of private hell. He had no quarrel with Marina, he just needed her to let him go.

"But I can't see!"

She was right. She had to be able to see to let him go. He eased up a little, allowing just enough light for her to navigate the room. He kept her tethered to his boyhood fear that the dark-monsters weren't really gone, they were hiding in the closet or under the bed. Even in the cedar chest, waiting there to spring out and devour him.

Marina stumbled across the room in what seemed like a crazed stupor and reached into another drawer in the same white cabinet where she'd found the penlight. Her shaking hands ran through the drawer, pushing aside a roll of gauze, tossing a forehead thermometer to the floor in her rush to find what she was looking for. What she retrieved was a remote-control device. She pointed it at the bed, a shaking finger pressed one button, then a second. His restraints released.

Raven pulled both arms free and sat up, rubbing his wrists where the plastic had held him.

Then he brought the curtain of darkness down in its entirety, consuming her in utter blackness. She fell to the floor, sobbing.

"You said you'd make it stop!" she cried.

"And I will. As soon as I get out of here."

"You won't get anywhere!" her voice was shaking, filled with rage beneath the terror. "There are guards all around this place. You *lied to me*! Let me *go!*"

"All right." He lifted the black veil.

She stood, tentatively, blinking at him through bloodshot eyes.

"I'm still inside your mind," he warned. "I can bring it back in a heartbeat." He'd kept a foothold in her mind, like a fishhook that he could pull on if he needed to, but he didn't know how long he could make it last. As it was, it had taken a lot out of him, both mentally and emotionally. To maintain it, *he* had to experience it. The difference was, he knew it was a memory. *She* was experiencing it as something very real. It was far from pleasant. Not something he wanted to do again anytime soon.

She nodded, the rage draining out of her, the fear replaced by resignation. "What do you want from me?" she said in a tired voice.

Raven looked at her, feeling sorry for her. "Just come with me," his voice softening. "Tell the guards you're under orders to move me to a"—he paused, trying to come up with the right words—"secure location." He shook his head. "Or whatever you think will convince them. Be convincing, or I'll have to . . ." He left the rest unsaid. She nodded.

He wasn't at all sure that any of this would work, but it was the best idea he could think of. If Carson were here, he'd probably have a better idea, but Carson wasn't here, and Minerva . . .

Raven.

There was a tickling at the back of his mind, a familiar thought-voice he'd thought he'd never hear again.

Raven, are you there? Were you real? In the dream. Please answer. I need to know. I need to know you're okay.

It was Minerva's.

On the other end, she waited, hoping against hope that the dream had been more than a dream. That he had come to her, just as he had when she revived him the first time.

Raven felt his heart beat a little faster. There was hope, after all.

Yes, I'm here. And yes, it was me. Thank you, my love, for finding me. Thank you for never giving up.

Diner

"Are you sure you didn't get the entire code?" Carson whispered.

He was sitting across the table from Minerva in Youngstown, Ohio, after they had checked into another nondescript motel, well off the interstate. He'd insisted they keep moving in case someone was following, although he'd seen no evidence so far.

The Pettway Diner was a hole in the wall, but the food was good, and Carson was hungry. He hadn't eaten a real meal in a couple of days.

They were headed west because Carson wanted to move farther away from New York and FIN headquarters—back toward California, where Henry was waiting, where they both felt more at home.

If some epic battle was coming, it would be better to fight it on their home turf.

With Phantom dead and FIN leaderless, it was bound to happen sooner or later. Someone would have to step into the power vacuum. How that person would proceed was anybody's guess.

Minerva had told Carson she'd made contact with Raven, so they decided to move slowly, giving him a chance to catch up. Carson didn't want to risk going back, so he'd wired some cash for a bus ticket and arranged to meet him at the diner.

When Raven walked in, Minerva had to fight the urge to run up and grab him in a bear hug. Carson had told her not to draw attention to herself, but he'd delivered no such warning to Raven, who all but ran to the table. When she stood, he pulled her up into his arms, lifting her a couple of inches off the ground.

"It's been forever," he said after they kissed and she scooted over so he could sit down next to her.

"Seems we have ourselves quite the reunion here," said the waiter, who came over and supplied him with a menu.

"Newlyweds," Carson scoffed, trying to play the whole thing down.

"And who are you, the father of the bride?" the waiter scolded.

"You guessed it," said Carson.

"I'll have the barbecue chicken," Raven announced. It didn't hurt to indulge his revived taste buds now and then. Now that he had found Minerva again, he felt like celebrating.

"You got it." The waiter declared, taking the menu back from Raven. "I'll have it to you in a few minutes."

Carson shook his head. "Now as I was saying before we were interrupted..."

"What's this?" Raven asked, addressing Carson but looking at Minerva. "Not even a hello? I guess I shouldn't expect any courtesy from a killer." He bit his lip.

"Stop it," Minerva said. "We have to get along. I know you don't like him, but we don't have a choice. Besides, he did send you bus money."

"The seats were cramped," Raven muttered.

"Oh, boo-hoo!" Minerva said, pushing out her lip in a pretend pout, hoping he might laugh.

He didn't.

Carson ignored the exchange and started again in a low voice: "As I was saying, about that code: Are you sure you didn't get all of it?"

"What code?" Raven interjected.

"The code I found inside Neil's mind—that's Phantom, the head of FIN."

"For god's sake, keep your voice down!" Carson enjoined.

"Sorry."

The waiter returned with three waters in translucent gold-plastic glasses, covered with small bumps to make them easier to hold. He didn't say anything this time and gave no sign that he'd overheard anything.

Minerva shook her head. "I only got up to nineteen or twenty characters."

"What does this code go to?" Raven asked.

Carson ignored him. "How many characters were there, in all?"

"I don't know what it's to," Minerva said, answering Raven rather than Carson. "I wasn't in there long enough to figure it out. I was interrupted." She gestured toward Carson with an open palm, then turned to him. "And to answer *your* question, there were thirty-seven characters. At least I remember *that* much."

"What does it matter how many characters there were?" Raven asked.

"It matters because codes aren't always what they appear to be," Carson said. "Sometimes, it's not the code itself that needs deciphering, it's the package the code comes in. A codebreaker who's preoccupied with the obvious will miss the real message."

"Like opening a Christmas present so fast you don't even notice the wrapping because you're in such a rush to get inside?" Minerva offered.

"Something like that, yes."

"So, you're saying the number thirty-seven might somehow be significant?" Raven asked.

"Maybe. Maybe not. It's hard to say," Carson said. "The code itself might have been straightforward. It was complicated enough, from what you described, but the fact that it was so complex might mean it was a ruse."

"Talk about second-guessing second-guesses," Minerva said.

"We have no way of knowing without more information."

Minerva exhaled in exasperation, wishing she'd had more time to ferret out the rest of the code itself. If Carson hadn't interrupted when he did, she could've gotten more information. And Neil might not be dead. She still felt guilty about that, even though Carson was the one who pulled the trigger.

From her excursion inside the man's head, she knew he wasn't a bad man, just someone caught up in something he felt obligated to see through. He might not even have known what the ultimate endgame was, but he had faith in the process—a faith perhaps misplaced, but not out of malice.

"Did you see anything else?" Carson asked.

"Well, there was a stuffed blue bunny with a missing eye and what looked like the same emerald that Raven has around his . . . Wait, what happened to the emerald?"

Raven bit his lower lip and looked down at the table. "Will Scadlock stole it from me."

"What?" Carson said. "Who's Will Scadlock?"

"You'd know him as Will Scarlet—if you know your Robin Hood."

Carson shook his head vigorously, as if trying to dislodge some cobwebs.

The waiter returned with Raven's barbecue chicken and a plate of ribs for Carson. "Here you go!" the waiter said. "Is there anything else I can get for you folks?"

Carson waved him away with his hand,

Minerva spoke up to provide some manners. "No, thank you," she said, glaring at Carson as the man stepped away. The scent of the ribs and chicken were tantalizing and Minerva inhaled deeply. She'd learned to enjoy smells as much as tastes since being revived. Without any actual hunger, the scents were just as satisfying.

"It's a long story," she said, addressing Carson's question about Scadlock. "A word of advice, though, if you *do* happen to run into someone who looks like Robin Hood—I mean the real Robin Hood—he hates that name. His real name's Roger."

"I'll keep that in mind," Carson said, unsure of whether she was serious. She looked it, but she had been trying to use humor to make him lighten up. Bad humor. And this was pret) bad.

Carson picked up a rib and bit into it, pulling the meat from the bone. "Do you think the emerald and the code have anything to do with each other?"

"I don't know," Minerva said.

"We have to find that necklace," Raven put in. "It's extremely powerful, and very old. Josef referred to it as the Philosopher's Stone."

Minerva turned to look at him directly. "You saw Josef? What about Jules?"

Raven cleared his throat. "Umm, I was going to tell you about that."

Minerva's eyes narrowed. "What happened?"

"Well, you see." He didn't know quite how to bring it up. "My grandfather—that is, Josef—and Jules, they kind of threatened my parents."

"Go on."

"I didn't have any other choice. I don't know what they would have done to them if I hadn't . . ."

"Hadn't what?"

". . . promised to bring them back."

"You didn't. Tell me you didn't."

Carson, who hadn't said anything to this point, dropped the rib. They'd gone to such great lengths to keep Jules from coming back, and now, it seemed, Raven just opened up the front door and allowed her to waltz right in, along with his grandfather, apparently.

"Don't worry. I left them in New York. I actually managed to get away before they saw me. I'm sure they knew I had to have been there to bring them back, though. At least they can't hurt my parents. And they can't hurt us, either, if we're on the road to California."

"Unless they follow us," Carson said. "Are you sure they didn't see you?"

"Yes, I'm sure. I didn't see them anywhere."

Carson nodded. "That's good. For now. I wish we didn't have to deal with Jules again, but there's nothing we can do about it, except hope she stays in New York."

"Yeah, and Josef, too," Minerva said. "He's even worse."

Raven looked down at his plate and the half-finished breast of barbecue chicken. Somehow, it had lost its appeal. "Amber can help us with them," he ventured. "Where is she, anyway?"

Minerva looked away, avoiding his eyes.

"Min?"

"I lost her, Raven," she said in a whisper.

"And you can't . . . get her back?"

She shook her head slowly.

Carson's looked down at the table in front of him but said nothing. He left the rest of the ribs on his plate, too. "Check, please," he said, motioning toward the waiter. It was time to leave.

Billiards

It turned out Minerva did remember something else from inside Neil's mind. She hadn't thought anything of it at the time, but it was that old baseball jersey in navy blue and gold. It was hanging off to the side in the maze of mental corridors she'd tried to navigate as she sifted through the FIN director's thoughts. She hadn't paid much attention to it at the time, not being a baseball fan or thinking it had any bearing on what she was looking for. But now, thinking about it again, she realized she might have been wrong—because of the number on the back of that jersey: 37.

"Did you notice anything else about it?" Carson asked.

They were sitting in a pool hall in Columbia, Missouri, their next stop after Youngstown. They were making good time, traveling mostly at night, and there was still no sign of anyone following them. The hall was filled with the sounds of billiard balls crashing into and clattering off one another against a din of mostly drunken voices in the background. They could barely hear themselves over the racket. The three of them huddled together around a small round table with a dirty ashtray as its centerpiece. It was getting on toward midnight, and most of the patrons had at least a few beers, shots, or both in them by this time. This was helpful. No one was paying attention. They could speak freely.

"No," Minerva said. "I wasn't even paying that much attention to it, and I could only see the back of it, the part with the number. But I do remember it was 37."

Carson nodded. "Then my hunch was probably correct. The string of characters you couldn't quite memorize is meaningless. It's 37 that's important."

"A password?" Raven asked.

"No," said Carson. "It's too short. Part of a password, maybe."

"And even if it *is* a password, we still don't know what it's to," Minerva added. "Maybe we're making too big a deal of this. Maybe it doesn't mean anything."

Carson drummed his fingers lightly on the table. "Maybe," he said. "But everything else you saw was important to Vincent on some level, wasn't it?"

"Yeah," Minerva said. "That's how most people's memories work. They think about what's most important to them more often than other things, so that's what you see first when you get inside their heads. The same thing happened with Amber . . ." She stopped herself. "Anyway, I'm pretty sure everything I saw was important, at least to Neil."

"What about the stuffed rabbit?" Raven asked. "What do you think that means?"

"No clue. It might have just been really important when he was a kid, so he thought about it a lot and it was just left over in his memories. Who knows? Maybe it does mean something. I don't see how we'll ever know."

"There is one possibility," Carson said, staring at the ashtray as though it were a crystal ball.

"Which is?" Raven prompted.

"There is one place where we might find some more clues to the riddle— inside Vincent's home."

Raven leaned back and put both hands out in front of him, palms outward toward Carson. "Oh, no you don't," he said. "You're not taking us on some wild goose chase back to New York just because there *might* be a clue to something that *might* be important in some dead guy's house."

"I don't think we'd have to—go to New York, I mean," Minerva said. "The bunny was probably something he had when he was a kid, and I don't think he lived in New York back then. I remember something else. I saw a street sign with the name Lafayette on it."

"Lafayette's in Louisiana," Raven put in. "My parents took me there once when I was like five."

"I don't think that's the one." Carson said. Wheels were clearly turning inside his mind. "What did you say the colors of that baseball uniform were?"

"Blue and gold. Dark blue."

"University of Notre Dame," Carson said. "That's in Indiana. And there's a Lafayette in Indiana, too, just down the road from there. Did you see anything that might indicate Vincent was Catholic?"

Minerva nodded. "Rosary beads."

"That's enough for me." Carson said, leaning back in his chair.

Raven stood up abruptly and glared across the table. "That's it," he declared. "You don't get to decide this stuff all by yourself, Carson. Indiana's half a day's drive back the way we came, and you don't know whether it's the right place. Even if it is, what do you plan to do? Search every house in the city until you find the right one? Get real."

Raven was expecting Carson to confront him. Instead it was Minerva. "Look," she said. "I've had enough of you being always pissed. I get it. You don't like him. And you don't have to. I wouldn't, either, if I were you.

"But he's not stupid and he's worth listening to." She shot Carson a glance. "Sometimes."

Carson couldn't help but display the faintest hint of a smirk.

"What? You're his best friend, now?" Raven demanded.

"No, but I'll take help wherever I can get it. Besides, do we have anything better to do?"

Before he could answer, however, a bar patron with a long, scruffy beard, wearing a Stetson and a dark brown leather jacket, stepped between them. Raven could smell the beer on his breath before he even got there. He turned toward Minerva. "This fellow botherin' you?"

Nice going, Minerva told Raven telepathically. *The last thing we wanted to do was draw attention to ourselves.*

But Raven was busy staring angrily at the back of the man who stood between him and Minerva. "Excuse me," he said, tapping the man on the shoulder. "But shouldn't you be talking to me?"

The man held his position and kept looking directly at Minerva.

Don't you dare start anything, or I swear . . .

I didn't start this . . .

If you take this guy on, he'll just kick your butt.

Raven knew she was probably right. The cowboy was about four inches taller and weighed probably forty pounds more.

Raven eyed the man's back and wondered how much damage he might do with a well-placed kidney punch.

Before he could do anything, Carson stood and stepped forward. "We're all here together. This is none of your concern."

"Oh, ain't it?" The man puffed out his chest like a cartoon rooster.

Carson kept his voice level. "No, it's not."

The man's eyes narrowed. "Don't think you understand, friend. I come here every night after work to relax. But if a pretty lady can't relax, *I* can't relax. So, I reckon you're spoilin' my evenin'. I think you oughta leave."

Carson smiled. He did it so rarely that he looked funny when he did it, and in this case, it looked even weirder because it was so obviously forced. "We're going," he said. "If you'd just move out of our way . . ."

"I meant you. An' him." The cowboy turned his head slightly toward one shoulder to indicate Raven. "Not her."

"I'm afraid—" Carson began, but the cowboy wouldn't let him finish.

"I ain't got any way of knowin' what you're gonna do t'her once you get her outta here, now do I?" he said.

"I suppose not," Carson said. "But I don't have any way of knowing what you might do if she stays." There was a cutting tone to his voice.

The cowboy might be able to kick Raven's butt, but Raven knew who he'd bet on if the guy picked a fight with Carson. Drunken oaf versus trained assassin? Not much of a contest there . . . except that a bunch of people in the bar seemed to have started gathering around, and most of them had a lot more in common with the cowboy than with Carson.

"Now that ain't none of your concern now, is it?" the cowboy taunted. It was clear he knew the answer Carson was expected to give.

"No, it's not any of his concern." It was Minerva who answered in a tone that seemed more conciliatory than offended. Was she flirting with the guy?

Don't you dare do anything. Raven heard her voice inside his head. *I've got this.*

Raven balled up one fist but kept it at his side.

"Of course, I'll stay here with you, sugar," she said. "A big strong man like you can protect me anytime he likes."

The man puffed his chest out even farther.

Aren't you laying it on a little thick?

Minerva ignored him and . . . *was she actually batting her eyes?* She looked like some floozy barmaid in a bad Fifties western.

"You got mighty pretty eyes there, missy," the cowboy said.

He'd taken the bait.

Sleep.

Minerva sent a memory of her own sleepiness into the man's mind. Combined with the alcohol in his system, he was already asleep. Within seconds, he fell like a human avalanche, collapsing in a heap on the wooden floor. The people who had gathered around them let out a series of gasps, curses, and whoops, depending on their level of intoxication.

"Someone call 911!" one of them shouted.

"Why?" laughed another. "Can't you hear that? He's *snoring*!"

Sure enough, the cowboy was curled up on the floor like a pig in a blanket, and snoring like one, too.

In the confusion, Minerva grabbed Raven's hand and led him hastily to the door. Carson followed. They were out of there before any of the others realized they were gone.

"What now?" asked Raven as they reached the car.

"Looks like we're headed for Lafayette," Minerva said. "Unless you want to *argue* about it."

Raven kept his mouth shut. Besides, Minerva was right. They had nothing better to do.

Realty

Lafayette, home to about 70,000 people, was a sleepy town in eastern Indiana with a photo-ready historic domed courthouse, a beautiful old brick church, and plenty of tree-lined streets. None of those streets, however, shared their name with the city. They were looking for a *street sign*, Minerva reminded them.

"I don't think we've got the right Lafayette," Raven said, not trying to hide his I-told-you-so tone of self-satisfaction.

"I noticed," Minerva said. "So, what now?"

"GPS, anyone?" Raven suggested.

"Too risky," Carson said. "There are ways to track people using GPS, or even smartphones. Unless we've got access to secure technology, it's best to do things the old-fashioned way. Let's buy a road map."

They stopped at a Marathon station, and Carson gave the cashier a five-dollar bill in exchange for a fold-out map of Indiana that had detailed close-ups of the major cities. "Lafayette Street," he said aloud but to himself. "There's one in Anderson and one in Fort Wayne." Finally he announced, "Fort Wayne's closer, and bigger. We'll try that."

Raven bit his tongue. It wouldn't do any good to argue. Minerva seemed to side with Carson more than she did with him, and there was no point in debating things if he knew he'd be on the losing end of a two-to-one vote.

He was surprised to hear Minerva speak up when he didn't.

"Maybe Raven's right," she said. "Maybe this is a wild goose chase."

Raven smiled a little. "I know you don't want to go back to New York, Raven, but shouldn't we be more worried about Jules and Josef?" Minerva asked.

Carson didn't answer right away. "You may be right," he said finally. "I thought they'd follow us, but I haven't seen any sign. It wouldn't be a bad

PARALUCIDITY

idea to keep an eye on them. Still, we're right here. It can't hurt to take a day or two and try to crack the code."

"All right," Raven said, resigned. "Just so long as we don't wind up in Lafayette, Louisiana, after this."

"Agreed," said Minerva, and Carson nodded, too.

Heading north from Indianapolis on I-69, they took the ring road east when they hit the outskirts of Fort Wayne, then turned north again on U.S. Route 27, also known as Lafayette Street. Even though it was a federal highway, it was just a four-lane road with plenty of cross-streets. It made its way through neighborhoods dating from the middle of the last century. Some of the homes were two stories; others had wrap-around porches. There was no way of knowing which, if any, had ever been occupied by Vincent.

"What now?" Raven asked.

"We could go to the assessor's office, but you leave a trail if you make a public records request. Besides, it takes time."

"So?"

"So, if there's anyone who knows about property, it's a real estate agent. They pay more attention to closing deals than they do to names and faces— especially when those names and faces belong to people who don't end up buying. All we have to do is find one who's been around long enough to know the history of the place."

Kekionga Colonial Realty seemed like as good a place as any to start. Fort Wayne had been named Kekionga, capital of the Miami tribe, before European colonists had settled. The name seemed to indicate the company had been around a long time. But it didn't guarantee a sense of history. That became apparent when they arrived at the office and were greeted by a clean-shaven early thirty-something millennial with slicked-back hair and a pasted-on smile. He stepped toward them briskly as they walked into the office, extending his hand.

"Philip Nordstrom," he announced, grabbing Carson's hand almost before he had a chance to raise it. "What can I help you find today?"

"We're looking for a historical property," Carson said. "The Vincent home. Have you heard of it?"

The realty agent released Carson's hand and scowled. "Price range?" he said. "Number of bedrooms? Maybe I can narrow things down for you."

Carson tried not to return the man's scowl. Was he *that* dense? "I've already narrowed it down," he said. "We're looking for a specific property. The *Vincent* home. Have you heard of it?"

"I'm sorry," the man said hurriedly. "Our listings are all by address, property number, number of bedrooms, square footage—"

"I understand," Carson interrupted. "You obviously can't help us. Can you direct us to someone who can, or should we take our business elsewhere?" He started to turn back to the door, but Nordstrom stopped him with a loud, "Wait!"

Carson stopped and turned again to face him.

"We have an agent who's out in the field now, Louie Crichton. He's been around forever. His wife works at the library. If anyone could steer you right, he could."

Carson inclined his head slightly toward Nordstrom. "Thank you. We'll wait." He strode over to one in a row of plastic chairs that lined the wall and deposited himself, with Minerva and Raven to his right.

They didn't wait long before a man stepped through the door, walking briskly despite a slightly stooped posture. He wore a bow tie and looked to be in his seventies at least, with thick but wispy white hair that looked like it had been transplanted from Albert Einstein and dark skin that stood out in contrast. He ignored them as he entered; he seemed intent upon finding his way to the back of the office when Nordstrom waylaid him.

"Louie, this family has a question for you."

Family? Do we look that domesticated? Minerva wondered.

A lot of people looking for homes are families, Raven replied. *You're about as domesticated as a mountain lion.*

Thanks. She grinned at him.

"Of course, of course," said the newcomer, turning on the heels of his brightly polished brown dress shoes to face them. "And you are . . .?"

Carson stuck out his hand and the man took it eagerly. "The Murphy family," he said. "This is my daughter and son-in-law. It will be their first home, but we're interested in a property with particular historical significance."

"We have quite a few around here, sir," the man said, nodding as he considered. "Some date back to the nineteenth century. May I ask what style of home you're looking for? What kind of amenities?"

"We'd like to have a look at a specific property—the Vincent home, if it's available. Even if it's not, we'd be interested in potentially making an offer well above its current valuation."

The man's eyes widened, his smile became perplexed. "Oh, I've heard of the Vincent home," he said haltingly. "But it isn't in our listings. Hasn't been for some time."

"Then it's not on the market?"

"Not exactly. It was, but . . ."

"Someone purchased it?"

"No, not that either. You see, the Vincent property is abandoned. Another office in town tried to sell it, but they couldn't find a buyer."

Nordstrom looked up from behind the reception counter. "Are they talking about the old place up on 27? The haunted house?"

His colleague nodded.

"Haunted house?" Minerva asked. "What makes you say it's haunted?"

"Because it is," Crichton said, as though he had just confirmed that the sun had come up in the east that morning. "Weird things have been happening there for as long as anyone can remember. Doors opening and closing by themselves. The sound of voices from places where no human being could ever fit, like from inside kitchen cabinets or the middle of walls. Recorded music when the power was out. Shadows stretching across the wall when the light was coming from the other direction, then disappearing as soon as someone noticed."

Minerva listened closely. She'd been fascinated by ghosts since she was a little girl. All the more so now that she'd crossed to the "other side" herself. Still, even though she was a memortal and she could fade without the attention of Raven's memory, she didn't think of herself as a spirit floating around in some spooky state between the dead and the living. Her body might be revived, but it was as solid as anyone's. She sure as hell couldn't walk through walls. Nor was she confined to a haunted house, cemetery, or anyplace else the way ghosts supposedly were.

Once, a few years earlier, Jessica had taken her and Archer to a nineteenth-century house in San Diego that was supposedly haunted. Jessica had oohed and ahhed at the tales about the place being haunted. Minerva was fascinated, too, but she hadn't run across any ghosts, and when Jessica had pointed out the "spirits of the dead" in an old photo, she'd seen nothing more than spots of light that had leaked into the camera lens.

Since then, she hadn't really believed in ghosts, but she didn't think all the people who said they'd seen them were just making things up, either. Maybe some of them were seeing light spots on photos. Maybe others had the gift and didn't realize it, and they really *were* seeing dead people, the way she thought she'd caught glimpses of Raven before he'd returned to her for good. Besides, the stories were intriguing, and she couldn't help but wonder what was behind the tales Crichton was telling them.

"Who owns it?" Carson asked.

"Why, the Vincent family still does, I expect," Crichton said. "It's not on our list of active properties, but I think it's technically still on the market. There might even be a realty box and key on the door. I can check, hold on."

He turned away and walked over to a computer station behind the reception desk, where he proceeded to punch something into the keyboard.

"This is better than I hoped," Carson whispered to Minerva. "If hardly anyone's been there since Phantom left the place, we might find just the kind of clues we need to crack the code."

"Do you think that's why they called him Phantom?" Raven quipped. "Maybe he was a ghost himself."

"I don't think so," Carson said. "The last time I saw him, he was very much alive—then very much dead. No in-between about it."

"Here it is," Crichton announced. "The last time it was formally listed was seven years ago, but I was right: There's no record of it ever being taken off the market."

Minerva spoke up: "We'd like to see it."

"Are you sure?" Crichton prompted. "I don't know what kind of shape it's in. It might need a lot of work ... if the ghosts will let you do it." He chuckled, but there was a hint of nervousness behind his laugh. He believed the home was haunted. He'd said so, without the slightest hint of uncertainty. And he obviously wasn't keen on the idea of heading over there and cooling his heels while "prospective buyers" took their time inspecting the place.

"We're sure," said Carson. "We'll follow you in our car. Agreed?"

Crichton raised his shoulders in a sort of half-shrug. "Suit yourself," he said. "But I think you're wasting your time. No one has even made an offer on the place, and it was listed pretty low back in the day. If I remember right, the owner even dropped the asking price a few times before he gave up."

"It's our time to waste," said Carson, "and your job to waste it. Now, if you don't mind."

Crichton rummaged through a drawer behind the counter, and his hand emerged with what the three of them assumed must be the key to the lockbox. "Yep, it's still here," he announced. "C'mon, let's get this over with." He chuckled again, and this time the nervous undercurrent was a little more pronounced.

"Yes, let's," said Minerva. "I'd like to meet these ghosts."

Haunted

Minerva didn't know what she'd expected to see when they arrived at the Vincent house. She remembered seeing a spooky old mansion in a movie called *Addams Family Values* that Jessica had rented for Halloween one year. That was pretty much what a haunted house was supposed to look like, she guessed. She'd seen other movies and old TV shows where they looked about the same. A haunted house was supposed to be two or three stories, with gray stone or rickety wooden walls, a gabled roof, and maybe even a tower. The windows might be broken or boarded up, and there might be a few stone gargoyles up in the rafters. Maybe there was a vintage luxury car in the driveway—one that no one ever drove and looked like it had seen far better days.

The Vincent house was nothing like that. It didn't look much different than any other homes on its block, except for the fact that it was clearly abandoned. Tall weeds had replaced whatever lawn had been there, and some of the paint appeared to be peeling. Other than that, there was little to distinguish it from other homes built in the era before the Second World War. It did have a gabled roof, but apart from a small loft, it was a single story. The paint wasn't gray, but a shade of yellow that had probably been brighter when it was first applied. A wrap-around porch encircled the house, with a swing bench bolted to the ceiling at one side of the front door.

Crichton referred to an old pamphlet for the place that described it as "A classic in Midwestern comfort. Modern livability with a nostalgic sense of style."

Whatever that meant.

The floor plan had nearly three-thousand square feet, with a floor heater, a big kitchen, and three "spacious" bedrooms. "There's also a laundry room, a sun room, and three baths," Crichton said, still reading from the pamphlet, trying to sound like a salesman, despite his personal misgivings. He wasn't very convincing.

Retrieving the key from the lockbox, he inserted it in the lock and opened the door to let them in.

The most remarkable thing about the interior was that it was still mostly appointed with what they guessed were the furnishings Vincent had left there when he departed. Either he'd been in a hurry to leave or he hadn't had room for them in his new place.

"Maybe he bought new stuff because he thought these things were cursed," Raven joked, patting the cushion of an old blue sofa with the palm of his hand, watching a cloud of dust rise in the air.

The blinds and curtains had been drawn, and it was overcast outside anyway, so it wasn't too easy to see their way around.

"I want a better look at this place," Raven said, pulling back the living room drapes to let at least some light in. It was getting toward late afternoon. They didn't have much more than an hour of daylight.

"So, what would you like to see first?" Crichton asked. His hesitant tone told them he hoped they'd tell him they weren't interested and had seen enough already.

No such luck.

"Would you mind if we looked around a little on our own?" Carson asked. People in real estate sales liked to hover far too much, and he wanted to make sure they could speak freely.

"Go right ahead," Crichton said, sounding relieved to be off the hook from venturing any farther into the depths of the old home. He handed them the old pamphlet he'd brought with them. "This should be able to answer any questions for you, and if not, I'll tell you anything I can. I'll just wait out on the front porch, okay? Take your time."

Carson nodded.

"Thanks," said Minerva, but he'd already turned around and made his way hurriedly out the door.

"He's really scared of this place," Raven said. "I don't see anything to be afraid of."

"Neither do I," said Minerva. "But then again, people wouldn't be afraid of memortals unless they knew what was inside, would they?" She winked at him and flashed a mischievous smile.

"I guess not," he laughed, then raised his chin in exaggerated fashion and declared, "I ain't afraid of no ghost."

This time it was Minerva's turn to laugh. Even Carson allowed himself a brief chuckle before asking, "Do you recognize anything?"

She looked around. "Not really," she said. "But I would think the more personal things, if he didn't take them with him, would be in one of the bedrooms."

"This pamphlet says the home was in the same family for three generations," Carson said, "so it's likely he grew up here. We might find some of the things you saw that looked like they were from his childhood."

They walked down a corridor that led away from the entry and living room, into the interior of the house. One door led off to the right, another to the left, and there was a third at the end of the hallway.

"A master bedroom and two others," Carson speculated.

"Only one way to find out," said Minerva as she pulled open the nearest door, the one on the right.

There wasn't much. A bed without any bedsheets, a nightstand with a cheap ornamental lamp that had been knocked over at some point and a digital alarm clock whose face was blank.

"Guest room?" Raven asked.

"Yeah, I don't see anything here," Minerva said after a quick look around.

They tried the room across the hall. There was a little more there. It had been a boy's room most recently. There wasn't a bed. The only piece of furniture was a small table in one corner with a coloring book on it. Minerva picked it up and leafed through pages until she came to one with an outline picture of a cat and a porcupine. "People like us seem furry and purry," the text read, underneath a picture of a half-colored-in cat curled up contentedly by a fireplace. Then, under the porcupine, who had a sad look on its face and a tear in its eye: "But people who look different aren't icky and prickly." She turned the page to see the two animals smiling at each other, with a big heart drawn over their heads. "We're all the same underneath."

"Nice message," she said. "Wish people were really like this. I always did like animals better."

She turned the page and felt like she nearly jumped out of her skin: There was nothing there. It wasn't that a page was blank or missing, or that a picture hadn't been colored. There was no *there* there. Just a swirling mist of nothing that looked like a bowl of pea-soup fog, that didn't move when you looked straight at it, but when you started to look away it seemed to roil and seethe like an angry ocean. Minerva felt dizzy, like she might fall in it . . . or like the "nothing" might reach out and grab her.

She slammed the book shut.

"What is it?" Raven asked, moving close and putting an arm around her.

She was shaking. It wasn't like her to be unnerved like that.

"Didn't you see it?"

"Sorry, I wasn't looking," he said. "I was watching the corner of the room over there. It seems weird, darker than it should."

"Just shadows, I think," Carson said, glancing over. "There's not much light in here."

Raven looked closer, and Minerva followed his eyes. "No, he's right," she said. "It's too dark. You should be able to see something, even in this light, but it's like everything disappears . . . the light and everything else."

Carson pulled a small penlight from his pocket and clicked the end with his thumb, shining a bright beam of light toward the corner in question. It appeared to be just a corner; nothing strange about it. "You're letting that talk of this place being haunted get to you," he said.

Minerva glared at him. "No," she insisted, "look at this."

She opened the coloring book again, but this time all the pages seem to be intact. At the place that had startled her before, a fully colored figure of a Dalmatian puppy stared back.

Minerva gathered her composure but didn't say anything. She knew what she'd seen. Just because it wasn't here now, that didn't mean it hadn't been there before . . . or hadn't been *not* there. The memory of it still felt like *nothing*—a "nothing" with substance. Like a black hole or some kind of void, reaching out to clutch at her, trying to pull her into it. The fact that she remembered it, and vividly, reassured her that she hadn't imagined it. If there was one thing she could count on, it was her memory.

She looked at the far wall to the room's dominant feature. A mural that seemed to depict an epic battle, pitting men with iron helms and chain mail against a ravenous wolf that looked larger than life. Whoever had created it had been meticulous in detail, down to a notch in one of the axe blades and each individual link in the warriors' mail. The mural appear almost three-dimensional. Minerva moved to it, looking more closely. It was disturbing in a way, hardly the kind of thing you would expect to find in a child's room.

"See anything familiar?" Raven asked.

She paused for a moment, then shook her head. "No," she said, "but there's something about it. It seems almost too real." She reached out and ran her fingers over the surface of the wall; it was so smooth it felt fluid.

"If you don't recognize it, we should move on," Carson said. "There's another bedroom to explore, and I don't want to be here after dark."

"You scared of ghosts too?" Raven needled.

"Not at all," Carson replied, his voice serious. "We just can't afford to stay here too long. Minerva's right: We need to worry about Jules."

"And Josef," Minerva added. "You're right, Carson. Let's move on to that other bedroom. I don't see anything in this one, and it's creeping me out."

They left the room and were halfway down the hall when they heard a sharp series of knocks coming from the other side of the door they had just closed.

"Don't tell me you didn't hear that," Minerva said, looking at Carson.

He didn't say anything but went back to look. Pulling out his Baby Glock just in case, he opened the door slowly, hugging the wall outside, and peered around the corner quickly.

There was no one there.

Carson scanned the room thoroughly; there was no indication of movement. Nothing had been disturbed and everything seemed quiet. He shut the door again and returned to the others. "All clear," he announced, as if that's exactly how he'd expected it to turn out.

"Just the wind, eh, Carson?" Raven chided.

Carson shot him a look that said, "Watch it, smartass," which was lost in the shadows of the hallway. "Let's see what's in the last room."

The double doors at the end of the hallway opened onto a large master suite. Like the first two bedrooms, it was sparsely furnished. There wasn't a bed, and most of the space was taken up by at least a dozen large cardboard boxes. An armoire against the wall to their right and a cedar chest in the middle of the room were the only two pieces of furniture. The room was darker than the others, the only window facing east, away from what afternoon sunlight made it through the clouds and Venetian blinds.

"Looks like he left in a hurry," Raven said. "Wonder why he left all this stuff here."

"Maybe he just decided to store it here when no one bought the place?" Minerva suggested.

It seemed like as good an explanation as any.

None of the boxes had been taped shut, so it wasn't hard to sift through the piles of old clothes, books, towels, and linens, along with a few knick-knacks.

"Look what I found," Minerva said, holding up a stuffed blue bunny with a missing eye. Raven held open a white plastic kitchen bag they'd brought with them, and she dropped it inside. "I'm going to check the armoire," she said.

She walked over and pulled on the twin doors, which opened easily. Inside were some more clothes, including a baseball uniform. The same one she had seen inside Vincent's head. Carson directed his penlight toward it. The words "Notre Dame" were emblazoned across the front, with a number on the back. 24.

It didn't make sense. What had happened to the 37? Had she seen it wrong? Had two memories gotten crossed up in Vincent's subconscious?

It was making less and less sense.

Maybe she'd be able to figure it out later. She brought the jersey to Raven, folded it up loosely, and dropped it into the bag.

"Maybe this is a dead end," Raven said. "We aren't any closer to figuring out the code than we were when we got here."

He turned his attention back to the box he'd been looking through. It was filled with envelopes, but he couldn't make out the writing in the fading daylight. "Hand that light here for a sec, will ya?"

Carson did, and he shone the penlight on the envelopes. Most of them were unopened and looked like they were junk mail.

"Make anything of this?" Raven asked, handing him a stack of mail topped by an Easter Seals solicitation and a campaign mailer for the 2008 election.

"Yeah, actually, I do," Carson said. "Look at the address."

Raven looked closer: The envelopes had all been sent to 137 Lafayette St. There was their 37. It looked like the answer to the code had been staring them in the face the whole time.

"What does the 1 mean, though?" Raven asked.

"Thirty-seven is a prime number," Carson said. "And the word 'prime' means 'first.' So, you get 137. Just by being here, we might have found our way inside wherever it is that Neil's code was the key to—unless there's another meaning we're missing."

Bang! They heard the sound of a door slamming down the hall, and all three of them jumped in unison—even Carson.

"How you folks doing in here?"

It was Crichton. They all exhaled.

"Fine," Minerva called down the hall.

"Just give us a few more minutes," Carson said.

"Glad to," Crichton called back. The front door creaked opened, then closed again behind him. It didn't slam this time; it probably hadn't before, either. The sound had just cut through the silence, shattering their concentration.

The three of them took turns looking at one another in the dim light, asking the same unspoken question: If this was where the code was supposed to lead them, what was so important? A stuffed bunny? An old baseball jersey? Maybe it was all just sentimental. Maybe he simply regretted leaving it behind.

If that were the case, why had he gone to the trouble of setting up and remembering an elaborate code that was meaningless? A decoy to keep anyone from finding his family home at 137 Lafayette Street in Fort Wayne, Indiana?

No, there had to be something important.

Yet there didn't seem to be anything noteworthy, except for the Viking mural in the other room. That was anything *but* ordinary.

"Maybe it's like that Da Vinci novel. One clue leads to another?" Minerva suggested. That didn't even sound convincing to her ears. The jersey was here, so was the bunny.

This was the place.

"Maybe the answer's back there," Raven said, pointing down the hallway, "in the kid's room. You said you saw some weird stuff, right?"

I don't really want to admit that I was spooked, but do we really have to go back there? she said in her thoughts.

197

Not if you don't want to, but the way you acted before, maybe it's worth another look.

You're probably right. It's just . . . have you ever felt like you were about to be swallowed up by something?

Carson couldn't read their thoughts, but he might as well have: "I think we should go back to that second bedroom," he said. "You two seemed to think there was something not quite right about it, so I want to have another look."

I guess that settles it. Minerva gave an inaudible mental sigh.

Raven took her hand. It wasn't often he got to play the protective boyfriend, mainly because Minerva was so badass. She'd saved his skin more often than the other way around. But something about that room had really rattled her. That alone was enough for him to decide it needed a second look.

Want to wait here? he asked.

Like hell!

That's the Min I know. Even so, she didn't let go of his hand. He loved that about her, too.

Carson pulled his out gun and took the lead as they headed back down the hall. Opening the door, they found it exactly as they left it, only darker. The clouds outside had gotten thicker, and the sun dipped lower. So there was even less light than before. They could hear the sound of a light wind in the branches of the willow outside the window.

Minerva put out her hand and Carson gave her the penlight. She took the coloring book and leafed through it rapidly, but found nothing out of the ordinary. Still, it was probably worth taking it with them, she decided. She motioned to Raven, who held out the bag, and she dropped it inside. It couldn't hurt to have a closer look at the thing in better light.

They heard the sound of a car engine starting.

"That's Crichton's car," Raven said.

"Guess he isn't interested in making a sale," Carson answered, then fell silent.

The three of them listened.

They stood in the center of the room, back to back, as if they'd been surrounded by some invisible army. They searched the shadows for any sign of movement, anything out of the ordinary. The wind beyond the walls of the house quickened, then abated for a few heartbeats, only to kick up again moments later—restless, like some anxious spirit swirling about, seeking entry, yet trapped beyond a barrier less tangible and more unyielding than the walls of the old home.

The house itself answered, its foundation settling with a groan.

They waited.

Finally, Carson spoke. "I still don't see anything. It's getting late. We should probably go."

"Yeah," said Raven. "Do we have everything?"

"I think so," said Minerva as she opened the bag he had given her to check inside.

She shook her head violently, as if trying to break free of an attacker, taking a step backward. There was nothing there. Nothing at all. It was the same *nothing* she had seen before. And it was clawing at her desperately, pulling her down into invisible quicksand. She tried to pull back, but leaned forward despite herself, compelled by a cacophony of sound that seemed like a thousand voices trying to speak over one another. She couldn't make out much of what they were saying beyond the frantic tone they seemed to share.

"Help me!" she heard one of the voices cry.

"Save us!"

"No one's remembering! Someone . . . please . . ."

Min, what is it? Raven's own mental voice was frantic. *Look at me. What's happening?*

His mental voice jarred her loose from the hold of the others. She hadn't felt anything that powerful since . . . ever.

Not even when Jules invaded her mind or when she'd felt herself losing her identity to Guy of Gisborne. This was like that, only amplified a hundred-fold. It was like she was being mobbed by starving cannibals trying to eat her soul.

She fell backward as she felt Raven grab the bag from her hands.

She felt dizzy and disoriented.

"What just happened?" she asked, aware that her voice was quavering.

"You tell me," said Raven. "It almost looked like something in that bag was trying to suck you in."

"That's what it felt like," she said.

"I think it's that book," Raven said. "Something happened the last time you looked at it, too."

Carson nodded. "It's probably what Phantom was trying to protect. Let's get it out of here and have another look at it tomorrow, after we've all had some rest."

Minerva took another step away from the bag. "*You* can look next time," she said. "Whatever's in there is . . . I don't know . . . it's like . . ." She wanted to say "evil," but that wasn't quite it. She didn't believe in the idea of evil, anyway.

She steadied herself. She didn't know much of anything about what was inside that bag—not yet. But knowledge was always the best defense.

"Maybe I will look at it again after all," she said as they left the Vincent home at 137 Lafayette Street. "I just need a little while to recover, okay?"

No one was about to argue with her.

Leverage

Duke Malone was not a patient man. This could work to his advantage, because he knew how to get things done. He'd started young, sweeping up at his uncle's barbershop, a single-chair hole-in-the-wall in an older neighborhood where small businesses like a corner drugstore and a vintage two-pump service station shared blocks with pre-World War II homes.

One thing he'd learned at Jimbo's Barbershop was to listen. He'd listened to the conversations between his uncle and the customers, who treated Jimbo Malone as if he were their confessor or their bartender. He'd developed a keen ear for what was important and what wasn't, learning to filter out the B.S. and to focus on the important things. He'd gotten so good at it that he'd picked up tips on what horses to bet at the track, who was cheating on whom, and which mechanics were scamming their customers.

Also, *how* they were scamming their customers.

And whether it was working.

He'd only been twelve when he started sweeping the floor, and he hadn't understood half of what people said, but he'd remembered it all. He'd realized early on that he had a good memory. Good wasn't the word for it, really; uncanny was more like it. That was part of the reason he was impatient. He expected everyone to be as observant as he was. Their memories to be as reliable as his. When they weren't, he didn't tend to have much sympathy.

He'd dispose of them.

"Pulling the weeds," he called it. But sometimes, weeds could be helpful, even if they were a pain in the ass. Take DeJohn Sutcliffe, for instance. He'd told his boys that Sutcliffe was expendable; he would be more trouble than it was worth to keep him alive. He'd been wrong. Things had gone according to plan in the beginning. Then all hell broke loose.

Sutcliffe might have been able to help him rectify the problem.

If he'd still been alive.

But not only was Sutcliffe dead, now Vincent apparently was, also. His photo had come onto the screen of one of those cable news shows. The announcer reported that Vincent, the former head of the Nuclear Regulatory Commission, had been found dead on Long Island, a bullet through his head.

Malone was back at square one.

The way FIN operated, there was no way of knowing who Vincent's successor would be. Malone had lost his leverage. The teenage boy he'd been holding was worthless now, so Malone had him killed. It was regrettable, but necessary.

Killing Sutcliffe, on the other hand, had not only been unnecessary but costly. If Malone had shown a little more restraint, he might have been able to procure the man's services to gain access to the new director of FIN, whoever it was. He didn't have that option now, but Duke Malone wasn't the kind to let a debt go unpaid or a score go unsettled.

Henry Marshall had crossed him, big time, the Duke wasn't about to let him get away with it. He needed to send a message that, whatever the courts might do, no one got the better of Duke Malone. Not without paying for it.

But there was a bright side to all the trouble Marshall had put him through. There was usually a bright side, if you knew where to look—and how to listen. What he'd heard in this case is what had led him to Marshall's connection with FIN in the first place, and that had presented him with a fine business opportunity. If he could manage to infiltrate FIN, he'd have access to all sorts of classified information that would give him a leg up on the competition. And, if he played his cards right, help him gain enough influence to expand his operations.

FIN might be a shadowy operation, but with the right skills and for the right price, you could find out just about anything. What Malone's hired ears had found was that FIN, under the guise of the witness protection program, had created a new "life" for Marshall out by the Salton Sea, under the protection of a deep-cover agent who Marshall himself probably didn't even know was a plant.

Rosa Carbajal was now calling herself Paige Daly, but she'd gone by a lot of different names, and from what Malone had found out, she'd been undercover, on one job or another, for more than a decade. She'd even married a guy named Ted Frias, a midlevel operative with the Cardenas Cartel, to set him up for a federal sting. But that plan had gone sour when she had panicked and Mike Gonzalez, the leader of the Lost Hills Condors biker gang, had taken it upon himself to play the knight in shining armor.

FIN had kept Rosa embedded with the Condors to keep her out of the way while they tried to clean up the mess. If the Cardenas group thought she really *was* a biker girl, FIN might be able to use her in an operation later. In the meantime, she could keep an eye on the Condors, who had a reputation of their own for causing trouble. But even that had blown up when the police caught wind of her whereabouts and arrested her for questioning in the Frias case, at which point FIN had reassigned her again, this time to keep an eye on Marshall in a pseudo-witness protection setup.

Malone had learned a lot of this thanks to Sutcliffe's adept hack of FIN's computer operations. It wasn't something the Duke could replicate, which led him back to the mistake he'd made in disposing of Sutcliffe too quickly.

Fortunately, he'd been able to infiltrate the Condors with one of his own, a man named Davonte Jameson, who'd been working with him for some time as head of a small biker club in Brawley. Jameson had even called his club the Sand Dukes in honor of Malone—something Malone didn't care for. But he'd allowed it because he had an ego, and "Sand Dukes" had a nice ring to it.

With Jameson inside the Condors, Malone hoped he could glean some information from Rosa/Paige that would help him get back inside FIN. It might also allow him to have his revenge on Marshall.

Jameson had already told him that Rosa and Marshall appeared close, romantically speaking. If there were true, it might be something he could use as leverage . . . if he chose to keep Marshall alive. That was a big "if" at this point and he didn't want to wait too long to make a decision.

He was, after all, not a patient man.

Secrets

The others were asleep. Paige led Henry outside the barn where the Condors were holed up. Stars winked silently from above, peering down out of a cold dark sky. Something skittered past a few yards off, a desert cottontail disturbed from hiding by a coyote that had come sniffing around. The coyote didn't seem to notice them, preoccupied as it was, and lost no time in dashing after its quarry.

Henry was only too happy for an excuse to get outside. He'd awoken inside the barn to find a scorpion sleeping beside him not three feet from his head, basking in the moonlight that drifted down through an opening in the rafters. Besides, it was nice to be alone with Paige, out here beyond the odor of the barn—and the bikers. Not that the two of them smelled much better: Henry hadn't thought he'd start to feel homesick for the trailer in Bombay Beach, but then again, everything was relative.

"There's something I have to tell you," Paige said.

"What is it?"

She moved in close to him and kissed him on the cheek, then whispered in his ear. "You know I got feelings for you, right?" she said.

He nodded. "Yes, and you know I do for you."

"Good. Well, kiddo, there's something I ain't told you. About me."

He sat up a little straighter. Part of him wanted to tell her it didn't matter, but he was curious, and a little worried. He felt vulnerable enough acknowledging his feelings for her, and the idea that she'd been keeping secrets wasn't exactly reassuring, especially when she was telling him this soon in their relationship. This was a relationship, wasn't it? They hadn't even been together, in the intimate sense, yet. But he felt close to her. Part of him had hoped she'd taken him outside the barn to . . . well . . . even if there were coyotes prowling around and there was too much sand for comfort, he would have put up with it. Since they'd been together, he'd found himself drawn to her almost constantly.

He was overthinking things. He tended to do that.

"Go on," he said.

"You know how I told you I'm in the witness protection program, like you?"

"Yes."

"Well, that's not totally true. Your friend, Carson—"

"You know him?"

"I've never met him, but I know about him. He works for the government. So do I. I was assigned to keep an eye on you."

"You were what?" Henry pulled away from her and looked her in the eye. He wasn't sure what he was looking for, other than a sign of something he hadn't seen before. Mockery, maybe. Or betrayal. Worse still, coldness. But he couldn't see any difference. Her eyes seemed as warm as ever, and as he shifted his position, restless and about to get to his feet, she put her hand on his and held it there. He relaxed, just a bit, at her touch.

"So, this whole setup really *was* an act?"

She shook her head, "No, hon. That's not what I'm saying. Do you think I'd be telling you this if it was an act? I'm blowing my cover here 'cause I trust you, and 'cause I need you to trust me if we're gonna make it through this. If you ever tell anyone what I just told you, it's over for me. They'll turn me over to the cops for Ted's death, and Mike won't be able to protect me 'cause they'll fake the evidence. Just like you made things up to get Duke Malone indicted."

"You know about that?"

"Yeah, and a lot of other stuff, too. I know about you and Carson and the Rus girl and her back-from-the-dead boyfriend, and about Amber."

"Amber," Henry said. "What do you know about Amber?"

Paige smiled. "You liked her, didn't you?"

"She and I were colleagues. I . . . got to know her, and I always admired her, but there wasn't ever anything between us. Not really."

"But you wanted there to be."

He opened his mouth to say something but thought better of it. If she was willing to tell him her secret, he should be willing to admit to this. "At one time, yes," he said. "But not anymore."

Paige squeezed his hand. "I believe you, kiddo. I can see it in your eyes. So we're square, eh?"

He nodded.

"Good. I'm glad we cleared all this up, 'cause we won't have much chance to talk. I think there's someone here who's watching us, and I'm worried that if we stick around, it might not be too good for our health, if you know what I mean."

"Who?"

"Davonte. I barely know him, but the Condors have a code: 'If you ride, we'll ride with you'—unless you're in the Diamond Dogs or Hillside Hellions." She saw the confused look on his face. "Clubs that don't get along with Mike and the boys," she explained. "It's a long story. But Davonte's club has always been cool with Mike, so they're, well, not tight, but it's all good between them. I told Mike I didn't trust him, but he laughed it off."

Henry looked worried. "Do you think he might tell Davonte about your suspicions."

"No," she said firmly. "What I tell him stays between us. Always has. He's got his own personal code, not just the Condor code, and he always liked me, the way you liked Amber. I think he still does, but he knows the score. He's still protective, though, and I can't say I'm sorry for that. I'd have his back just like that if he asked me, too. I just don't think he can protect me now, and I worry about you even more, kiddo. 'Cause, let's face it: He doesn't really like you very much."

He felt like laughing at that, just because it was so obvious, but he stifled the urge. "So, what do we do?" he asked instead.

"Ever been to New York?"

He had been, actually. He'd traveled there for a week-long medical conference a few years back. He remembered it well because it was personal. The conference had focused on an experimental treatment for leukemia. He'd become a doctor after his mother had been diagnosed with the disease, and there'd been nothing he could do to save her. That was why he'd insisted on attending the conference, even though a colleague had been first in line for the trip.

He'd never really gotten over his mother's death. She'd always been stronger than anyone else he'd known. Seeing her lying there, weak and frail like that, seemed unreal, impossible to him. He'd known she was dying, and there wasn't a damn thing he could do about it. No matter how often he implored the doctors to save her, they would only say that they were doing their best. It was never enough. No matter how he tried to ease her discomfort, to make it better, nothing seemed to help.

He'd been holding her hand when she passed, shortly after midnight on that last day. He'd known it was coming, but not then, not at that moment. Not on that night, when she had smiled and said, "See you in the morning." But her eyes had stayed shut, no matter how long he'd pleaded with her to open them.

"Hey, kiddo." Paige was waving her hand in front of his face. "Where'd you go?"

"New York," he said, repeating her last words, then focusing again on her face. "No, somewhere else, a long time ago. Somewhere I don't want to go back to again."

"Where?"

He took a deep breath. "My mother's deathbed." His face was a mask, but he could tell from the softening in her eyes that she read the pain. Part of him didn't want to share it with her. Another knew he had to. He hadn't told anyone else about being there when his mother died. It occurred to him that he might never have mentioned it to anyone if it hadn't been for Paige.

"Yes, I've been to New York," he said. "When you mentioned it, it brought back memories of a conference I attended there some time ago. Reminded me of why I became a doctor. I dropped out of school back home and came over here to study after my mum died, with the money she left me. That chance was all I had left. I was determined to make the most of it. I'd let her down once, and I promised myself I wouldn't do it again. So I went into medicine. I didn't want anyone else to be let down, the way she was." He paused, looking down, then back up at her. "Sorry," he said. "You didn't need to hear all that. All you asked about was New York. *Why* did you ask about New York?"

"'Cause that's where I think we need to go. My contact in FIN told me before this all went down that if everything went to hell, to go to this address in New York and I'd get more instructions."

"Wouldn't it have been easier just to phone this person?"

"We try to stay offline as much as possible. Once we get an assignment, we're pretty much on our own unless we screw it up beyond repair. I don't even know my contact's name, just a code name: Phantom27iR5."

"What's yours? Your code name, I mean."

"Badger68pP1."

"And this Phantom will be good with things if I tag along?"

"He'd better be," Paige chuckled. "You're the whole reason I'm here in the first place. I'm not letting you out of my sight, if I can help it. You're too valuable."

To you or to this Phantom? he thought, but he didn't say it out loud. Instead he asked, "When do we leave."

"No time like the present, kiddo," she said. "Ready to spend the next three days on the back of a Harley?"

It didn't sound comfortable, but he nodded.

"Good. Then c'mon, baby, 'cause I'm ready to ride."

It seemed like a good time to leave, with everyone asleep; they could only hope that the sound of the engine starting wouldn't wake anyone. As it turned out, though, Davonte Jameson was already awake. Sitting just inside the back entrance to the rickety old barn, he'd heard snippets of what Paige and Henry had been saying to each other, enough to know that they intended to sneak off to New York. He couldn't let them go without a little company, even if he wasn't exactly planning to ride alongside them. The tiny tracking device he'd affixed to the underside of the Hog's rear fender would ensure he didn't lose them.

He waited until they'd gotten a small head start, then revved up his bike and followed. It was going to be a long ride.

Youngstown

They spent the night in Youngstown, at the same motel Minerva and Carson had stayed on their way west. Despite Raven's reservations, they were headed back to New York. It was the only way, Carson had argued, of stopping Jules and Josef.

The motel was just four hours east of Fort Wayne, and they could have made it all the way through to New York by sunrise, but they all agreed it would be best to greet the new day with fresh eyes. Besides, Minerva wanted to stop and look in the bag. She'd forced herself to shake off the lingering feelings of anxiety over her previous encounter with whatever it was, or *wasn't*, for the sake of satisfying her curiosity.

When they unlocked the door to the motel room, the first thing she did was sit down with the bag in her hands. Steeling herself for what she was sure she'd see, she opened it and looked inside. It was almost a letdown to find the items they'd put in the bag just sitting there, undisturbed, as if nothing had happened.

Hesitantly, she reached inside and pulled one out after the other. The coloring book, blue bunny, the jersey. She put the bunny on her nightstand and set aside the jersey for the moment to focus on the book.

Slowly, she began leafing through the pages, some of them all colored in, some partly completed, others untouched. Flipping them gradually faster until she came to the page with the cat and the porcupine. The page after that had been the "ghost page." She didn't know what else to call it—the swirling mist of nothingness that had tried to pull her in.

She turned the page.

A Dalmatian puppy gazed out at her, a fire chief's hat on its head. Annoyed, she turned the page. A blue and purple bear held up a fish in its paw. The fish, which the owner of the book had colored gold, was staring at the bear with an angry look on its face, demanding, "Put me back!"

No ghost page there, either.

She turned the page again. A black-and-white skunk was handing a pink flower to a bunny that had been colored blue. Another picture of woodland creatures, this one uncolored, followed on the next page, and on the page after that. She finally reached the end of the book. From start to finish, it seemed nothing more than a child's coloring book.

"It's not here," she said.

Raven studied her face for a moment, but it was Carson who said what they both had been wondering: "Do you think you just imagined it?"

Wrong question.

"I don't *imagine* things, Carson. I *remember* them. And I always remember them exactly the way they were. You should know that by now."

Raven was glad Carson had been the one to ask. Raven had the gift, too, but he'd never been quite as sure of it as Minerva, even though he'd been the one to awaken it in her in the first place. Everyone was fallible. Everyone made mistakes. He knew that about himself, but Minerva's memory was the one thing that had never failed. She wasn't prepared to even consider the possibility that it might.

"She's right," Raven said. "It wasn't her imagination. I remember that weird shadow in the corner of the room where we found the book. And remember, you heard the knocking from behind the door after we left it."

Carson shook his head. "That was just a shadow. We put the flashlight on it, and it looked normal. And that knocking was probably just the house settling, or a raccoon running around in the attic. There wasn't anything in the room when I checked."

"Not so fast," Minerva said, putting the coloring book aside. "What if it isn't the coloring book that's haunted—or whatever you want to call it. What if it's the room?"

Raven nodded slowly. "Makes sense. Each of us saw or heard something weird there."

"So now you both think the place really *was* haunted?" Carson said. "Sorry, I don't buy it."

"I'm not saying that. It wasn't like there were any ghosts in the house. Hey, I don't even believe in ghosts. It was more like something was *on the other side* of that missing page, or that shadow, that wanted to get into the house but couldn't. Like a gateway of some kind that had been blocked, and whoever—whatever—was on the other side wanted out. Or in. I don't know. But it couldn't get through, and it wanted me to go there. It was trying to pull me in. I felt like it almost did."

"Pull you into what?" Carson asked.

"I don't know."

"Why?" said Raven.

"I don't know that, either. All I know is it felt kinda familiar in some ways. I can't tell you how exactly."

Carson stood up and started pacing. The look on his face seemed to say he believed she'd seen something, even if she couldn't describe it. He didn't believe in ghosts, either, but he was standing here talking to a couple of dead people, so what did he know? "There's something we're missing— some piece of the puzzle that will make sense of this. I just can't think of what it is."

"I think it might have something to do with the gift," Minerva said.

"Do you think that's why we *saw* things in the room but Carson didn't?" Raven said. "Maybe the knocking he heard *was* just a raccoon in the attic. Maybe he couldn't see the empty shadows when he was in the room because he doesn't have the gift."

"It's possible," Carson admitted, "but we still don't know how your gift plays into it, or what's on the other side of this gateway, if that's what it is."

"No, we don't," said Minerva. "But if Jules and Josef figure it out first, guess what?"

"They'll exploit it," said Carson. "Which is why we have to get to New York as soon as possible. But I, for one, need a good night's rest. We'll get out of here at first light, agreed?"

"Agreed," said Raven.

They could reach New York in less than seven hours if they drove straight through. What they'd find when they got there was anybody's guess.

Arena

Roger took aim and fired. The arrow pierced the apple on top of the figure forty yards away, a scarecrow with a pumpkin's head on which the apple had been perched. The pumpkin had been carved in such a way that its face resembled someone gasping in surprise, its open mouth gasping in silent horror and its eyes wide with astonishment.

Will stepped up and clapped him on the shoulder. "Well done!" he said loudly. Then, in a whisper: "You are supposed to bow to the crowd, I think."

The people in the stands clapped heartily in rhythm as they chanted, "Robin! Robin! Robin!"

"I loathe that name," he said under his breath, and he didn't like the way Scadlock was egging them on, either, removing his cap and indicating Roger with a sweeping gesture.

"Lords! Ladies!" Will shouted. "Have you ever witnessed such a feat of mastery with bolt and bow? Truly, our kinsman, good Robin, is a magician with the rarest of gifts."

Roger grabbed him by the collar of his tunic and yanked him close, causing him to stumble across the dusty soil of the arena.

The crowd roared its approval.

"I said, I *loathe* that name," he seethed in Will's ear.

"All part of the show, Robin . . . I mean Roger," Will whispered, then winked at him.

What was it with Scadlock? Everything was a joke to him—either that or an excuse to down a mug of ale and go chasing after the nearest woman, not necessarily in that order. As a devotee of the Holy Mother, he wondered why he put up with it. Probably because, for all their differences, they shared one essential thing in common: the gift.

His attention was drawn away from Scadlock by a sudden gasp from the crowd, whose heads turned in unison at the entrance of a man on a black horse riding toward them, the reins in one hand and a bow in the other. An amplified voice rose from all sides of the arena at once: "Ladies and gentlemen, the sheriff of Nottingham!" The announcement was met by a series of boos and catcalls, and the crowd started stomping their feet on the metal grandstands.

"What is that infernal voice?" Roger demanded rather loudly, though no one but Will could hear him over all the racket.

"The voice of God, perhaps?" Will teased.

"The devil is far more likely," Roger scoffed. "God would know the difference between the true shire-reeve and that imposter."

"At least they think *you're* the real thing."

"Well, I am. So are you." Even so, Roger knew the whole pageant was a charade, a performance in which he was pretending to be someone pretending to be him. Play-acting was the work of the devil, and he was complicit in it. He silently cursed himself.

The man on the horse turned away at the last minute and rode toward the center of the arena. Without stopping, he let loose of the reins, reached over his shoulder, pulled an arrow from his quiver—and nearly fell from the saddle. This prompted another gasp from the crowd, who "knew" it was all part of the show, even though it wasn't. The man was clearly not an accomplished rider.

Righting himself, he nocked the arrow, aiming at the pumpkin head that remained undisturbed below where the apple had been. He missed badly.

The crowed whooped and roared.

"Idiot," Roger remarked under his breath.

"I think you are expected to taunt him," Will prompted. "Then demonstrate how vastly superior your own skill is."

Roger took an arrow from his own quiver, nocked it and aimed straight for the sky.

The crowd gasped.

"You can't do that!" shouted the man who had confronted them before, carrying a clipboard—which he was still holding. It seemed like it was attached to him. "You could hit someone!" he cried. "We're not insured for . . ."

Too late. Roger sent the arrow soaring skyward in an arc that drew all eyes to it like a rainbow on its way to an elusive pot of gold. It rose high into the air, reached its apex, then hurtled back toward earth, piercing the scarecrow's pumpkin head straight through, sending pieces flying in all directions.

The crowd went wild.

The man dropped the clipboard.

And a pair of uniformed police officers, waving their arms, stepped through the far gate into the arena and started toward them. This was not part of the show.

The crowd wasn't quite sure about that, but the fact that the police weren't dressed in period outfits gave them pause. They went silent, unsure of how to react.

"Oh, bother," said Will. "I think you were *too* good, Robin."

"My. Name. Is. ROGER," Roger declared, and this time everyone heard him.

"That's a good start," said one of the officers. "We'll need your full name and ID, sir."

The officer's partner turned toward the crowd and said, "I'm afraid that's it for today folks. Show's over. Everyone please head for the exits in an orderly fashion."

The man with the clipboard came running up to them along with Terri, the director of the faire, who had vouched for them back at the entrance. The goodwill she had shown them was the only reason Roger had gone along with this ridiculous pretense—that and not wanting to spend the night in jail.

"They're employees," she said to the officer. "What have they done? I know their act is a little . . . unconventional. But . . ."

"This has nothing to do with their act," the officer replied. "Someone's made a complaint against them, accused them of grand theft."

"Now there be a stroke of irony," Scadlock quipped. "We *are* thieves, but I assure you we have not stolen anything since our arrival."

"We have a report that says otherwise," the officer said. "And you're wearing the item that was reported stolen."

He pointed at Will's neck.

At the emerald necklace.

Will reached up and put his hand around it reflexively.

"I'm sorry, but we'll have to take that for the time being, and I'm afraid you'll have to come down to the precinct and answer a few questions."

"Are you arresting them?" Terri asked.

"Not necessarily," the officer said. "We'd prefer that they come with us voluntarily, but if it comes down to it, we do have probable cause. The owner of the necklace supplied a detailed description—both of it and of you gentlemen. Now, if you don't mind coming this way."

Roger and Will both looked at Terri. She was the only person here they knew and, to be frank, they were both decidedly unfamiliar with how things worked around here. They needed some guidance from someone, and she was the only person who'd shown them the least bit of courtesy.

She nodded. "You'd better do as they say," she said. "We've got a lawyer. He mainly deals in liability issues, but he's on retainer. I'll see what he can do."

Roger bowed slightly. "My thanks, lady," he said, allowing the officer to take him by the arm and lead him away. The other officer did the same with Will, who was, nonetheless, reluctant to part with the necklace.

"Hand it over," the officer in possession of his arm said. "It's stolen property."

Will let go of the necklace, reluctantly, and wondered as he did so who could have reported it missing. It wasn't even from here, and no one knew they had it. No one except . . .

Key

Josef twirled the emerald in his hands, allowing the chain to cascade through his fingers like a gentle waterfall. There was nothing gentle about Josef, there never had been. He took what he wanted. Anyone who asked questions was a nuisance at best. This was the reason he'd never really loved Jules. Even though she shared his own ruthless nature and despite her obvious physical attributes, she asked too many questions. He didn't have time for that.

Unfortunately, he had even less time to figure out how the world had changed since his own death more than thirty-five years ago.

Some things never changed. The sheer ignorance of human beings, their blind terror at their own mortality, and his readiness to exploit those failings to his own advantage.

But other things were far different. The players had changed. So had the technology. He needed Jules to help him navigate these changes, until he understood them well enough to be done with her.

This was especially true because of her access to FIN, a top-secret government agency that hadn't been around during Josef's lifetime, but which seemed to have surpassed the CIA in terms of both importance and effectiveness.

The previous head of FIN had tapped Jules as his successor. That man was dead, which meant she now had access to all the codes and clearances necessary to control the organization.

He would put up with her questions for the time being, answer them cordially, and, even though it sickened him, lead her on romantically.

He'd always been willing to do whatever it took to reach his goals. That's why he'd been so successful—that and the chance discovery of the Philosopher's Stone, which he'd found hidden among a collection of old scrolls and keepsakes in the attic of a Jewish rabbi's home. That had been in 1938, the year he'd joined the SS. It was the same year the Reich passed a law allowing for the seizure of Jewish assets, so he'd been perfectly within his rights as a member of the Wehrmacht to enter the home and take what he wanted.

He'd known right away that the stone was something of value, but he hadn't realized its true potential until he opened the scrolls that he'd taken from the home along with it.

"Behold the Philosopher's Stone, a gift from the Ancient of Days," it read. "Within it lies the power to restore what was forgotten, to reveal the mysteries of the antediluvian world, yay, to unlock the very gates of Sheol."

Sheol was the Hebrew afterlife, a drear place of shades and darkness that bore little resemblance to the Christian concepts of heavenly cities with streets of gold and blasts of fanfare from trumpets.

To the ancient Hebrews, there had been no glorious heaven or damnable hell, only a place of indistinct nothingness, walled off from the world of the living by the grave and accessible only through memory. Another scroll showed him how to access that memory, which it described as the "divine gift God gave to man for the purpose of remembering the ways of God."

The scrolls had contained instructions on how to harness the power of memory. To unlock the "gates of Sheol" and revive the dead. Using his medical knowledge, he'd figured out a way to transfer that power into human beings, by embedding tiny, almost microscopic pieces of the stone in a subject's hippocampus, the brain's center of long-term memory. He'd only learned later that some people were born with the gift, and that it was linked to eidetic memory.

Josef's mistake had been, in a moment of weakness, giving the stone to Mary Lou Corbet in an attempt to demonstrate his trust and, yes, his love for her. She'd taken it with her to the grave. From there, into the Between. He'd only succeeded in getting it back because people who managed to return from the other side were able to bring with them whatever they were holding or wearing at the time of their transference.

The "merry men" had used it to revive themselves, to bring themselves into the present. Now, at long last, he had the stone back in his possession. The question was, how best to use it to his advantage.

"What exactly can this thing do?" Jules asked. She was sitting next to Josef on a sofa on the thirteenth floor of a high-rise in midtown Manhattan.

217

"Many things."

"Such as?"

Josef didn't know how much to tell her, but he had to give her something. "With the correct knowledge, whoever has the stone has the ability to impart its powers to whomever he wishes. You must have the correct knowledge, of course—an understanding of medicine and the knowledge contained in the scrolls I found with the artifact."

"What happened to the scrolls?"

"I burned them, which ensured that I alone retained the knowledge of how to use the stone in that manner. But anyone can use it to move to this realm from the Between, as our friends from Sherwood demonstrated."

"They got here without the help of anyone?"

"Yes."

"But doesn't that mean . . .?" her voice trailed off.

"What?"

"Doesn't it mean they aren't actually revived? If no one has to remember them, they won't fade. They're actually alive."

He hadn't thought about that. There was another possibility, though. Perhaps they were remembering each other. Both had the gift. Maybe that was the cause.

But Jules had a point. The stone itself, in its pure form, might be able to accomplish things people with the gift couldn't.

It was an intriguing idea. He was surprised he hadn't thought of it himself. The stone might well be able to bring people back to life, not just revive them in a state dependent on memory.

"And if they're actually alive—"

"They can be killed," Jules said. "And we can be rid of them for good. You said the stone acts like a key that opens a portal between here and the Between, right?"

"It does."

"Well, here's the thing, keys can be used to unlock doors, but they can also be used to lock them. Can you remember anything from the scrolls that says how to do that?"

Josef considered. Of course, he remembered every line. He, too, possessed the gift. But he'd never considered the possibility Jules was suggesting. All his energies had been focused on finding a way to bring people back from the other side, not to keep them there. But now that he thought about it: *Seal the gates of Sheol with this stone. Bind the shades of yesterday with its power.*

"Yes," he said finally. "I believe so."

"So, all we have to do," Jules concluded, "is find a way to send our enemies back to the other side, lock the door and make sure we control the key."

"It would seem so."

Jules always had been sharp. He decided he'd been right about keeping her around, at least for the time being. He was starting to formulate a plan and he had a feeling she would be useful in helping him implement it. What if there were an actual door between the two worlds that could be thrown open to allow the souls of Sheol to return to life? He could call forth thousands upon thousands of the dead at a single command. He could summon the dead from the Wehrmacht, perhaps even from the Golden Horde or the legions of Rome. He could establish a Fourth Reich, with himself as the new Führer.

He could send his enemies back the other way, seal the door and imprison them there.

This was coming together better than he had planned. All he had to do was find that door.

Adjusting

Roger had been nervous about parting with the necklace, but Scadlock had convinced him. Now that they were actually back to the real world, they didn't really need the stone, did they? Neither wanted to spend much time behind bars, and without their fellow outlaws to stage a jailbreak, they thought it better to take the offer the police had given them. They'd been told that the person who'd reported the theft of the stone wouldn't press charges, as long as the necklace was returned. Roger and Scadlock were both worried about who that person was. It had to be either Josef or Jules—most likely both—since they were the only ones who knew they had it.

How had they managed to return to the real world without it? And what did they still want with it now that they were back? Those were questions neither Sherwood outlaw could answer. What they did know was they would have to fit in better than they did in their outlaw garb. They stood out like a sore thumb in the twenty-first century. Fortunately, they had help: Terri Yerma, the director of the Faire, had decided to lend them a hand now that they were out of jail. It turned out the Faire only ran a few weekends, and Terri had decided to take some time off from her regular job, which involved something called web design.

"How does one earn a living from that?" Roger had asked. "Where we hail from, spiders spin their own webs. Nobody pays for them."

But she had explained that she worked on a different kind of web. An invisible device that allowed people to communicate with others all over the world just by typing words onto a computer screen. Terri used some kind of code to create pictures, portals, and other things in what she called cyberspace. An invisible realm that existed to support communications between humans via electronic signals. They didn't know what electronics were, either. She had to explain that, also.

At some point between their own time and now, fire had been replaced by something called electricity, which could be trapped within small glass globes or tubes that gave off light. The mysterious substance was used to animate everything from sun dials that worked without the sun to the screens that provided access to the web.

"Where have you two been that you don't know about the web?" she'd asked. "Have you lived your whole lives in Renaissance Faires?"

Scadlock was skeptical about telling her they really *were* from Sherwood Forest, thinking she would never believe them. But when Roger pointed out that everything she was telling them had been hard to believe, he agreed to be up front about it.

"We hail from the Shire Wood, in the one thousand, two hundred and seventy-first year of our lord," Roger declared.

She blinked at them a couple of times, then smiled. "That explains it," she said easily. "Or I guess quantum physics would explain it, if I knew enough about it to understand that stuff."

"So, you accept our explanation?" Roger said.

"I accept everyone's explanations," she said. "Who am I to judge the universe if it winds up picking up a couple of outlaws from the thirteenth century and depositing them in the twenty-first?" She laughed, but not as though she were ridiculing them. Rather, she seemed to find the whole thing amusing and enjoyable. "Imagine me meeting Robin Hood and Will Scarlet in the flesh. I'm one lucky girl."

"That's Roger. Roger Godberd."

"And Scadlock, not Scarlet."

"As you wish, milords," she said, adopting the style of speech she'd used at the Faire, which seemed almost as foreign to Will and Roger as the dialect she normally spoke.

The Faire, she told them, was a re-enactment set in the time of Queen Elizabeth, who had occupied the throne three centuries after their own time. The people who had visited them in the Between had only told them so much, and they hadn't mentioned anything about this. The idea that a woman had occupied the throne was even stranger than learning about the web or electricity. In their day, men alone ruled. The idea of a woman lording over men seemed, to use Scadlock's term, inconceivable, and in Roger's, was "against the holy law of God. No offense, Lady Terri."

She scowled at them. "Well, you'd better get used to it, guys—there's a woman on the throne of England now. There has been for more than sixty years." Her scowl evaporated and gave way to more laughter. "You really *do* have a lot to learn."

"What I would like to learn, if you please, is what we are supposed to do now?"

"Let's pretend you're tourists on a vacation," Terri said. "I'll drive you down to New York and show you the sights. Central Park. The Statue of Liberty. Wall Street. Give you a taste of the Big Apple."

"I have visited York," Will said. "I did not realize someone had built a new one."

"To which apple are you referring?" Roger asked. "And how large is it?"

"I have a fondness for apples myself," Will chimed in, "most especially when they are used as a basis for cider. Hard cider, of course."

Terri looked like she was about to say something, then appeared to think better of it, shaking her head. "You'll just have to see it. New York isn't anything like the old one, trust me. And sorry, Will, but they don't grow apples there, for cider or anything else. But before we go, I'll have to take you shopping. What passes for Ren Faire garb won't cut it on the streets of Manhattan, unless you're going to a con or something. Probably not even then, unless you want to get mugged."

Con?

Mugged?

They couldn't seem to understand half the words she was saying; not too many people had come through the Shire Wood who spoke the way she did. Minerva and Raven came from this same time, but neither of them had used words like that.

Terri instructed them to get in what she called a car. They'd ridden in one of those to the police station, but they still weren't used to the idea of traveling without the benefit of a steed. Terri told them her "car," which she called a 2001 Accord, had the power of 150 horses. That seemed impossible. Even so, they had to admit it was more comfortable than what the police had referred to as a "squad car."

They were headed east on 76 through Pennsylvania when something roared by them as though they were standing still. A moment later, another something about the same size, going about the same speed, followed.

"What was that?" Will asked.

"That," Terri said, "is an accident waiting to happen. Or a ticket."

"What he means to ask," Roger added, "is what manner of vehicle that is?"

"Oh, right," Terri laughed. "That's a Hog. Two of them, actually."

"Those don't look like any hogs I've ever seen," Will said, raising an eyebrow.

Roger was incredulous. "You say your wagon has 150 invisible horses, yet it cannot match the speed of two hogs?"

"Wanna see what this puppy can do?" Terri asked.

"Puppy?"

"Challenge accepted, gentlemen. Hold on to your hood, Robin."

"Roger."

Chicken

Paige felt Henry's fingers digging into her sides as she leaned forward. It was like they were riding into a hurricane. In a way, they were. The wind buffeted her face and whipped around her in a fury as she zigzagged through traffic heading east on the interstate, trying to lose Davonte—or at the very least, stay ahead of him. He'd hung back out of sight as he shadowed them across most of the continent, but now, suddenly, he'd decided to make a move. Maybe he was trying to run them off the road, maybe he was trying to spook them. Maybe both. Paige wasn't about to stick around to find out. She leaned left, then pulled herself upright in an instant as she veered between a semi and a pickup, silently thanking her guardian angel that Henry had enough sense to follow her lead. They'd come more than two thousand miles and he'd developed a pretty good feel for how to react to her movements.

If he hadn't, they'd be dead. At this speed, it wouldn't matter that they were both wearing helmets; they'd be asphalt pancakes if they wiped out.

Davonte had the advantage. He was riding solo, so he didn't have to worry about a passenger who had to move in tandem.

Fortunately, Paige had been around bikes constantly for the four years she was with the Condors. She knew what she was doing. But that didn't make it any easier to find gaps between lanes—and vehicles—as traffic grew heavier on the highway. Looking over her shoulder, she saw Davonte following, deftly shadowing her every maneuver as he tried to close the gap between them.

"Don't fall off, kiddo!" Paige shouted, hoping Henry could hear her above the wind and traffic noise. She cared way too much to lose him now. "You're the doctor. I can't patch you up if we take a header on this goddamn highway!"

For once in her life, she wished for the sound of police sirens. If the cops saw someone speeding, they always seemed to let the first person go and latched onto the second guy who whizzed past them. More time to react. Easier target. Simple. But she had no such luck this time; the highway cops were probably off lurking behind a bush or billboard in some small-town speed trap, looking for an easy way to fill their quotas. Whatever they were doing, they weren't here. "Where's a cop when you need one?" she muttered.

Paige checked her rear-view mirror and saw Davonte roaring up the left lane.

Brake lights flickered ahead, both a blessing and a curse. As they slowed, they were less likely to wipe out, but it also meant Davonte could move in closer, maybe even catch up. Paige's eyes flashed to the right, looking for a way to get over. If she could find her way up onto the shoulder . . . No luck. A temporary barrier hugged the slow lane as they entered a construction zone. Probably the reason traffic was slowing in the first place.

Another check of the rearview mirror showed Davonte was catching up to them.

"Screw it!" she said under her breath, then louder: "Don't let go, kiddo!"

She swerved to her right and roared up alongside the concrete wall. It whizzed past them in a blur. Henry winced in the hope that his right leg didn't get crushed, somehow maintaining both his balance and his grip on Paige. He didn't realize he'd been holding his breath until Paige roared in front of an eighteen-wheeler that was all but stopped on the highway. The brake lights up ahead were no longer flickering. They were a solid, persistent red.

The big rig came to a stop; everything ahead was gridlocked. A glance behind revealed traffic slowing as it approached where they were. Davonte had followed them into the right lane and was only a few car lengths back now, but his bike was wedged in tight behind a Chevy Silverado and just ahead of a UPS truck. A Winnebago Sightseer hemmed him in to his left, leaving him no way of getting any closer.

From where she sat, shielded by the big rig, Paige could see Davonte, but she didn't think he could see her. He was sitting up on his seat, craning his neck to peer ahead, assuming that she'd kept going in the right lane. Unlike Davonte, however, Paige wasn't entirely pinned in. She had an avenue of escape, but it was back the way she had come. If she was careful, she could maneuver her bike across in front of the big rig, then double back on the other side, riding into traffic.

It was worth a shot.

The long trailer shielded her and Henry from view as they reversed course, and she was suddenly glad for the absence of the police patrols she'd been wishing for earlier. As luck would have it, the big rig was followed by a similarly bulky, double-decker car carrier, which was transporting new cars to a dealership advertised on the side: Billy's Big Deal Buick/GMC. Right behind that was the Winnebago. Paige could hear her bike's engine, but she doubted anyone else could amid the sound of idling engines, blaring car horns, and shouted four-letter words. She hoped by the time she snuck past she'd be behind Davonte, and that he wouldn't have noticed her—either by sight or by sound—heading back westward.

Sure enough, as she broke beyond the tail end of the Winnebago, she could see Davonte over her left shoulder, inching forward now but still surrounded by the three large vehicles.

He hadn't seen her.

But now she had another challenge: The farther west she got, the lighter the traffic became, and the more people started honking at her as she rode into traffic, weaving in and out.

"Shouldn't we get off the road?" Henry yelled.

But there was no place *to* get off. She sure as hell wasn't going to turn around and head back toward Davonte again, even though cars were now racing in her direction at close to forty miles an hour and she was dodging in and out of what seemed like a moving minefield of traffic at nearly the same speed. She knew she couldn't keep this up for long, and she started saying the rosary in her head, a childhood habit she reverted to whenever something seemed out of control.

This definitely qualified.

"Shit!" She veered to her right, into and across the fast lane, to avoid a vintage Cadillac equipped with fins that looked like they belonged on the Batmobile, then slowed as she saw a blue Honda Accord heading straight for her. If she tried to get out of the way, she risked skidding out and sending them sprawling onto the concrete median. Not an option. But the alternative? Keep going and hope like hell the Accord could get out of the way: She couldn't afford to lose this game of chicken, or they'd both be dead.

She heard the squeal of brakes as the car vaulted up onto the median, turned on its side, and threatened to flip before gravity caught it at the last moment and pulled it back down on its wheels with a crash.

Paige was able to slow her bike enough to keep it from flipping entirely out of control as she hit the median going the opposite direction, right behind the car, and bounced at a crazy angle. She felt Henry's arms fly loose of her midsection as he tumbled to the ground and rolled. She laid down the bike and jumped off before it could pin her leg, tumbling past Henry, who now lay motionless a few feet away.

She pulled herself to her feet and ran over to him, kneeling down beside him and looking into his eyes.

They were still open, blinking in what looked like confusion at the sky above him.

"Are you okay?" she asked.

He nodded, "I think so, but from the feeling in my thigh, I suspect I have one jolly good case of road burn."

She glanced down at his right leg. His jeans were shredded like they'd been through a giant cheese grater. There was plenty of blood where some of the fabric used to be. It wasn't spurting, but it was a lot worse than a simple case of road burn. She could tell it would get infected if it started clotting and matting against the dirty torn fabric that lay over it. "We need to get that cleaned up," she said.

Henry winced as he nodded, one corner of his mouth turning up in a wry half-grin. "I know. I'm the doctor, remember?"

"Hey!" A petite woman came running across the median. She couldn't have been more than five feet tall, but she carried herself like an amazon looking for a fight.

"Hold on, sister," Paige said, getting to her feet, staring down at the other woman.

A head shorter and maybe weighing half as much, the woman wasn't backing down.

"No, you hold on. And I'm not your sister, sister! That's my car over there." She pointed at the Honda in the median. "You were going the wrong way on the goddamn interstate. You could have got us all killed!"

"Honda," Paige whispered under her breath. "Their cars are as flimsy as their bikes."

If the other woman heard her, she didn't acknowledge it. "C'mon. Cough it up, 'sister.' Driver's license, address, insurance info—"

"Whoa, hold on. Do we really have to involve the police?"

"Yes, we do. I'm not paying for the damage to my Carly—"

"Seriously? You named your car Carly?" Paige rolled her eyes.

"—and neither is my insurance company. Yours is."

"Look, I'll make it right, but we've got to get going?"

"You're not going anywhere with your bike looking like that," the woman said, gesturing toward the twisted motorcycle.

She was right. The front tire was flat and the frame was bent. It might not have been totaled, but it was nowhere near ridable.

Paige responded with an expression somewhere between a smile and a grimace. "I don't suppose you could give us a lift. Whoa! Who the ...?" She looked past the woman in front of her at the sight of two men dressed in robes, advancing toward them. One of whom was pointing—yes, it *was* a bow and arrow. "You've got to be messing with me," she said. "What are you people, refugees from a Ren Faire?"

"Now that you mention it, I do *run* a Renaissance Faire," the short woman said. "These are my friends, Roger and Will."

"Your friends might wanna change into something less—hell, I don't know—ridiculous. And stop pointing arrows at people. It ain't nice."

"Ummm. Hey." Henry waved at them and gestured toward his leg. "Think there might be any way to get me to a doctor before this leg falls off?" A bit melodramatic, sure, but it *did* hurt.

Paige smiled at him, then turned back to the woman and extended her hand. "I'm Paige," she said, quieting her voice and changing her tone as she forced the edges of her lips to keep curling upward. It took some effort.

The other woman hesitated a moment then reached forward and grasped her hand. "Terri Yerma," she said in a clipped voice.

"Terri. Good to meet you. My friend here is hurt. He needs a doc, and we can't get him there on my Hog. The cops are gonna be here any minute, which would not be too good for you, either, seeing your friend there is still aiming his pointy thing at me."

Terri turned halfway around and waved at Roger, palm-down toward the ground, to lower his bow.

He didn't.

"Sorry. They take their act too seriously sometimes." She frowned. She wasn't happy about being in a car crash, but she wasn't about to just leave this injured guy there by the side of the road. She hesitated a moment, then decided to swallow her anger. "If my car's still running, there's room for you two. You can give me your insurance info on the way."

Paige nodded. "Think one of your friends can help get Henry in the car?" *If they stop scowling long enough,* she thought.

"Hey, Will, wanna give this guy a hand?"

Will jogged across the median and bent down over Henry, slipped his hand underneath his arm and helped him to his feet—one foot, anyway. He hesitated to put pressure on the injured leg. Once he was standing, he tested it and found it could bear his weight. Nothing seemed to be broken, at least.

"Thanks," he said.

They all piled into the car, which, fortunately, was still drivable. They had to climb through the doors on the driver's side. The metal on the passenger's side had been damaged so badly, they couldn't get either of the doors open. Amazingly, there was no serious damage to any other part of the car. The rims weren't bent, and the alignment didn't seem too far off. Best of all, the engine started when Terri turned the key. Now if they could just get past the traffic and where they needed to go without any more delays.

"Where's the nearest hospital?" Terri asked, pulling back onto the interstate.

"I think Henry'll be okay," Paige said reassuringly. "Nothing broken, is there, kiddo?"

"No. As long as I get some disinfectant and gauze bandages, I'll be good, love."

Terri shot a sidelong glance at Paige. "I thought you said . . ." She stopped speaking when she felt the pressure of a small knife held at her throat.

She tried not to swallow.

"Your friends in the back better not try anything," Paige said.

"Okay." Terri's tone was suddenly lower, and meeker. "Where are we going then?"

"New York."

"That's fine. We were going there anyway," Terri said, letting just a touch of sarcasm sneak through her worried tone. "You could've asked."

"Just drive."

Front

Carson opened his notebook and stared at the screen.

He had risked going online to track down Vincent, but since then he'd kept off the grid, electronically speaking. He didn't want to tip anyone off about his location, now that he had Minerva and Raven back. Everyone always seemed to be looking for the two of them, and now that they both had gone missing, it was a good bet someone would guess they were with him.

Whether they found Jules and Josef, or the other way around, only mattered as far as the element of surprise was concerned. That was significant, but if he went back online, he'd be able to get more information using the codes that Sutcliffe had provided, more information was always better than less.

"What do you think you'll find?" Minerva whispered as she sat across from him, sipping gingerly at the edge of a cup of hot caramel latte. They'd stopped at a place called Caffeinated Wi-Fi, a busy corner coffee shop just outside the city.

Carson stared at the screen of his laptop, squinting. He didn't want to admit he was getting older and needed reading glasses. "I'm not sure," he said in answer to her question. "I'm not even really sure what I'm looking for. Anything that might give us an edge." He looked up across the table at her. "Besides, I don't have your perfect memory. I can't remember how to get back to the place I found Vincent."

Minerva stifled a laugh.

"So, the great Bradley Carson isn't perfect," Raven mocked. "Imagine that."

Minerva elbowed him gently. "Be nice. We can't all be perfect . . . I mean gifted." She winked at him. "Why would we want to go back there?" she asked Carson. "We're not trying to find Neil. He's dead. We're looking for Jules and Josef."

Minerva turned back to Raven. "Where did you leave them when you popped back from the Between?"

"Central Park," he said. "I hid behind a tree when they came through, so they couldn't see me. I saw them looking around for a little bit. It was kind of funny, really."

"That's no help," Carson said. "We won't be able to trace them from there. Wait. I think I've got something here."

"What is it?"

Carson's eyes narrowed. "There's no firewall." He was talking to himself more than answering Minerva's question. "I shouldn't be able to reconstruct the hack DeJohn used to breach FIN security. It's hard enough to do that once. With a change of leadership, it's standard procedure for the new director to erase any previous footprint by changing servers and setting up a new firewall. That's at minimum. No one's touched this."

"What does that mean?"

"It means there's been some sort of breakdown. Phantom's death must have thrown everything into chaos. One good thing about having such a loose network is that it's hard to trace things back to any one person. But the flip side, if something does go wrong and that one person is eliminated, it's hard to coordinate picking up the pieces."

Minerva frowned. "So, who's giving the orders now at FIN?"

"I don't know who is—or if anyone is, for that matter."

"So, what now?"

Carson slammed the laptop screen shut. "We have to get to Phantom's office now," he said. "If there's been a breakdown in command structure . . ."

"You're saying no one is in charge?" Raven asked, incredulous.

"That's what it looks like. At least for now." Carson deposited the laptop in a canvas bag as he stood.

Minerva saw where he was going. "But someone needs to be, right?"

Carson nodded sharply. "And we have access to those codes. That someone might as well be us."

⌐

"This is the place."

"What do we do now?" Raven asked. "Just walk on up into FIN headquarters, put our feet up on Vincent's old desk, and make ourselves at home?"

"It might not be *that* easy," Carson said, "but it might not be as hard as you think."

When Malone had tried to blackmail Vincent, he demanded Carson's security clearance be restored. The point of that, Carson was sure, was to make it look like he was the person making those demands. It was too obvious. He doubted Phantom would have fallen for it. But that didn't mean he didn't comply. There had been too much at stake. His son's life *had* been threatened.

Carson hadn't tested his clearance since then; he didn't want to give away his location. But if they were waltzing into the FIN command center, that wouldn't be a concern . . . if this still *was* the command center. It might have been moved following Vincent's death.

That's what he would have expected. But he would have expected the server to have been swapped out, too. It hadn't been.

He checked himself. This was *too* easy. Maybe whoever was in there was expecting him, trying to lure him through the front door.

Malone? He had gained access to Vincent's computer, so he had the motive. But did he have the means? If he'd killed Sutcliffe, as Carson was sure he had, he would have denied himself the services of the best black hat in LA, probably the best west of the Mississippi. To say Malone would have been hard pressed to duplicate DeJohn's work would be an understatement. Carson himself couldn't have done it, which is why he'd employed Sutcliffe's services in the first place.

No, if someone was trying to bait him, it probably wasn't Malone.

He shook his head. He was overthinking this. With Phantom dead, Malone was the only one who would have known the status of Carson's security clearance.

"Follow me," Carson said.

Minerva and Raven stepped into the gold-lined glass revolving door that separated the interior of the high-rise from the outside.

"Good day," said a man dressed in a dark gray uniform with burgundy accents. He stood from his seat at the security station, a small desk in the center of an expansive foyer that was empty except for the four of them. "How may I help you today?"

"We have an appointment," Carson said.

"May I ask with whom?"

"You can ask, but I'm not at liberty to tell you," Carson said firmly.

"Sir, this is a place of business. The individuals who rent office space here do so on the assumption that they will not be disturbed—except, of course, on their own authorization. Now, if you'd like to tell me which of our tenants you're here to see, I'd be happy to relay the message that you've arrived and escort you to those offices."

Carson planted both fists on the reception desk and leaned forward. "The individual I'm scheduled to see left me with explicit instructions *not* to discuss his identity or the nature of the business I'm here to conduct. It was my understanding that I would be provided access upon confirmation of my identity at an automated console."

The guard raised an eyebrow.

"You know," Minerva said, pointing at the guard. "Kind of like the keypads you see outside a trailer park? I'm sure you've been to one of those. You look like the type."

The guard glared at her. "Miss, I can assure you that—"

"What? That you've never been in a trailer park? That you don't know what the hell I'm talking about? Look me in the eye and tell me that."

He stared directly into her eyes, and felt his eyelids starting to grow heavy. He fought to keep them open, but before they were even shut all the way, the muscles all over his body started to relax, and he put his hand out to steady himself against the security station. It didn't help. Within seconds, his eyelids had fallen shut and he fell to the floor, his knees buckling and his legs giving way beneath him.

"Thanks," said Carson. "Neat trick there. Same thing you did to that cowboy back in Missouri."

Minerva shrugged. "I just remember what it's like to fall asleep, and I plant the memory in their minds to knock them out."

It seemed strange that the lobby of the E. Wyndham Putnam Building, as it was called, was staffed only by a single security guard, especially if it housed FIN's base of operations, but that was partly by design. No one was supposed to know that FIN had any presence here. It was just another of the agency's sometimes extreme measures to keep a lower than low profile.

But that didn't mean security was lacking.

When they got to the elevator, it didn't respond when Raven pushed the call button. The door to the stairwell was locked, too, but that was just as well, since none of them wanted to traipse up thirty flights of stairs if what they were looking for turned out to be at the top of the building. Raven glanced at a directory, a series of gold-plated rectangles with names in black lettering that indicated attorneys, accountants, and offices of businesses whose names none of them recognized.

"You won't find what you're looking for there," Carson said. "I doubt any of those people even exist."

"You mean this entire building's a front?" Raven asked.

"I wouldn't be surprised. Do you see anyone else here besides us?"

They didn't. And they hadn't ever since they arrived. "So, there's thirty floors on top of us, we have no idea where we're going, and the elevator isn't working."

"It's working," Carson said. "At least I think it is. Allow me."

He reached forward and pressed his thumb to the call button, which lit up at his touch at the same time the door swung open, allowing them all to step inside.

"Neat trick yourself," Minerva said, nodding her approval. "What floor should we try?" She looked toward the lighted numbers.

Carson shook his head. "I don't think those are floor numbers," he said. "I think it's a keypad. It was my fingerprint that activated the call button. Now I have to enter my security access code, and the elevator *should* take us exactly where we need to go." He shielded the keyboard with his hand.

"Don't trust us?" Raven asked.

"Protocol. And force of habit. But it won't help you to know this kind of information, and it could get you killed . . . or . . . in trouble. Sometimes I still forget you're dead already."

Carson must have done something right, because the elevator responded to the series of numbers he entered by lurching slightly underneath them, then starting upward, ascending with surprising speed until it stopped somewhere between the twelfth and fourteenth floors. Like many high-rises, the E. Wyndham Putnam Building didn't have a thirteenth floor:

The architects had skipped that number out of superstition. In this case, though, it seemed that the floor was really there, just not indicated on the lighted numbers over the elevator doors.

Those doors opened onto a brightly lit hallway, carpeted in dark red and lined by simply designed, translucent light fixtures trimmed in gold. There didn't seem to be any rooms on either side of the corridor, just a pair of double doors at the far end.

"What do we do now?" asked Raven.

"What else?" said Minerva. "We go in."

Off-Ramp

When the traffic finally cleared, Davonte pulled off the highway and into a service station at the end of the off-ramp, cursing himself the entire way. Malone wasn't going to like this. He briefly considered saying "to hell with it" and just blowing the whole thing off, but he'd heard what happened to other people who treated Malone like that. It wasn't pleasant.

He cut the engine, pulled out his smartphone, and dialed.

A woman picked up on the other end.

"Is the Duke there?"

"He's busy."

"Too busy to talk about Henry Marshall?"

There was a brief pause. "I'll get him."

Davonte was put on hold and forced to listen to an old Air Supply tune reworked as elevator music. He could hardly tell the difference. To his relief, it was only a short time before the music cut off and a voice came on the line.

"Malone here. What is it?"

"Duke," he said. "Davonte. Hey, listen, I'm here in Pennsylvania and—"

"Don't tell me. You lost them."

"I'm sorry, man. I mean, yeah. I picked up the signal again, but it turned out they'd got behind me, and when I went back to check it out, her bike was there but it was all messed up and there were a bunch of cops standing around it, y'know?"

"So."

"Yeah?"

"You lost them," Malone repeated.

"Without that tracker, I got no clue where they went. I'm sorry, man. What do you want me to do?"

"Nothing."

"Nothing?"

"That's right, nothing. I'm not wasting any more time with you. I don't have to. I'll have time to deal with Marshall, later. Something else has come up . . . a business opportunity."

"What?"

"Not your concern, you useless little fuck. I'll deal with this myself. I'm going to hang up. If you ever call this number again, you're dead.

"You're dead anyway, but I'll leave you to think about when and how it's gonna happen. Just knowing that you'll be looking over your shoulder for the rest of your short life will give me almost as much satisfaction as giving the order to . . . Well, you get the idea."

"Duke, I—"

The line went dead and Davonte flung the phone across the parking lot, watching it shatter on the asphalt in front of one of the pump islands. A gray-haired woman filling up a late-model Chevy Malibu turned to look at him for a second, then turned back around, pretending she hadn't seen him.

Not that it mattered, Davonte didn't care how much trouble he got in to. Duke Malone trouble made every other kind seem meaningless. The only thing worse at this point would be if someone were holding a gun to his head.

He froze.

Someone *was* holding a gun to his head.

"You're a hard man to find, Davonte."

Davonte started to turn his head. "Don't."

The gray-haired woman pulled the gas nozzle out of her car, fumbled it, and watched it clatter to the pavement. Flustered, she scurried around the car a lot faster than her physical appearance suggested she could, got in, and slammed the door. A moment later, she peeled out of the gas station and onto the road.

"Let's go around back, Davonte."

It wasn't a suggestion.

Davonte went around behind the station, the gun still flush against his temple, his arm held fast, twisted hard against his back. He was a big man, and strong, but the man behind him was bigger, stronger. Davonte thought he recognized the voice, but he couldn't be sure.

The back of the station was deserted, up against a vacant lot buried beneath weeds, old newspapers, rusting tin cans, and other, less sanitary objects. The wind kicked up briefly, then died, the only sound apart from the traffic.

"Inside."

Davonte opened the door to the restroom.

"You're not feeling well, are you?" the voice said. "On your knees, asshole. Pray to the porcelain god."

Davonte did as he was told, and he breathed an involuntary sigh of relief when he felt the barrel ease away from the side of his head. It was the last breath he ever took. In the next moment, he felt a muscular forearm snap around his neck and yank him backward, constricting his windpipe. He struggled, gasping, arms flailing, but the man who held him was determined. There was no breaking his grip. Moments later, Jameson's body fell limp.

The man released him. His head bounced off the side of the toilet bowl and joined his lifeless body on the floor.

Mike Gonzalez turned and walked out of the men's restroom at the Sheetz gas station, shutting the door quietly behind him. No one screwed with Mike Gonzalez. And no one fucked with Paige.

Checkmate

Another print-scanner and keypad awaited them at the doorway to Phantom's office. Carson activated it, pressed his thumb to it, and entered his access code. A light flashed green at the top of the panel. Carson nodded to Raven, who reached down to grasp the door handle. He felt the mechanism slide easily and soundlessly into the open position. He pushed slightly and the door opened inward.

"Welcome."

All three of them stopped, half in and half out of the office.

"Come in, come in. We've been expecting you. In fact, you took a little longer to get here than we expected. But better late than never, isn't that what they say?"

"How . . .?" Carson didn't bother to finish his sentence. One look at Jules sitting there behind the desk and he knew how. He'd been so worried about Jules' gift and how she might use it, he'd forgotten who she was. First and foremost, she'd been his contact in FIN, the one who had assigned him to have Minerva's memory erased back when all this all started.

The fact that Jules had been doling out assignments meant one thing. She was higher on the food chain than Carson, and Carson was no flunky. That's why he had the highest security clearance you could get. But even in an organization as meticulously decentralized as FIN, there had to be some sort of pecking order. Even if you didn't know your superior's real name or location, you had to answer to someone, and he had answered to Jules, who had answered to . . . who? He had no idea. It might have been Vincent, for all he knew. And the fact that here she was, sitting in Vincent's chair in Vincent's office would seem to indicate that she had been pretty close to the top of the pyramid.

Close enough, anyway, to assume control in the event of Vincent's death.

"I really do have to thank you for getting poor Neil out of the way, Triage," she said, chuckling mischievously as she drew out his code name on her lips. "Lucky me. I got back just in time to take advantage of it. Of course, you couldn't have known that Neil had named me his successor. No one was supposed to know, really, except for me and Neil. I guess this means you can call *me* Phantom, now. I always did like the name. It suits me even better, don't you think? I am dead, after all."

Josef laughed. He was there, too, leaning against the side of the desk, as pleased with himself as some Nazi parody of Beau Brummell.

Minerva stepped between Carson and Raven, too angry to worry about what Jules might do to her. "You orchestrated this to get us here?"

"Well, you did want to find us, didn't you?" Josef mocked.

"We were just trying to help by making it easy," Jules added.

"Why?"

"Because," Jules said, "as tiresome as we both find you, it turns out we still need the two of you. Carson, not so much, but he's done his part by bringing you here."

Raven wheeled on Carson. "You mean you were in on this?"

"No," Carson said, but Raven was unconvinced.

"You've been working with them all along, haven't you? Just waiting for the chance to turn and hand us over. Whatever's convenient, right? What did you get out of this, Carson? How much did they pay you to sell us out?"

This is a nice bonus, Jules thought. She and Josef had worked out how to communicate silently between them in much the same way Raven and Minerva. *I hadn't expected them to turn on each other so quickly.*

Yes, this is turning out to be easier than I thought, Josef agreed.

"I'm not your enemy," Carson growled at Raven under his breath. "They are."

Minerva glanced at Raven, her expression a mix of sympathy and impatience. Whether Carson had betrayed them or not, what he was saying now made sense: The biggest threat they faced was standing in front of them.

"Congratulations," Minerva said, turning back to Jules. "You're really, really clever. How nice for you. But now, since you have us here, would you mind telling us why you need us?"

"You have something we want," Josef said.

"Which is?"

240

"Information," Josef said. "We've been in touch with a certain Duke Malone. Name ring a bell?"

"Malone," said Carson. "What does he have to do with this?"

"Before our friend Neil met his untimely end, he'd ordered FIN's cyber geeks to trace a hack to our system," said Jules. "A very good hack. So good that they couldn't figure out where it had come from, before Neil . . . left us. But they kept working on it, and by the time I took over, they had it all figured out. The man responsible for the hack was none other than Duke Malone."

Carson raised his eyebrows, unimpressed. "I could have told you that."

Jules ignored him, and Josef spoke up: "Once we knew the origin of the transmission, we were able to make contact with Mr. Malone and offer him a deal. A deal he was happy to accept. He would assist us in exchange for access to some low-level FIN intelligence that could give him a leg up on his competition."

"Assist you how?" asked Raven.

"With his expertise in certain areas. As I'm sure you know, Mr. Malone was able to kidnap Mr. Vincent's son and blackmail him into revealing where your friend Henry was. It was quite impressive, really. Unfortunately for Malone, your friend managed to escape. And when you," he nodded to Carson, "put a bullet in Vincent's skull, Malone had no more use for the boy. Rudy, I think his name was."

Minerva's eyes flashed. "He killed the kid?"

Josef nodded in mock regret. "Sadly," he said, "Rudy is no longer with us. But another boy, by the name of Archer, is. Or, to be more precise, with some of Mr. Malone's associates."

Minerva went rigid, her spine held in an invisible vise by fury on one side and terror on the other. When she spoke, her words came haltingly. "You . . . have . . . my . . . little . . . brother?"

Jules nodded. "Yes, dear, we do. But don't worry. He's perfectly safe. He'll stay that way as long as you cooperate. But if Malone's people don't hear from us in seventy-two hours, they'll know you didn't. That would be a shame."

Minerva tried to speak, but she couldn't move her lips. She'd never considered that Archer might be in danger. Jules might be bluffing. Malone might not have him at all. But she knew they were counting on the fact that she wouldn't take a chance. They were counting right.

241

"What kind of information do you want?" Carson asked, his voice sounding muffled and distant to Minerva beyond the wall of her panic.

"Thanks to you," Josef said, nodding approvingly toward Raven, "and to your grandmother, we are in possession of a key."

"The emerald?" said Raven.

"Correct."

"I told you he was a bright boy," Jules mocked.

"So, you did," said Josef. "In any case, we retrieved the stone from those merry friends of yours and learned something that even I hadn't guessed might be possible. Once Jules gained access to Phantom's personal database, we discovered he had done a great deal of research. He concluded that the stone acts as a sort of key to the Between. In a nutshell, it can unlock a portal between the two worlds and allow the dead to enter this realm without relying on anyone with the gift. We believe Vincent knew where this portal is located. We believe you do, too."

"How would we know that?" Carson asked warily.

"You really ought to be more careful, Triage," Jules said. "Talking about things like passwords out in public. Not something I'd expect of someone with your experience. I think you said something about the number thirty-seven. And Lafayette, Indiana, if I'm not mistaken."

Carson cursed himself silently: They *had* been followed. And whoever it was, did one hell of a job staying out of sight, yet close enough to overhear everything they'd said in that pool hall in Columbia, Missouri. He'd gotten sloppy. Again. No wonder Raven thought he had betrayed them. He'd been so careless, he might as well have.

But if they thought this portal of theirs was in Lafayette, Indiana, they had it all wrong. There was still a chance they could—

"Not Lafayette, Indiana," Minerva said, her low, trembling voice shattering Carson's thoughts like a shotgun blast.

Min, what are you doing?

She ignored Raven's thoughts and looked at the floor. Her tone had been defiant moments earlier, but now any trace of defiance seemed to have vanished. Raven had never heard her voice like this before, quavering, sounding almost lost, drained of hope or purpose. "There's nothing in Lafayette, Indiana," she said.

Jules leaned forward. "Then where?"

Min!

"If I tell you, you'll let Archer go?"

"Yes."

Min, you can't be serious. You don't even know if she has Archer, and if she does, what makes you think she'll let him go if you do what she wants?

She's not bluffing, Raven.

How do you know? Did you find a way inside her mind without her realizing?

It's not her, it's Archer. He and I always had a connection. I don't know if it's because of the gift or just because we grew up depending on each other so much. Since all . . . this . . . happened, I've been so focused on thinking about you—about keeping you alive. Then Amber, too. Since that, I haven't felt anything from Archer. It's like I stopped worrying about him. God, how could I have let him down like that?

You didn't let him down.

Yes, I did. If I'd been paying attention, I would have known he was in trouble. I might have been able to do something. But the minute she said his name, I knew she was telling the truth. I felt him again. He's scared, Raven, and it's all my fault.

"This is bullshit," Carson said. "You don't have her brother, Jules. What kind of fool do you think I am?"

"The best kind," Jules said. "One who doesn't know he is one."

"You think you've won, Jules. But this isn't checkmate."

"It's okay, Carson," Minerva said. "I'm through fighting." She turned to Jules, careful not to look her in the eye. She was in no shape for that sort of confrontation. "I'll take you where you want to go," she said, a hint of defiance creeping back into her tone, "but you should know, I'll be able to tell if you've kept your word. If anything happens to Archer, I'll . . ."

A half-smile climbed up one side of Jules' mouth, as if to say, "You'll what?" But she left that unspoken, instead nodding calmly. "You have my word, and I'll keep it."

"Then so will I," Minerva said. Her voice was barely above a whisper.

She turned to Carson. "I'm sorry, Bradley," she said in a tone that suggested something between pity and regret. "Or whatever your real name is." Until then, she'd always called him Carson.

He looked at her, searching her eyes for her meaning, and that's when he felt it, an uncontrollable drowsiness, blanketing his limbs and wrapping him in an invisible cocoon. He'd done it again. He'd gotten careless, and she'd taken advantage of that fleeting instant when he'd let down his guard. If he could make mistakes like this, it was probably better that she was going on without him. She could take care of herself, he tried to reassure himself, as he sank to the floor in the middle of the room.

That reassurance didn't come before he was lost inside a deep and dreamless sleep.

Elevator

When Carson opened his eyes, he was alone and, frankly, surprised to be alive. Minerva must have made Jules and Josef agree to spare his life as part of their bargain, or maybe they simply thought he was too inept. That's how he felt about himself at this point. But his training told him self-pity could get him killed more easily than anything else. It was a distraction, poisoned bait in a deadly trap. He brushed it aside and got to his feet, his ears picking up a faint sound somewhere in the building.

Security guard? That had to be it. Jules and Josef weren't going to leave him here to just waltz out the front door. There had to be more security than he'd seen on his way in.

He wondered if Jules had revoked his clearance again, now that it had served its purpose. He walked to the doorway and pressed his thumb to the print-reading console. Sure enough, a red light flashed.

Access denied.

He was stuck. No clearance meant no elevator access, and there didn't appear to be a door to the stairwell on this floor.

But what was that noise? It was getting louder . . . a thumping or pounding. It seemed to be coming from the elevator.

Carson approached it slowly, groping for his gun before he realized that Jules and Josef had deprived him of it. The closer he got, the more certain he became that the noise was, in fact, coming from the elevator. Something was inside, and it was trying to get out. At this point, even unarmed, he had nothing to lose. He stepped up to the doors and tried to pry them apart. He wouldn't have stood a chance of moving them by himself, but someone on the other side was doing the same. Within a few moments, he felt the doors start to give. Straining, he pulled in both directions until a small gap appeared, then widened slightly as he and his accomplice on the other side forced the doors apart.

Check that. Accomplices, plural. There were two men inside the elevator.

At last, the doors came apart and Carson stepped back.

The pair stepped out and stared him up and down, trying to get a fix on who they were dealing with. They looked decidedly out of place: Each wore Levi's and a T-shirt, one of which had a big stylized "S" encased in the shape of a diamond, while the other read, "Like what you see? Just don't look in the mirror."

"Is a man named Phantom in this vicinity?" the second man asked in what sounded like some variation on a thick British accent.

"No, he's not," said Carson. "I didn't get your name. I'm Carson."

The other man stepped forward. "William," he said, then added, pointing at the "S" on his shirt, "This is for my family name."

"I don't think that's what it stands for," Carson said.

"Roger," the other man said, not pointing to his own shirt. "We were sent to find Phantom."

William and Roger. He'd heard those names before, but he couldn't remember where. He brushed it aside; he'd figure it out later. Carson looked past them, through the half-opened doors and into the elevator carriage. In the floor was a trap door that looked like it had been forced open. Beyond that, a cable descended into blackness for a dozen floors below them. "You *climbed* all the way up that?" Carson said.

The one who'd called himself William held out his hands, which had been rubbed nearly raw by the experience. "A sturdy oak is much less taxing," he said. "But we are both accustomed to a good climb. It was a challenge." He smiled.

Carson shook his head. He didn't want to know. Whoever these two were, they weren't FIN, and they didn't seem to know anything more than their stated objective. To find Vincent. Someone had obviously sent them on an errand, maybe because they could climb thirteen floors up an elevator cable. It was a handy trick. Carson was in decent shape, but he wasn't sure he could climb up that far. As he thought about that, it occurred to him that, unless he found another way out of here, he would probably have to climb *down* thirteen floors.

"Who sent you?"

"If you are Carson, then I believe we were sent by a man of your acquaintance. I heard him mention that name," Roger said. "He is here, along with his maiden."

A man of his acquaintance? That could have been anyone. And who talked like that? Who called women *maidens* in this day and age?

"Are you sure this 'Phantom' is not here?"

"Yes," Carson said. "I don't think there's anyone else around, either. Jules—the woman who left me here—sealed this place off so well they don't need guards."

"We managed to make it through," William said, grinning.

He had a point.

"Then there is no purpose in remaining," Roger declared. "Your friend is waiting below."

Stone

"Henry? How did you get here?"

Carson looked at his hands, they were as raw as his rescuers'. He imagined theirs were worse, after the climb back down, but they didn't seem to be complaining.

"Long story," Henry said. "I didn't fancy I'd ever see you again. The whole thing was odd, really. After that bloke knocked you out back at the jail, they put me in witness protection, just the way you said."

"Sorry about that," said a woman who was standing beside him. "They sent Mirage to get you out of the way because we just couldn't trust you. Nothing personal." The woman stepped forward and stretched out her hand. "Paige Marie Daly at your service," she said.

Mirage. That sounded like a code name. "They?" Carson asked. "You mean FIN?"

The woman threw back her head and laughed. "Who do you think?" she said. "Word was out you'd gone rogue, so Phantom gave the order to have you sidelined."

Carson's eyes narrowed. "You reported directly to Phantom?"

"What, don't I look impressive enough for ya?" A broad grin spread across her face, but Carson couldn't tell if it was meant to convey humor or a challenge. "Look, Triage, I was told that if everything went to hell in a handbasket, I was supposed to come back here and get debriefed by Phantom. Well, everything *did* go to hell, without even waiting for the handbasket. But it looks like you got here first. Since you're still standing, I *assume* you're back on his good side. Am I assuming right?" Carson's eyes traveled down her arm to her side, where she was holding a small pistol.

"Not exactly," Carson said. "Phantom's not here. He's dead."

He decided to leave out the part about being the one who had killed him. There was no use making her mad. She had a gun, and he didn't. "Where did you pick up these two?"

"We kinda ran into them on the highway. Actually, we didn't *literally* run into them, but we almost did." She laughed again. At least someone thought this whole thing was amusing. "Their friend over there gave us a ride." She gestured toward a petite woman whose ponytail was almost as long as she was tall. "She runs a Renaissance Faire that these two guys hooked up with. They played Robin Hood types."

"That's *not* my name," Roger growled under his breath.

"They seem to take it seriously," Carson remarked, and suddenly he knew where he'd heard their names before. William and Roger. Raven had mentioned those names in a brief conversation he'd had about Robin Hood. These were probably the same two. He eyed them with renewed suspicion, but they looked harmless enough, and they seemed clueless about everything.

Carson turned back to the woman. "Aren't you worried about compromising security by talking openly in front of these people?"

Paige shrugged. "I brought Henry into the loop because I figured he deserved to know. Besides, I kinda like him." She put an arm around him and pulled him toward her. He pulled back, and they met in the middle.

Carson raised an eyebrow.

"The others don't have a clue what I'm talking about, so if I say anything in front of them, I'm sure it goes in one ear and out the other," Paige continued. "I don't understand half of what they say, either."

"I'm not sure it matters anyway," Carson said, "with Phantom dead. You said things went to hell. Well, they did."

"So, who's calling the shots?" Paige asked.

"We are."

The two of them turned around and saw Roger aiming Paige's pistol at Carson's skull. "I assume this mechanism works by pulling the small handle?"

"Hey!" said Paige. "How did you get that?"

"Roger and I are thieves," William said. "We have a knack for pilferage."

"Which is why we find it vexatious when something is stolen from *us*, as occurred not many days ago," Roger said, then grumbled under his breath, "Overlooking the fact that we stole it ourselves to begin with."

Paige stretched out her hand and took a step forward. "Just give me the gun, and we'll all be copacetic," she said.

"I would advise you to come no closer," Roger said, raising the gun slightly. "I may not be familiar with this mechanism, but I assure you that I am more than adequate when it comes to hitting a target. Now, if you please." He shot a sidelong glance at Carson. "I believe you mentioned someone named Jules."

"Jules?" Carson was confused. What did she have to do with these two jokers?

"You spoke her name in passing when we first encountered you," Roger said.

"It is not a common name," Will put in, smiling.

He smiled far too much for Carson's liking.

Carson didn't remember saying anything about Jules, but maybe he had. Still, that didn't explain how they could have possibly known her.

"We believe she and her companion have what was stolen from us," Roger said.

"Which is?"

"An emerald necklace."

"A valuable antique," Will added.

Carson couldn't believe it. Somehow, these two were mixed up in this business with the stone. What had Raven called it? The Philosopher's Stone? He'd never heard of it before, and he wished he never had. The thing was turning out to be nothing but trouble. "Look," he said at last, "I think I know what you're talking about, and I'm pretty sure it's the same Jules. Unless I miss my guess, she *does* have what you're looking for. And I have an idea where to find her."

Will smiled again. "Then why do we tarry?" he announced. "Lead on, my good squire. We shall retrieve that which we are seeking!"

I'm not a squire, Carson thought. *But these two do have a gun pointed at us, and they might be useful in dealing with Jules. And Josef.*

"I suppose I'm driving again," Terri said.

Paige laughed. "Yeah, I suppose you are."

Shadows

They pulled up in front of the home at 137 Lafayette Street and cut the engine. It looked just the way it had when they had been here the first time. Quiet, deserted, a place both forgotten and foreboding. The key was still in the lockbox, but they didn't bother with it. Raven simply wedged a broken piece of fence post into a crack beside one of the windows and jimmied it open.

There was no use in delaying. Minerva led them directly to the room where she and Raven had seen the shadows . . . where the book had opened like a monster trying to swallow her.

"I think this is what you're looking for," she said. "Your portal."

Jules and Josef looked around, their eyes searching eagerly for any clue to what they were looking for.

"It looks like an ordinary room," Jules said.

"Except for this." Josef walked to the mural that dominated the room, the battle between a single giant wolf and an army of warriors beneath a swirling gray sky. They could almost feel the bite of the cold from the snow-capped mountains rising up against the iron clouds. "Remarkable," he said, reaching out a hand and running the tips of his fingers lightly across its surface. "It almost calls to me, summoning me toward it."

Shadows danced in one corner, propelled by light through tree branches beyond the window. But in another corner, the shadows seemed to almost ooze out of the wall, unaffected by the light and receding back into an endless abyss. Those were the shadows Raven remembered.

"There," he said, pointing to it, and the others' eyes followed the line of his index finger to the corner.

"Yes," said Josef. "I believe this is the place. The gateway to the Between." He reached into his pocket and pulled out the stone. It gave off a faint, green glow.

"So, what happens now?" asked Jules. "We've got the key, we've got the door, but where's the lock?"

Josef studied the shadows, then turned back to the mural. "I don't know." He held the stone up high in the air, then walked over and pressed it against the mural. Nothing happened. He hesitated, then tried to walk toward the shadows. When he reached them, they seemed to dissipate, leaving only a blank and empty corner.

"Something's wrong," Jules said. "We're missing something."

"Let me try something," said Minerva. "Give me the stone."

Josef studied her closely, avoiding her eyes as he scrutinized her body language, but Jules was shaking her head. "Don't trust her, Josef. It's a trick."

He stayed silent for a moment, feeling the eyes of the other three upon him. "I don't think so," he said finally. "I think she is sincere. Don't forget: We have her brother." He held out his hand, opening his palm to release his grip on the stone.

"You're a fool," Jules spat. "First you gave it to that whore of yours, and now to this child."

Before she could object further, Minerva took the stone from him. "When I was here before, whatever is on the other side of . . . that . . . it felt like it was trying to pull me in."

"I felt that too," Raven said, "but it didn't seem as strong. With you, it almost seemed irresistible."

Minerva nodded.

What are you going to do? It was Raven's voice in her head; she could feel his concern.

I don't know. Maybe it's not enough to have a key and know where the door is. Maybe you need the right person to unlock it.

Couldn't you just use it to send them back to the Between?

You heard them. If Malone doesn't hear from them in less than seventy-two hours, he's going to kill Archer.

Raven didn't have an answer for that, so he asked again: *So, what are you going to do?*

I'm gonna try to open this door.

The stone glowed more brightly now as she held it, the light radiating around her. She held it up to the mural, which answered with a glow of its own. Dark silver, the color that dominated the scene, became almost fluorescent. She felt the pull, like before, but it was stronger in the other direction, toward the shadows.

Raven had said the stone was powerful, but she didn't know what it could do. When he'd given it to her, she had felt something she hadn't been able to describe. Now it seemed almost like a feeling of kinship. She'd thought it was because of the way she felt about Raven, because it had belonged to his grandmother, that he'd given such a special family heirloom to her. But now she realized it was more. It was as if she shared some part of the stone's memory, but only a very small part. As she held it, it seemed like it was indeed a key, but not just to the Between. To all the memories ever collected, in every corner of the world, on every plane of existence.

Being connected to the stone was like having access to it all. It was overwhelming. Like being in the world's biggest library without having a computer to look up where the books were located, nor even an old-fashioned card catalog. The pull was irresistible, like the pull of the coloring book.

She barely noticed as she started walking slowly, deliberately, toward the shadows, her mind consumed by the wonders of the stone.

Min, where are you going? Be careful . . .

Raven's warning barely registered. She kept moving forward, toward the shadows, but seeing only the stone's beauty. The shadows didn't recoil as they did with Josef; they seemed to undulate, to reach toward her in newly formed tendrils of liquid smoke. Instinctively, she stretched out the hand that held the emerald toward the shadows. They, in turn, extended toward her.

Min, this is crazy. What are you doing?

Stone and shadow met, and there was a spark that couldn't be called light or dark. The green glow became a flash that, like a bolt of lightning, was there and gone again almost before anyone could tell what had happened. The room itself seemed to be rolling like the way it feels to be tossed to and fro on a boat in a winter storm. The shadow reached out to touch Minerva when she extended the stone. It expanded . . . and engulfed her.

Raven lunged forward, grabbing for her, but his fingers closed on empty air. She just wasn't there.

"Min!" He shouted. There was no answer. Then with his mind's voice, *Minerva!* Still no response. He couldn't feel her presence. It was as if she'd been picked up and whisked off the face of the earth. Where had she gone?

The Between? Or did this gateway lead somewhere else?

Raven stared at the corner. The shadows started receding back into themselves, like a voracious predator that had eaten its fill. The stone hadn't gone with her. It had fallen to the floor where she'd been standing a moment earlier. It lay at his feet, the glow fading to almost nothing.

Raven snatched the stone up off the floor and cradled it in his hand, watching the glow slowly return—not quite as bright, but pulsating, almost like a heartbeat.

The shadows stopped receding, suspended, almost as if they were watching to see what he would do.

Josef and Jules were wondering, too. Josef stared at him—was that fear in his eyes? Jules had the same look. But before he could do anything, the door flew open and two men burst into the room. One of them held a small handgun to the head of a woman he didn't recognize. The other held a longbow, which he proceeded to point directly at Raven.

"Unhand that jewel!" Roger Godberd, demanded. "It belongs to us by right!"

Another man and a woman entered the room behind them, with Carson. And was that Henry?

He fixed his gaze on Roger and considered trying to enter his mind but quickly discarded the idea. Roger had centuries of practice. Besides, if Raven focused all his attention on him, there was no telling what the others would do. If only he could reach Minerva, they could work on this together. That's what they'd always done. When they worked together, they'd always found a way out of the worst predicaments. Even when they'd both been stuck in the same body.

Min, where are you?

No answer.

"I said, unhand the jewel," Godberd said again. "Or I shall separate it from you with this arrow!"

Raven knew what he had to do. He just didn't know whether he could manage to do it before Roger's arrow found its mark. The arrow couldn't kill him, he was a memortal, after all, but the force of its impact might dislodge the jewel from his grip. That was something he couldn't risk. He had to move before it was too late. In an instant, he sprang at the liquid shadow in the corner, reaching out with the stone in the same motion. In that instant, he felt something whiz past his left ear, followed by a gasp of disbelief: "But at this range, I *never* miss!"

It was the last thing he heard as the emerald tumbled from his hand, as if wrenched loose by some unseen force. He felt a maddening sensation in his mind that he could only describe as being turned inside out.

Then he woke up.

Wolf

Now it was Josef's turn to snatch up the stone. As he did so, Roger rushed toward him.

"That stone belongs to us," he shouted.

Josef let out something that sounded like a growl, but it was eclipsed by the sound of another. This one much louder and emanating from the far wall. The surface of the mural, which had always seemed more lifelike than should have been possible, shimmered like a mirage across an asphalt road on a torrid summer day. The wolf crouched on its hindquarters and sprang, snapping and snarling as it leapt from some other world into their own.

The animal was immense, its teeth sharp and stained with blood, its paws scraping the floor as it landed in the midst of them. It stood nearly four feet tall at its shoulder, and those shoulders were far broader and more heavily muscled than any of them could remember seeing on a dog. It had to weigh over two hundred pounds.

Terri screamed and ran out of the room, followed by Paige and Henry, both of whom had been standing near the door. Carson hesitated, then ran after them. The remaining four found themselves trapped, with the animal between them and the exit.

"What the hell *was* that?" Paige shouted as they all hurried down the hall and out the front door. She realized she was shaking. It was at least some comfort to see that Henry was a lot paler than even his usual British complexion made him look.

"I don't know what it was," he said. "But I'm glad we're out of there."

Carson ran out ahead of them. Terri was already in the car and gunning the engine, her face pale, her hands shaking.

"Can you drive?" Carson asked, getting in beside her.

She nodded quickly; it almost looked like a nervous tic. She'd been caught up in this madness by chance. It had become too much. Taking on a role at a Ren Faire was one thing, but dealing with the real Robin Hood, two government agents, and four people who had returned from the dead was something else. Not to mention a giant wolf.

"I don't think so," he said. "Let me drive. Don't worry, I'm not going to steal your car. You'll be fine once we're away from here. Then you can drop me off down the road. There's something I have to do."

She nodded again and allowed him to switch seats.

"C'mon, kiddo," Paige said, running toward the car. "Let's get over there before they leave without us."

"And before that thing comes after us," Henry added.

"I think it's got its hands full."

An instant after she spoke, she heard a gunshot from inside the house. Will had turned his pistol on the giant canine and fired. The bullet found its mark where the left foreleg met its body, but it had no effect. It rushed at Will and leapt for his throat—only his agility and presence of mind allowed him to roll out of the way before it struck.

"Fools!" Josef shouted. "It's revived, like us. You can't hurt it with a gun."

The wolf landed at the far end of the room, then turned and crouched, growling in a corner. Before any of them could react, it lunged at the closed window with the full force of its weight, shattering the old plate glass into countless shards as it cleared the barrier and landed on the lawn. It looked back briefly, then bounded away down the street, out of view.

"What *was* that?" said Jules.

"What it was," said Josef, "is evidence that our friend Minerva succeeded in doing as she promised. The gateway is open, and from the look of that mural, there's an army on the other side. An army of memortals."

"You still believe we can control them?" The tone of Jules' voice made it clear she was having doubts.

"I'm counting on it," he said. "With this stone, they'll be ours to command."

"*If* you know how to use it," Jules scoffed. "It seems to me it was Minerva who opened the portal. You looked like a helpless child."

Josef brushed her words aside. "I spent years studying this stone. I know what it can do, and how to use it. Observe."

Picking up the stone, he held it out in front of him, pointing it at Will and Roger. "I bet you two are growing homesick for old Nottingham, aren't you?" he said. "You've made quite a nuisance of yourselves. I'm not one to hold a grudge. Now that the portal's open, you're free to head back where you belong."

"We have no intention of going anywhere," Roger snarled. "By the Holy Virgin, it is not up to you to dictate when and where we go."

"I beg to differ." Josef thrust out his hand toward them and a beam of green light shot out at the two merry men. In that instant, they were gone.

"Impressive," Jules said. "I may have underestimated you."

His eyes narrowed. "I forgive you," He said through pursed lips. "Just don't do it again."

Déjà

Minerva hated that smoke. It drifted into the back seat from the front of the car, making her gag. She didn't want to cough because she knew it would draw attention to her, and every time that happened, her mother seemed to blame her for something. She'd get in trouble for not taking her dishes into the sink, even though she *had* and it was her mother's own dishes that had been left in the living room to draw ants. Or she'd be blamed for ruining her mother's date with the latest of her "prospects," as she liked to call them, even though Minerva had been sound asleep the whole time. "It's all your fault," she'd say. "Once he found out I had a kid, he didn't want no more to do with me. You're just bad luck, that's all."

Minerva waved at the smoke that assailed her, trying to keep it away, and when that didn't work, she put a hand over her mouth to keep from coughing. She tried to distract herself by watching the trees and telephone poles as they sped past outside the window of her mother's '94 Acura Legend, or by playing the alphabet game, trying to find each letter of the alphabet, in order, on license plates and street signs and billboards.

A boy two years older than she was rode in the back seat beside her, a shock of black hair falling lazily down over his forehead.

He grinned at her. "She's just like a dragon with all that smoke, isn't she, Min?" he said conspiratorially. It was barely more than a whisper, but even that was too much of a risk.

"Shhhhh! She'll hear you!" she said.

He just chuckled. He never seemed to worry too much, probably because he had such nice parents. Minerva wished she had nice parents. But she just had the one, and the one she had wasn't nice. "Where are we going?" he asked.

"Mom has to buy more cigarettes."

"Oh."

Minerva closed her eyes—the smoke was getting to them, too. Now she had a headache. Her mother complained about getting those sometimes, usually after she drank too much wine or bourbon. Minerva had come down with an ear infection once, and her head hadn't felt good when she had a cold, but she had never felt like this before. She felt like something was inside her head, trying to get out.

"What is it?" the boy next to her asked. His name was Raven. She thought it was a weird name for a boy, but she kind of liked it. She liked him, too. They had known each other for a while now.

"My head hurts," she said. She opened her eyes and looked at him. It was the weirdest thing . . . somehow she was able to see what he would look like all grown up.

"Stop looking at me like that," he said and pushed her shoulder, but he wasn't mean about it. He was never mean to her, just silly sometimes. Somehow, she knew he would always be like that.

I feel like I've been here before, she thought, and to her surprise, she heard another voice in her head say back to her: *Me, too.*

Did you say something?

No.

She kept looking at Raven, and he was looking back at her. But not like a kid, more like a grown-up, like he was worried.

You have to stop it, Min.

Stop what.

Remember I told you? The accident is a lie. You have to make it a lie.

What accident?

Minerva put both hands up to the side of her head. The smoke was still really bad, but that wasn't what was making her head hurt. She felt like she was forgetting something, but she never forgot anything. The one thing she could always count on is that she could remember. Even the things she didn't want to remember. Like her mom yelling at her or the time she'd fallen down when she was trying to dance at that Fourth of July picnic. Look how that had turned out. Her mother got mad then, too.

The sound of the car squealing startled her. Her mother had been going too fast again and jammed on the brakes when the light changed at just the wrong time.

I remember that, too.

I know. Now remember what comes next. You have to stop it.

How?

With your memory. It's the key to everything. Remember how I taught you to feel your legs, to walk again? It's like that.

I don't remember that.

That's because it hasn't happened yet, but you can still remember it. You have to try, so you can stop it.

You're not talking like a little boy.

"Want some gum?" Raven asked.

"What?" Minerva was confused. "Mom won't let me," she said, but she felt like someone else was talking.

Her head was hurting even more. It was like she was being pulled outside herself to watch everything that was happening.

And Raven was talking to her in her head.

"Anytime now," her mother said, tapping her fingers hard on the steering wheel, as though that would make the light change faster. It didn't. The cross traffic just kept coming in a steady stream.

We're not really here, are we?

We are but we're not. It's hard to explain.

Why can't I remember?

Because it hasn't happened yet.

Then how do you know?

Because I came here from outside your dream, like before.

Then this is a dream?

Not exactly. There's no time.

The headache was getting worse. She could feel the pressure pounding at her from the inside. Something wanted to get out, a memory of something that hadn't happened yet. That's why she couldn't remember.

It was making her sick.

The light finally changed, and Minerva's mother put her foot down hard on the accelerator. The car lurched forward into the intersection, wheels screeching, then gaining traction as the car flew down the road.

"Geez!" Raven exclaimed.

"Did I just hear you take the Lord's name in vain, young man?" Jessica Meyer looked over her shoulder. Her expression was all self-righteous.

Minerva saw her mother take her eyes off the road and heard herself say, "Mom." She was about to add, "the road," but said something else instead. "I'm sick." This time, she was saying it, not just hearing it.

"Suck it up, buttercup. You'll be okay till we get home."

"No, Mom, I won't. I'm gonna throw up."

"Hell," Jessica said. "Not in my car you don't." She veered over to the right lane and pulled alongside the curb, stopping the car and jamming the gear angrily into park. The ashes fell from her cigarette, and it went out. The pack was empty. Now she'd have to wait even longer while Minerva either threw up or realized she didn't have to. "Get out and be quick about it."

Minerva wasn't listening. The pounding inside her head was growing more painful; she bit down, accidentally biting the side of her tongue. She barely noticed it amid the pain inside her head.

She closed her eyes again, it felt like she was spinning on a teacup ride in a pitch-dark cavern. She tried opening them, but it was just as dark. She wasn't sure whether her eyes were open or closed.

She wasn't sure of anything.

She felt dizzy, and she fell, but there was no floor to catch her. A near-deafening wind sounded in her ears, but she couldn't feel the air. She tumbled over and over and over through empT space until she finally landed—on something soft.

Home

Minerva finally managed to open her eyes. The first thing she saw was the flame from the candle she'd kept lit on her nightstand.

Memories flooded back, but she no longer knew the difference between memories and dreams . . . or fantasy.

Here she was in her own bed, where this whole thing had begun, without the slightest clue about how she'd gotten there. Or how long she'd been asleep.

It felt like a very long time.

She reached down in a sudden panic to feel her legs. The skin responded to her touch. She wriggled her toes and propped her knees up in front of her. Whatever else had been a dream, her recovery from the paralysis had been real. But wait— Had that crash even taken place? Did she somehow manage to go back and change it? Was that what Raven was talking about?

Raven.

She had to keep remembering him, or he'd fade. If she'd been out too long . . . No, she didn't have to worry about that. He'd been there with her, in her dream. Maybe it hadn't been a dream at all.

My mouth hurts.

Minerva put an index finger in her mouth and felt the inside of her cheek. "Ouch."

She pulled the finger back out and looked at it: There was blood on the tip of it.

There shouldn't have been.

I'm revived. This isn't supposed to happen.

The door opened, and she sat up in the bed. "Hey, ever hear of knocking?"

Archer came bounding in the way he always did, wearing a Charmander T-shirt and those ridiculous corduroy pants Jessica bought him.

"You're awake!" he said, running over to the bed and practically jumping on it.

"And you're okay!" Minerva said, throwing her arms around him in a bear hug.

"Why wouldn't I be?"

"I'll ask the questions here," she said in her teasing big-sister voice. "Why wouldn't I be awake? It's morning, right?"

"Afternoon," Archer corrected. "You keep it so dark in here I can't tell the difference. You've been asleep for a long time. Your doctor friend said you were in a coma."

"My doctor friend? Wait. How long is a long time?"

"Yeah, your friend Henry. A couple of weeks."

"Someone mention my name?" Henry said, striding into the room. "Ah, sleeping beauty awakens. It's about time. Let's have a look at you, shall we?" He pulled out a stethoscope and pressed it against her chest. "Breathe in and out for me. That's right. All sounds normal. Now, let me have a look in those pretty eyes of yours." He picked up a light and shone it in her eyes one at a time, first right and then left. "Hmmm. There may be something going on there, but I don't want to take you back to the hospital so soon. Best to let you rest here a little, now that you're awake."

"*Back* to the hospital? I was in the hospital?"

"Until today, in fact. We had to keep you there on fluids to keep you hydrated. You don't need to lose any more weight."

But I don't need *food.*

"We brought you back here because you were out of the coma. Still asleep, but out of danger. I was confident you'd wake up today. And I was right. Usually am." He chuckled.

"Where's Raven?" she asked. "Is he here?"

"Waiting right outside. He was knocked out too, at first, but unlike you he came to right away. He stayed in your room with you the whole time you were in the hospital, talking to you. I heard some of it, and I have to say it didn't make much sense to me. You gave us all a real scare."

"I want to see him."

"Of course. I'll get him now, love."

Henry left the room with Archer, and a moment later Raven all but sprinted into the room and over to her bedside, taking her up into his arms. He kissed her on the cheek, the forehead, on her ears . . . all over her face. Lastly on her lips. That kiss lasted the longest. "You did it," he whispered. "You saved yourself. You saved us."

"What are you talking about?"

"I've been telling you all along, the accident was a lie. You finally figured it out. None of us could do it for you; you had to do it on your own. Look!" He reached over by the side of her bed and picked up a safety pin that was lying on the nightstand, opened it up and stuck it in the ball of his middle finger. He squeezed it, and a drop of blood oozed to the surface and stayed there in a tiny liquid dome. "That stung."

That should be healing.

No, it shouldn't.

You can still talk to me in my mind?

Of course. This isn't some lame TV show where you wake up at the end and find out everything was a dream.

She opened her mouth again and spoke what came next. She needed to hear him actually say it. "Then . . . are we . . . ?"

"Alive? Yeah. Both of us. Sometimes things happen that are never supposed to. I can't explain it, but the accident was one of them. I've always known that, ever since you brought me back. The stone I gave you . . . I didn't know it at the time, but I think it was meant to help you undo the accident."

Minerva reached out and took his hand. The connection they had was still there. It hadn't been taken away now that they were fully mortal again.

They still had the gift.

"So, has everything changed now?" She'd seen those science fiction films and heard all about the butterfly effect, where changing one piece of history had the potential of changing everything.

"No, it's all the same—except for us. It's just that one thing that was wrong. Nothing else. It's like a rope that got tangled around itself. Once you undo the knot, the rope's still there, with the same beginning and the same end. It's just that the kinks have been worked out."

"Archer?"

"That was Carson's doing. I hate to admit it, but I might have been wrong about him. The guy went in with Paige and took out Malone and two of his bodyguards. Got Archer out of there without a scratch. A 'routine extraction,' he called it. I think he was being modest, but whatever, it worked."

Minerva put her arms around Raven again and held him close, feeling their hearts beat against each other, fully alive. Together without any sort of death separating them for the first time since the accident . . . the accident that had never taken place.

That must have been why Raven had had all those memories when she'd revived him. Going to high school, getting a job, college, even though he'd been dead through it all. He was never supposed to have been dead in the first place.

It was just a knot in his timeline.

"That means I don't have to worry about remembering you all the time," she smiled. "I suppose I'd better be nice to you, now that you don't *need* me to keep you alive."

"Who says I don't?" he said and kissed her. "Besides, you're always nice to me."

"I'm glad you think so."

Carson came into the room just then. He didn't look happy, but then he never seemed exactly overjoyed about anything. Even with that, though, his face looked worried. "Sorry to interrupt."

Minerva put her hand up to her neckline to draw her nightgown more snugly around her neck, and caught her breath.

"Where's the necklace? My emerald necklace?" she asked.

Raven looked at her, the same look of concern on his face. "I'm afraid you dropped it when you entered whatever it was that took you back to the accident. We don't have it."

"Then who does?"

Carson nodded toward Raven. "His grandfather does. Josef Mengele. And if we don't stop him, he's going to use it to conquer the world."

Minerva looked at Raven, then at Carson, then back at Raven again.

"Then I guess," she said, "we'd better stop him."

ABOUT THE AUTHOR

Stephen H. Provost is a journalist and author. He has worked as an editor, reporter, and columnist at newspapers throughout California. His previous books include *Fresno Growing Up: A City Comes of Age 1945–1985*, a history of his hometown; *Highway 99: A History of California's Main Street*; and *Memortality*, the first book of the *Memortality* saga. Provost frequently blogs on writing and current events at his website, stephenhprovost.com.

Printed in the USA
CPSIA information can be obtained
at www.ICGtesting.com
JSHW082155140824
68134JS00014B/248

9 781610 353182